Li
Chances

Judy Kay

outskirts
press

Outskirts Press, Inc.
http://www.outskirtspress.com

Paperback ISBN: 978-1-9772-3830-6

Library of Congress Control Number: 2021900518

Outskirts Press and the "OP" logo are trademarks belonging to Outskirts Press, Inc.

PRINTED IN THE UNITED STATES OF AMERICA

"Life's Chances"

This a Fictional story full of Mystery, Suspense, and Sexy Romance.

The names, places and characters have been created from the imagination of the author. I want to dedicate this book to the memories of the many lives who inspired and the people who shared their emotional ideas. I respect their admiration, their abilities and achievements.

A Special Thanks to my friend and editing lady (A.S.) who did not want to be named. We had so much fun. The hours we spent laughing and crying together always finishing the day "What's going to happen next? She couldn't wait. When we met for the next editing day she had already read ahead full of questions.

What are the chances that you could really have more than one true love in a life time? Does this happen to more of us than we realize? Yes, I quess it possibly has happened to more than one of you. Follow the story and see... You may be surprised that at one time or another, the same thing could happen or has already happened to you.

Chapter 1

GLORY MAY'S NEW LIFE started the day she and her mother decided to move into the small town nestled in the Shenandoah Valley just at the foot of the mountains with The Blue Ridge National Forest to the east and The George Washington National Forest to the west.

When her mother parked and stepped out of the van, Glory May was hanging out the passenger window. She was overwhelmed by the colors of the mountains in the background on this late September afternoon. The mountains seem to be calling her. She looked about taking in all the beautiful colors in shades of greens, yellows, oranges, and reds. The fallen leaves blew across the street in small whirlwinds.

Fall was in the air with the smell of the wood burning stoves hanging heavily on the breeze. She thought, "Could this be the only 'heat' she will find in this small country town?" Being from the city Glory May just was not sure about the purpose of moving here. It was cold here in the middle of miles and miles of nothing but *MOUNTAINS*? Her subconscious was asking, 'could she really even begin to say she may like it here?'

Glory May had promised her mom she would at least try. She meant well saying those words, but she knew life here was going to be so different from the city. She was already missing the tall buildings and noisy traffic.

Glory May's mom walked back toward the van saying it would be another twenty minutes drive before reaching the house according to the directions the gentleman behind the counter had given her.

"Twenty minutes!" Glory screamed. "This has been the longest ride - a ride from hell and back. I just want to get to the house and take a long hot shower. No... I want a bath with lots of bubbles covering me into a drifty cloud of forgetfulness about this trip!"

"Oh, Glory May, you are already in another world. Come back to reality. We will be there soon. You can get your shower, bath or whatever! Just let's get there!" her mom replied.

The ride had been long, hot and trying for both of them. Ms. Barnes was being tested to adjust after going through the worst divorce ever. She did not care to have a man in her life after the disaster of this last marriage. Maybe she should have sent both Glory May and herself to a school for nuns for years. The only good thing coming out of this marriage was the family house that was left to Glory May and herself through a Family Trust set up by Glory May's great grandfather before he passed away. His wife, Ms. Barnes and Glory May's great grandmother, had a living trust to the house and mountain land until she passed away. The final wish of Mr. Charles Millan Barnes was revealed to everyone after his wife's death. No one knew about the trust being given to another family member after his wife's death... until now. Mary Ann Barnes had not been to the house in years but she had so many memories of when she was a little girl running up and down the fields of the mountain land with her grandparents. Ms. Barnes was worried about what the house would look like now after so many years. This was the one thing the ex-husband could not get his hands on. This trust was just for Ms. Mary Ann Barnes and her daughter Glory May. Her hand settled on the envelope laying between them on the seat with the letter she received from the attorney's office. It stated: "Ms. Mary Ann Barnes, you are now the full owner of the family house and fifty-five acres of mountain land." Could this really be true? The chance for them to ever think of owning anything seemed very slim to none. Nevertheless, here they were...on the way down the road to their new home!

She drove the van down the town's main street. She saw several children playing on the sidewalk. A family dog was running around after them nipping at their heels. Ms. Barnes thought she would never be able to give Glory May a life of this kind. Glory May was going on thirteen but thinks she is twenty after living in the city. Ms. Barnes wanted things to be different for both of them. She was hoping to give Glory May a real family life with things at a slower pace here. Maybe it would calm her down some. She needed to get her daughter out of the city life. Now they both have a chance for a new start.

Ms. Barnes was not sure if she had remembered the way out the country road to their new home. That's why she stopped at the gas station to ask the attendant for directions. It had been years since she had been here. She was just a teenager herself with four children the last time they visited the house and farmland. Oh, the fun they had there! The wonderful memories began to rush through her head.

Glory May sat still half hanging out the van window. Even with the chill of the fall evening air blowing through her hair and across Ms. Barnes' shoulders, she was okay with that. Glory May had high hopes for their new home. She knew how much it meant to her mom for them to start a new life.

The twenty minutes seemed like a day. When they crossed the railroad tracks, they could see the top of the farmhouse off in the sunset. What a beautiful site! The sky was the most gorgeous colors of blues, pinks, and purples. You were not going to see anything like this in the city of smog. The sun was setting just behind the mountain of trees - just peeking through the branches, like a little girl behind her mom's dress tail. It gave off rainbow colors that almost caused their eyes to water as it vanished, suddenly behind the mountaintop.

Chapter 2

MS. BARNES ALMOST MISSED the turn into the driveway as they approached the big red mailbox at the corner of the road. She was so overwhelmed by the sunset! Glory May made a comment about the mailbox being the same shape as the big house! They drove up the hill into the driveway. The house was a little run down. Glory May automatically said, "MOM! We're not gong to live in this?!"

Ms. Barnes was very surprised to see the outside of the house was an aged gray instead of white. The paint had lost it brightness and the brilliance that she remembered from her last visit here. The railing up the front stairs was hanging by two nails, flopping in the wind. Some of the windows were cracked, but she didn't see any front windows completely broken. That was a good sign. Ms. Barnes knew the nights here would be cold even as early as September. She parked the van and told Glory May, "Come on, let's check out the inside." She jumped out like a school girl full of excitement. "We need to see if the heat is on before it gets too cold. Glory May climbed out of the van - not what she wanted to do. This city girl wanted to turn that van around and go back where the large city lights blinked through her bedroom windows as they danced across her floor when they went on and off through the night. Here as fast as the sun falls, it was pitch dark. It did not take long after the sunset. No city street lights… the night was going to be blacker than black she thought!

"Come on, Glory May, I need us to do this together," Ms. Barnes was demanding by now. She too was not sure what they would find inside.

They stepped one step at a time up the long stairway, both of them hand and hand. The old wood talked to them as if in pain with each step they took. It seemed like a million steps, although it was only eleven. They went up five steps to a small landing, which made a 90 degree turn, and up another six steps to the porch. At the top of the steps, the porch wrapped all the way around the house. Glory May could sense something else was also on the porch besides them. She told her mom, "Please, open the door. We can check out the outside in the daylight."

Ms. Barnes was grateful to reply. They would feel more at ease inside, with lights, heat and warm beds to sleep in. It had been a long trip for them both and her body ached from the van ride.

She reached for the doorknob and to her surprise the door was unlocked. Then she remembered she had called ahead. She needed someone to check on the house to make sure the water, electric, heat, etc. could possibly be turned on for them, not knowing what time they would arrive from their journey. Ms. Barnes had been lucky for someone had been keeping an eye on the house over years to help when Ms. Barnes' grandmother had gotten sick. Knowing she could no longer take care of the house before she passed, this made Ms. Barnes think the house would be just as she had remembered with everything in its place.

To Ms. Barnes' surprise, when she opened the kitchen door and turned on light switch, several of the neighbors had been there and cleaned up some. They even left dinner in the refrigerator with a note on the counter. *WELCOME HOME Blondie.*" The note gave Ms. Barnes a large knot in her throat as she remembered her grandparents would call her "Blondie." God knows why since her hair was as red as cherries.

They walked around the kitchen. The kitchen looked like new. The floors had been upgraded with cedar wood, which made the kitchen smell like cedar chips that you would buy at the City Flea Market around Christmas time. The floor had small knotty eyes that played hop-scotch around the room. The walls were a melon color with a wallpaper border of farmhouses, pine trees, and deer jumping over the barnyard fence. Glory May was thinking, "I'm going to be sick. What happened to white walls with black and white tile floors? What will the rest of the house look like?" Afraid to find out, Glory May sat down on the wicker rocker placed near the door by the window. She turned toward the window to see a raccoon facing her. It was looking through the window checking out the new family that moved in. Glory May screamed. The raccoon cracked a loud noise that made the hair on Glory May's neck stand on end.

Ms. Barnes laughed saying, "Child, you need to get used to those things. There will be lots of wildlife around here. Just remember not to leave the trash cans out for them to overturn or the trash will be all over the mountain side."

Glory May was beside herself. She had only seen a raccoon in the zoo. Now she was going to be living with them! A few minutes went by before Glory May could collect herself. She was ready to check out the rest of the house. She ran toward an open door to the front foyer. Facing the front to her left shoulder was another set of stairs. To the right was a large open room with bay windows set off to one side and a big picture window to the other side. Two sofas sat parallel to each other with one having its back to the windows and the other with its back facing a fireplace. Both sofas were placed just perfectly toward the picture window to give the room a scenic view with a touch of country class. A small white wooden dining room table with two matching chairs just peeking out from under the table was sitting near the bay window. In the far corner of the room was a piano with a tablecloth draped over its top. Glory May jumped at the chance to make some noise other than her footsteps across the wood floor. But Mom said, "Maybe tomorrow. Let's check out the rest of the house. We still need to at least unload our suitcases from the van."

Glory May looked at her Mom and said, "Don't think I'm going out there with the raccoons!"

"Glory May, you just came from the big city where there were a lot more, scary things than that raccoon!"

Both wanted to check out the rest of the house, but before going any further, they went back to the kitchen. Glory May turned on the outside porch lights and waited for her mom to start out the door. The porch light lit up the whole flight of stairs and half of the large front yard. This gave Glory May a small feeling of being back in the city with her lights - just no noise of city life. The raccoon was still there chattering. Not sure if he/she was trying to talk to them or to another raccoon. It did let them know how unhappy it was of their presence.

Glory May helped to get the large suitcases up the stairs to the kitchen door. They placed them inside and started down for another trip. Glory May left the kitchen door open as she always did in the city for her mom to yell "close the door - you weren't born in a barn." Now that statement really had some meaning. She went back to close the door and was surprised by the raccoon who had beaten her back to the door. "What now?" she yelled.

Her mom chased the raccoon down the stairs into the yard. "I'll close the van, we can finish unloading tomorrow," shouting as she shooed away the raccoon.

"Sounds good to me, I've had enough of that raccoon for one night," replied Glory May.

Ms. Barnes came back inside with another bag in her hand. "I just couldn't come back up the stairs empty handed. Glory May, I think this bag maybe yours. Let's try going upstairs to find our rooms."

"ROOMS?!" Glory May yelled. "Don't think I'm going to sleep

anywhere but with you tonight, Mom. This place is too new for me."

Ms. Barnes had a small chuckle for her daughter. "Look who didn't seem to be afraid of anything in the big city. Give yourself a few days, Fine Child, and you will not believe that statement came out of your own mouth. You will see life here will be good for both of us."

They climbed the staircase to the door at the top of the stairs. They had to look around for the light switch. They found it hanging from the ceiling by a long piece of yarn in the hallway. Ms. Barnes remarked, "I think we may need to make a list of repairs to be done around here."

'Lots of repairs' Glory May was thinking, but not out loud.

When they opened the door, to their surprise the light automatically came on and there were twin beds and a dressing table with lots of family photos on one corner. There was another wicker rocker facing the window, just like the one downstairs. A beautiful knitted blanket with the name **Blondie** hand knitted in a triangle in one corner was draped across the back of the rocker. It was folded just right for the name to stand out to say, "Welcome Home." Ms. Barnes went over, picked up the blanket and sat down on one corner of the closest bed. "Grandmother made this for me. I think I was about ten. I would have so much fun when I would come for a visit. I really need to tell you some of my childhood stories, Glory May."

Glory May by this time did not care. She just wanted to know where the bathroom was and fast.

Ms. Barnes walked back into the hallway. "Here, my dear, here is the bathroom." Ms. Barnes opened the door and started into the room to turn on the light. No light! "Just leave the door open - it's just you and me. You don't have anything I haven't already seen." She thought tomorrow we will check out all the light switches and get to know where they are, but for tonight let's see if we can just get some rest. "Hungry?" Ms. Barnes asked as the bathroom door closed and she headed back down the stairs toward the living room stoop, turning to listen.

"No, Mom, I'm tired. It's been a long ride in that bouncy old van. Can we just go to bed?"

Her mom was nowhere close to being ready for bed herself. So many childhood memories in this old house were running through her mind. But, she gave into her daughter's request and said, "Let's setup a light downstairs just in case we need to get up for something, until we get to know the house and where everything is.

Glory May was up to having on the lights. "Let's leave them all on," she replied knowing her Mom was not going for that one as her mom went down the stairs. Ms. Barnes went around the living room checking the lamps sitting on the end tables at each end of the two sofas. Only one had a light bulb that worked. She left it on while walking toward the kitchen. She checked the door, locked it and turned off the outside lights.

"Mom, please leave the light on. It is so dark out there." She heard Glory May shout.

Ms. Barnes replied, "Tomorrow we will go into town and buy some low watt bulbs to leave on overnight. But I'm not going to leave these flood lights on all night. I don't want to burn the place down the first night we are here. It will be okay! I will make sure of that, Glory May." Ms. Barnes went to the kitchen counter. There was a light over the sink. She turned on the switch, "Yes" she said, "This will work beautifully." They both walked back across the room.

Glory May observed the kitchen cabinets having roosters on the handles. Her mom loved roosters. Every year for her birthday Glory May would go from store to store looking for just the right rooster for her mom. "Look Mom, you now have somewhere to put out all your rooster collection." Glory May was speaking to her mom as she looked up toward the ceiling.

Ms. Barnes remembered as she turned, there were the shelves

her grandfather had made for his wife on which to set <u>her</u> collection. "I hope there is room for mine," she thought as they both entered the doorway to the living room again. "Okay, Glory May, upstairs. We both will sleep in the twin bedroom tonight. Then tomorrow we will start exploring the rest of the house and find just the right room for you to call your own."

Glory May pulled the large suitcase up the stairs and over to one side of the bed. This bag had her Game-Boy, laptop computer and some other technology game machines tucked in one side pocket.

Ms. Barnes looked at her and said, "Oh, no, you were too tired to stay up and check out the house, so off to bed with you. No Game-Boy tonight! Get the clothes you need and lights out."

"Lights out, Mom? You promised!" Glory May pleaded.

Ms. Barnes walked across the room to a nightlight in one corner by the dressing table. "I think with the lights on downstairs this will be enough up here. I have a flashlight if you need to go the bathroom in the middle of the night. Tomorrow I will find out what we need to fix the lights. Maybe it is just the bulbs. We will see."

Glory May did not want to change clothes. She did not feel safe in their new home and had completely forgotten about the bath. She laid down across the bed. Ms. Barnes came over unfolded the quilted bedspread to show the dancing bears sheets beneath. Glory May looked at her mom saying, "I can't wait to get my things out of the van and into a real room."

Glory May no more than laid her head on the pillow when she was out like the lights within this old house. Ms. Barnes gave her daughter a kiss on the forehead and stepped toward the door. Leaving the door open, Ms. Barnes went back downstairs.

Chapter 3

IN THE LIVING ROOM, Ms. Barnes walked around remembering when each picture had been taken. The pictures lined the walls and were on the piano and the mantel above the fireplace. Each had been taken over the course of her childhood during the times that she visited with her grandparents. She had so many wonderful memories of the neighborhood full of children her age. Grandmother was always inviting someone over for a tea party. This gave her grandmother a reason to bake her wonderful peanut butter cookies with chocolate kisses in the center of each one. Ms. Barnes remembered how the children would dress up in their grownup clothes and sit around the table by the piano as Grandmother would play tunes while they drank their tea and ate the warm cookies straight from the oven.

Ms. Barnes walked over and sat down on the sofa. She laid back thinking of how she wished Glory May could have had the chance to get to know her grandparents. Glory May's dad would not let them come to visit. He always wanted Glory May in the city with him and Ms. Barnes was not going to leave Glory May.

Things were very hard in the big city. Glory May's dad was not one of the most liked men in town. Well known, yes, but he was not the uptown business respectable person you would want to bring home to meet the grandparents. Her mom and dad hated him for taking their daughter to the city and away from the farm life. Several times, before moving to the city, they wanted her to leave him. She just couldn't, she loved him, and they didn't understand that he loved her and the children. He was constantly trying to give them a better life. Therefore, she stayed year after year after year.

Ms. Barnes drifted back remembering the day his busy business life came knocking at their door. The police wanted to see him then placed him in hand cuffs in front of Glory May. What was she to tell their children? Their daddy was going away! His business lifestyle had caught up with him. Now they were going to take him far away and let all his candy-coated friends go free. Weeks of the trial went by listening to one business person after another who had testified to say "they were an associate, a link or had some kind of connection to him." They were there to put the man she had loved and the father of her children away for years to come. What will she tell their friends, their family and their children? "My husband's a prisoner for something he didn't do" - like they would believe that one.

Now it's like a bad dream. She spent a year and a half of going from one jail to another, weekend after weekend to visit with him for two short hours each time. Everyone kept asking how she was going to do this for twenty years. Yet, she was determined to try because she loved him. Even with all the bad things they said he did, he had a soft touch about him that made her love him. Laying on the sofa she remembered the afternoon she had received a letter from the state prison department. Her husband was being moved again to another prison farther away. Over the last nineteen months, she kept hoping he would be transferred closer to home to help with the driving time. But, it did not happen. She read the letter with an enclosed map with directions to the new jail. They moved him again, she thought. She studied the map and directions. It would take eight hours driving non-stop to get to the new location. She would leave Glory May with her mom and dad. Glory May did not want to see her father. She had been mad at him for leaving her. As the time got longer, she got madder. So, Ms. Barnes traveled alone for a husband and wife visitation of one hour at this new jail location. She had to go through several minutes, which seemed like hours of new security procedures and added rules, and the total humiliation of a strip search just to be able to see her husband.

She watched the families seated in the courtyard with barbwire wrapping the yard in so many different directions she couldn't see straight. She waited for her husband to come through the gate. Finally, she spotted him coming escorted out by a guard. He looked weathered and tired. He sat down opposite her, facing her. About ten minutes into the visit, she knew something was on his mind. He didn't seem himself. She reached for his arm, he looked at her and said, "DON'T! Do not come back here again. I want a divorce. This is not the life, I want for you and the children. DON'T come back!"

Her heart dropped. Her whole life has been wrapped up in this man. She believed every word of his innocence. Now after nineteen months of visiting every weekend the different hell holes he had been transferred to – <u>he</u> wanted a divorce! Not one weekend had she missed, never once complaining to him about the trips, or putting their lives on hold and <u>he</u> was saying divorce?! What was he thinking? She needed to hear "Glad to see you, I love you." Something! Maybe "How's Glory May?" "How are the boys?" Something!? Anything! But this!

He only said, "Good-bye" touching her forehead with the tips of his fingers as he stood and moved toward the guard. He spoke a word or two to the guard who was dressed in a dark shirt with a badge on his chest and matching pants with an orange stripe running down the outside legs. Her husband walked through the door disappearing from her sight for the last time.

Ms. Barnes laid back against the sofa arm thinking, hurting, and remembering the disappointment… like it was just today. She felt totally destroyed when she walked toward the guard there on the opposite side of courtyard where smiling families entered. The devastation of the nightmare of collecting her personal things from the guard so she could leave as she exited the door came flooding back to her. She remembered walking - no, running - to the car with tears flooding her face.

Somewhere on the journey home to Glory May she lost all caring about anything. She stopped by a roadside restaurant (truck stop) when she saw a sign *"Happy Hour Some Where"* as the light was blinking off and on to light up the darkest of nights. She stopped the car, got out, and made her way inside. She sat down beside a truck driver sitting on a barstool near the far side of the room. She saw the only empty seat in the very crowded room.

He introduced himself. "My name is Kenny. You look like you need a drink lady. Your name?" he asked.

She just sat there. Over an hour later, finally Kenny said, "Hey, lady, really are you okay?" She sat there with his ordered drink in front of her she had not touched. Closing time came about 4am. She was still seated in the same spot as she stared at her reflection in the glass. Her hands gripped the glass waiting for someone to take it away from her. The owner asked, "Lady, do I need to call someone? Can we help you?"

No reply! Kenny was still there. She was not sure why. But the owner said for the last time, "Lady, we are closing. You need to go!" Kenny asked if they would make several sandwiches for the road before they closed. He would even pay extra for them. The waiter made ham and cheese sandwiches since their grill had already been cleaned. They gave Kenny a bag of chips and some soft drinks to go. Kenny helped her out the door toward the car. Three days later, she was still with Kenny.

Mary laid there remembering and she started to cry. She was ashamed of what she let happen to her. Gasping, she was fighting to stop the tears that rolled down her cheeks. She shivered as she tried to stop the tears. Telling herself today is a better day. I will never leave Glory May again. I must be the strong one now. She leaned over to reach for another one of Grandmother's knitted blankets and curled into a ball on the red and green plaid sofa.

Chapter 4

THE NEXT MORNING…. MS. Barnes awakened to the sunrise shining through the living room picture window into her eyes. In the distance, she could hear a neighbor's rooster. In her mind, she thought he was saying, "come on sleepy head, it's time to get started with a new day."

She looked around the room thankful she had only had a bad dream. It's okay - she was safe now. But Glory May? She jumped to her feet and ran to the top of the stairs. Yes! She stopped at the bedroom door where Glory May was still sound asleep.

Mary went into the bathroom and washed her face. She found a comb in the cabinet above the sink and combed her hair. Looking into the mirror she saw the lines around her eyes. The crow's feet gave her the wrinkles of old age and the puffy eyes were from crying herself to sleep. She wiped her face again pressing the cold wash cloth to her swollen eye lids one at a time and looking around the large room. Mary didn't remember this room being this way. It must have been changed over the years when she was not visiting her grandparents.

She backed out the door and started down the stairs again. Once back in the living room she walked around to fold the knit blanket and placed it back on the sofa. She walked toward the kitchen thinking she would need items from the store. She had better make a list. She checked the cabinets, refrigerator and the closet (that her grandparents always called "the pantry"). Mary made a list of groceries, remembering she needed light bulbs. She walked over to check the light fixtures hanging on the wall by the kitchen table in between the windows. They hung like lanterns on large brass & copper rods. There were two more fixtures hanging on each side of the stove just like the ones by the windows. Mary was remembering that her grandmother liked a lot of lighting in her kitchen because she would sometimes cook (bake mostly) until very late hours of the night. Grandfather didn't mind - he knew that breakfast would always have something special the next morning. To his surprise, it would always still be warm.

While checking out the kitchen she came across the coffee pot and luckily, in the pantry, she remembered seeing a can of coffee. She started the pot. The smell of fresh coffee brought back the wonderful memories she had of the kitchen. She took a cup and saucer from the cabinet and placed it by the coffee pot. She was not very patient waiting for that first cup. The coffee ran from the dripper over the counter as she tired to pour that first cup. "Jesus," she said out loud.

"You know it's not one of those instant stop drippers that you are possibly used to operating?" She turned around quickly to see Erik standing in the doorway. "I thought I was going to beat you to the punch! I was going to have coffee and some breakfast ready when you woke up this morning."

"*Erik,*" she dropped the pot running into his arms and giving him the biggest welcome hug - not even he was expecting. She stopped as quickly as the hug began. "I'm sorry," she replied. "I did not mean to do that."

Erik was okay with it. As kids, they had given each other many hugs. In addition, around this part of the country that's how you welcome friends into your home.

He went to the sink cabinet for a rag to clean up the coffee and coffee grounds off the counter. He bent down, picked up the broken glass pot, and cleaned the coffee off the floor.

"Jesus," Mary remarked again.

Erik looked at her and said, "You really need to find a new line, Mary Ann Barnes."

She was surprised at his remark, but understood. She really did need to correct some of her language. The last several months had just seemed to bring out the very worst in her. She expressed regret for the statement. He changed the subject to "well, what about that cup of coffee?"

"What now?" she said. It did smell good.

Erik had a bag in his hands when she stopped him short with the greeting. She was so surprised to see him she did not notice the bag. He had set it down on the floor by the kitchen sink cabinet as he went for the rag to clean up the coffee mess. He picked up the bag and said, "It's under control, sit down and enjoy your first day back. Welcome home, Blondie."

"It was you that left the note yesterday."

He could not lie. When he found out that Mary was coming back, his heart raced. He always had a very strong feeling for Mary. But never had he said anything to anyone about his feelings. He wanted to remain her friend knowing the one thing to break a friendship is making it a relationship. He always told her, "Friends Forever." When she got married and never came back to visit the farm, he thought he had lost his friend. The only time he heard from her was those special greeting cards (birthdays, Easter, Thanksgiving, Christmas, New Years, etc.). It was the same every time: 'How's the family? We are doing fine.' But he was always able to read in between the lines (that things were hard) even if she didn't say so on paper.

Both of them had things to celebrate and there was no better way than with a new coffee pot ready to set up. He took it out of the box and the wrapper and set up the pot on the counter. The smell of fresh coffee was flowing through the kitchen again in minutes. When the coffee was ready, Erik took two cups and matching saucers from the cabinet and filled them both. He pulled from his bag a small container of creamer. He asked, "Want to go out on the porch?"

Mary who had not been outside yet this morning answered, "The weather - is it chilly?"

"No," he replied. "It's beautiful, come on." They took their cups and out the door they went. "Sorry, we will need to sit on the porch stairs. I put away all the porch furniture before the snow sets in. But I can bring several pieces out of the basement if you like."

Mary said, "We'll see" (meaning she'd think about it). "Maybe later - just let me enjoy the morning and my visit with an old friend."

Erik had a small smile on his face. "How's the coffee? Not too strong I hope?"

"No" replied Mary. "It's just fine and thanks."

Erik wanted to ask a million questions, but knew the time was not right. So, he bit his tongue until he could taste his own blood in the next sip of the coffee.

"So, you think you could help with some of the tender loving care repairs this place needs?" Mary asked.

"Oh, I think it could be arranged for maybe an evening dinner or something," he replied.

"Good. I mean I'll pay you."

"You will not. Having you home will be payment enough. Your friends have missed you," he replied. Erik went on to say he wanted to do something to keep the place from falling apart. "But the attorney's office would only let me stop by to check on water lines making sure nothing had broken, or make sure no fire had taken place or that no one had broken into the place. So, I'm sorry it looks run down."

"That's okay! Glory May and I will have it looking as good as new in no time."

"I bet you will! It will give us something to do." Erik returned to sipping his coffee. "Ready for a refill?" he asked.

He got up, and reached for her cup. She had missed the touch of someone helping to do just the small things, like refilling a coffee cup. He returned shortly with two refilled cups of coffee. "Here, My Dear, coffee…light on the creamer, no sugar."

Mary said, "You remembered?"

"Of course, I remembered. How many cups of coffee did we talk your grandmother into instead of her sweet tea?"

They laughed together. Mary felt the relief. Finally, she was sitting here on her own porch stairs and thinking she was home at last! Yes, it would need some work, but together Mary and Glory May would make it look like new. Well, maybe not new - the house did have its own touch of class with the country look. Mary wanted to keep as much of that as possible. The look gave it character.

The time went by so fast. Erik looked at his watch. It was going on 11AM. Where had the morning gone? Knowing she needed to get into town she told Erik she needed to go upstairs and wake Glory May. They stood up and turned to go inside. Glory May was standing in the doorway of the kitchen.

"Good morning, Sunshine," Erik said.

Glory May did not remember Erik. She was just a baby the last time Erik had seen her – well, she was maybe 3 or 4 years old. Now Erik saw a slim teenager in the doorway with blonde curls down past her shoulders. "You have grown into a beautiful young lady!"

She still did not reply back to Erik. "Mom, I need you."

"Glory May show your manners. Erik was talking to you." The teenage girl was not ready to wake up to see her mom talking to a man she did not remember. She turned and went into the house. On the counter she saw the bag and checked out what was inside.

"Mom, do we have time for breakfast before going into town? Or have you already been there?" Glory May shouted not going to the door to ask.

Mary replied, "Erik brought the bag," as she stepped inside with Erik behind her. "He's going to make breakfast while we get ready to go in to town. How's that for a welcome to our new home greeting?"

Glory May was not happy. She turned saying "Maybe I'll wait to eat later."

"Glory May, you are not going to start with me." Teenagers, she thought.

"Go on ladies, upstairs with both of you. Put on those pretty little painted faces you girls like. I can remember how your mom would not leave the house without her make-up. I always thought it was not needed. She was always the prettiest girl in town."

"Erik!" Mary turned to him, "You're NOT helping?"

"No?" he replied, "Okay, I think I remember where to find everything." Mary laughed as she and Glory May started upstairs.

Erik possibly remembered more about where things in the kitchen were than she did. She was always the one outside with grandfather instead of in the kitchen with grandmother.

Upstairs Glory May told her mom she was not feeling good about having Erik there. Mary told her daughter that they had grown up together. "We are like brother and sister. Please, try to get along with him."

Glory May promised her mom she would try. She gave her mom a big hug and sat down on the bed to play the Game-Boy.

"Come on Glory May. We have things to do," taking the Game-Boy from her and laying it on the dresser.

They got cleaned up. Mary put on a purple shirt and blue jeans. Glory May was trying to decide between a tan sweater or a pink shirt with gray cotton pants having a hole in one leg around the knee.

"I need to patch those pants," Mary told Glory May. But as for Glory May she liked the hole - it was the style. They took turns in the bath with the mirror over the sink. Both were acting like this was the only bathroom in the house. How did they know? They still had not explored the house.

They came back down stairs together. Erik had done a wonderful job with breakfast. Bacon, eggs-in-a-nest, and orange juice placed on the kitchen table with three place settings including the silverware placed just right on each side of the plates.

"Erik, you did good!" Mary said in a very thankful voice.

"More coffee?" Erik questioned as he started across the floor to pull out the chairs for both ladies. He knew that Mary would take more, but not sure about the true blonde sitting at the kitchen table.

Glory May did not reply so Erik refilled both his and Mary's cups and returned to table. He sat down and looked across the table at the two ladies in his presence. He was trying to hide a smile that was a dead give-away of what he was feeling.

"Did you know your mom has been called 'Blondie' since she was big enough to crawl?"

Glory May didn't seem to care. Breakfast was good she thought. She was hungry since she didn't eat before going to bed last night. She finished her plate and started to get up from the table.

"Glory May, where are your manners?"

"Sorry, Mom, can I go now? Thank you for breakfast. By the way I prefer to be called Glory." She removed herself from the table. She went to the kitchen window and looked out across the porch. "Did you see that raccoon this morning? Man was he big! He looked like he hasn't been hungry for a while."

Erik laughed, "That's Sneaky."

"Who?" Glory questioned.

"That's Sneaky. Your great grandmother fed her. I guess you could say she's a family pet."

"How did she get that name? A raccoon for a pet?"

"Your great grandmother named her. She would move so quietly and in such a sly way across the porch that Old Lady Barnes would say she acted like a person with a secret - underhanded meaning 'sneaky.' That is how she got her name."

"You mean if I feed her, she will come to me?"

"Yes, maybe but you are new to her so it may take some time."

Glory seemed happy to have a pet named "Sneaky."

Erik went on to let her know, "She won't be out until this evening. She likes to eat just before going to bed. Your great grandmother would say, "She made a better watch dog than most dogs."

Glory gave out a little scatter laugh. "Oh Mom, that's just great! Most families like dogs or cats for a pet. We have a raccoon. Does she bite?"

"No, she will make a lot of noise, but she's just nosey. Feed her and she goes away until the next day when she shows up for her next meal again."

"Why did she seem so upset with us being here last night?"

Erik told Glory, "She lives under the porch. You disturbed her sleep."

Glory thinking, "It's a she? Won't she have babies?"

Erik asked if they had checked out the rest of the house?

"No," Mary replied. "It was late when we got here. We were lucky to get several bags into the house and find the bedroom at the top of the stairs. I must get the bathroom light fixed today."

"What's wrong with the light?"

"Erik, if I knew, it would be fixed."

"Oh, that's right you are the outdoors person. Things about the house never seemed to be of any interest to you," he teased.

"Go ahead make fun!" Mary laughed.

Erik replied he had a toolbox in the truck. He would take a look at the light. First, he needed help with the dishes.

"No," Mary said as she rose from the table, "you made breakfast. I will take care of the dishes."

"Deal," he said. "I hate dishes."

By now, Glory was out on the porch. She walked around the house on the porch from front to back and back to front. Stopping by the kitchen door she told her mom she liked the porch. She disappeared again toward the back to the house. The fun and family memories of gathering on the porch made Mary smile again as she stood lost in thought.

Mary got the dishes washed and back in their place. She felt the need to check on Erik to see if he needed anything, but she had a bigger need to check on her daughter. She walked out on the porch and around to the back. She found Glory sitting in the old maple tree swing. Mary smiled. She didn't think the swing would still be there. Little did Glory know about country backyard swings, but glad to see that her daughter seemed to like it. The old maple tree was turning fall colors and a lot of the leaves had already fallen from the tree. Glory was kicking them about with her feet as she swung. Mary remembered how beautiful the mountainside was this time of year. She always loved the fall and spring with the color changes that gave the mountainside a touch of glamour across its fields. Both of Mary's favorite seasons had a character all their own. She was thinking how much she had missed for so many years.

"Now going on 1PM," Erik said coming out the back door of the house. "Ready for a ride to town?" he asked.

Glory jumped off the swing, thinking (as most teens) ready to go anywhere that meant possibly other teens.

Mary replied she would get her keys and handbag as she started across the porch going into the house by the same kitchen door she had come out of.

Mary locked the house. She asked Erik if there would be room for all three to go in the truck, since the van was not yet unloaded.

"Of course," was the reply with yet another one of his smiles. He proceeded around to the passenger side of truck to open the door for both while saying "Ladies, hop in." Mary could feel the passion rekindling within her.

Glory wanted to sit by the door. Mary slid across the seat sitting with her legs apart to give Erik room to change gears.

"Erik, have you ever had an automatic vehicle in your life?"

"Once," he replied. "Didn't like it, kept it two months and sold it. Anyway, I need the gears for the nursery hauling"

"The nursery is still in your family?"

"Yes, it's all mine now." Erik had all sisters. They got married moved away but, one moved back – Vivian. Together they kept the nursery going learning all he knew from his father, grandfather and great grandfather. "It's been in the family for four generations. With any lucky maybe my son will make it five."

"That's right, I read he came to live with you. How is that going?"

"Fine. He is working today."

Glory suggesting she had an interest in the conversation asked, "Could he go to town with us? How old is he?"

"He's just turned fifteen."

Glory was now interested. "Mom, can he go to town with us?" Unknown to Glory the shop for the nursery was in town.

Mary (thinking aloud) said she was looking forward to seeing him. It has been a long time since she had seen Erik's son. "I think he was maybe five the last time I was here."

"That's about right," Erik replied. "We will stop by the shop. If he's not out on a delivery, he will be there. We usually only stay open a half day on Saturdays and by the time we get cleaned up we are out by 2PM."

Glory was squirming in her seat. "What time is it, Mom?"

Chapter 5

THEY CAME TO THE edge of town and both ladies were a bundle of nerves. Mary was not sure who she would be running into or how they would react to her being back in town and staying this time. She hoped there wouldn't be many questions.

Glory's nerves were giving her goose bumps in the hopes of meeting others her age. She had already been told about starting school within the next week or two. It would help to know someone before entering the halls of a new school.

They passed the First National Bank, the US Post Office, a small home town movie theater, the Real Estate/Attorney's Office, a beauty salon shop, the antique shop, Amy's Grocery Store and finally the sign said "Erik's Florist & Nursery." Erik pulled into the back parking lot and turned off the engine to the truck.

"Ladies - coming in?" By the time Erik was around to the passenger side of the truck Glory was already out on both feet. He continued to the truck door, took Mary's hand and said, "Vivian is working here."

Mary thought, 'Well, I would run into her sooner or later. May as well be now!' These two ladies had a history of not being on the same page at the same time. But Mary was not going to let this spoil her homecoming. In addition, since Vivian was Erik's sister, she would try very hard to let bygones be bygones.

They walked to the door of the flower shop. Glory was already looking around inside. Of course, she did not see the young man behind the counter. He was on his knees when Glory entered through the back door of building.

When the bell on the back door rang another time as Mary and Erik entered, Erik's son stood up. He was nearly six feet tall, dark coal black hair, and slim like Glory. "You must be Mary Ann," he replied with his hand out to welcome her. "My name is Cliff."

Mary reached to shake his hand, put instead he kissed it. She said, "Yes, but you can call me Mary."

'Well,' she thought 'this is Erik's son.' Turning toward Erik she said, "Well taught."

Glory came out from behind a large tree standing in the middle of the room. Tripping over the smaller flower pots at the base of the tree she said, "My name is Glory."

The young man wasn't paying much attention to the slimmer blonde. He was more interested in the mess she was making on the floor he just finished cleaning so he could go home for day.

"Cliff, we are on our way to Frank's General Store. Are you about ready to close up? If so, you can go with us. It would give you and Glory a chance to get to know each other," Erik quipped teasingly.

Cliff was ready to get off work, but really not ready to get to know the new girl in town. "Dad, I have basketball."

"Sorry," Erik replied. "I did forget. We can do this another time. Get out of here. I will help Vivian close up the shop."

"Thanks, Dad. Nice to meet you, Mary. See you, Glory." And out the door Cliff went meeting up with several guys his age standing outside the shop.

Erik told Mary, "Cliff's team won 10-6 last season. Hoping they do even better this year."

Vivian came out of the storage cooler. She had been replacing some of the stock they had sold that day. "Erik, good see you. I was going to call you. Some of the flowers seem to be getting too cold in one side of the cooler."

Erik told his sister he would take a look. He disappeared around the corner of the room.

Vivian said "Hi" to Mary but didn't have too much to say past that. That was okay. She introduced her daughter and asked as Erik re-entered the room how far the general store was from them?

Erik replied, "Two buildings down."

Mary said, "We will meet you there, if that's alright?"

"That's fine. I won't be long!"

Mary and her daughter turned to walk out as Vivian said, "We'll get together soon."

"Sure - no problem" replied Mary as she pulled the door closed behind them.

Walking across the parking lot Glory sensed something was troubling her mom. "What is it, Mom?"

"Oh nothing, Glory. Everything is just fine."

She knew it wasn't - she knew her mom. She knew she would talk about it in her own time.

They arrived at the store. It was like a Lowes, Target, or Walmart with a large grocery store all in one. Glory came from the city, but this was nice. "Glory, please, stay with me," Mary announced to her daughter. "I do not have the patience or the time today to look for you."

Glory wanted to explore, but also knew they had a lot to do at the house before dark fell for yet another day. They got a cart and started up and down the rows. Glory checked off the items on the list. She called out the next item listed as she placed them in their cart.

About thirty minutes later Erik came into the store, found the two of them and apologized for taking longer than he meant to do.

"That's okay. We're still trying to find some of our items."

Erik asked if he could help find anything, since he knew the store layout very well. He went up and down the aisles with them.

Glory's interest was more focused on games. "Basketball games? When are they?"

Erik answered, "On Friday nights, we'll go sometime if you and your mom would like."

"Sure!!" she said. Mary just laughed.

Standing in the check-out line Mary saw her old friend, Maggie. Not sure if Maggie saw, Mary held out her hand waving.

Maggie came running over and hugged Mary. "You did make it! I was going to call or stop by the house tomorrow if I hadn't heard from you by then."

"We're here. We just needed a few things from the store to get moved in. We still need to unload the van. There just haven't been enough hours in this day."

Maggie said, "I'd be glad to come by tomorrow and help out if needed."

Mary said, "Let me see - I will call you."

"Okay, see you then. Glad you're here safely. And just in time I understand. The rain will be setting in over the next few days," Maggie replied.

'Tomorrow,' Mary thought, 'maybe tomorrow.'

"Mary Ann, what's on that pretty mean face of yours?" Erik asked.

"Tomorrow would have been Grandmother's birthday - October 1st."

"Of course! Well, we will make it a special day. We will celebrate her birthday and your return. We will fill the house with laughter once again!"

She looked up with a smile. "You always did know the right thing to say at the right time."

She paid for the items and they loaded the cart to take everything to the truck. Glory was surprised to see Cliff at the truck when they got there.

"What happen to the practice game, son?"

"Cancelled. The coach was sick. Practice's rescheduled for tomorrow unless it rains. Can I come with you guys?" asked Cliff.

"Sure," his dad replied. "We could use two additional strong arms."

Glory was very quiet on the way back to the house. The two teenagers rode in the back seat of the double cab truck. Of course, Mary and Erik didn't stop talking and laughing until Glory saw tears coming from her mom's eyes.

Cliff handed her some tissues from the box on the seat beside him saying, "You two are worse than two teenage girls gabbing."

"That's okay, son, we have a lot of catching up to do."

They turned the corner and pulled into the driveway. Glory sat up leaning on the back of her mom's seat. "Look Mom! We have company!"

"It's your Uncle Spence."

"Who, Mom?"

"Uncle Spence, Aunt Jenny's husband."

"Oh, your sister who came to visit us in the city? Right?" Glory questioned.

"Yes, they both did!"

"Great! I thought no one here would know…Mom?"

"It is okay, Glory."

They parked the truck and Erik walked around to get Mary's door, but this time she had beat him to it. "Spence! Good to see you!"

"Jennifer asked me to stop and see if you needed help unloading the van. Maggie told her you did, but she couldn't get out here to help until later next week."

"That's Maggie - already giving orders."

"That's fine, everything is good, Mary Ann. Now we have help!"

Erik replied. "The van will be unloaded in no time. Once everything is in, it will be easier for you to start putting things away. You ladies take in the groceries. The guys will start unloading the van. Come on team, let's get this train moving!"

Mary smiled and started up the stairs. Where was she going to put the items from the van? She hadn't checked out the rest of the house! Too late - things were starting to come in from the van. She opened the side door with a hallway running toward another back door that led to the back porch. To her right was another door. She opened it and said, "Guys, put it in here for now. Just put it in there for now," she replied a second time, stepping away from door to let the guys by with their arms loaded. No one turned on the lights to the room. The hallway was bright enough for the guys to see. Each time they entered or exited the room the guys were talking, laughing, and making small talk as they continued to unload the van.

Mary replied, "Everything is going in there for now. It will make it easier to unpack."

The guys answered, "No problem." Chuckling. Erik said, "It will make it easy for you to put your things away."

Neither Mary nor Glory went into the room that night. They were glad the van was unloaded. Spence had closed the door to the room and to the hallway. He went into the kitchen where the rest were standing around the kitchen counter talking and waiting on Mary who was pouring drinks for everyone.

Glory asked Cliff if he would like to go out on the porch.

"Sounds good. Come on."

The two teens went to the porch. By this time Sneaky was in the yard. "Look, we woke her up," Glory screamed. She went back inside to get Erik. "Show me how to feed her."

Erik was glad to help! He went to the refrigerator and pulled out a piece of lunch meat and some chips from the bag off the table.

"Come on! Let's go! Sneaky is waiting!" Glory squealed. Sneaky was on the far end of the porch by this time roaring and shying away from all the noise.

Erik leaned over bending down and said, "Come Sneaky, show your new owner what you can do!" Sneaky sat up on her back legs and clapped her two front paws together.

Glory just smiled afraid if she made any noise Sneaky would run away. Erik put a piece of the food in front of her. Sneaky came up to eat. When finished she was looking for more. Erik called Glory over beside him giving her a piece of the lunch meat. "This is her favorite."

Glory got on her knees and reached out with the meat in her hand. Sneaky took two steps backward. Glory said, "Come on, girl. I won't hurt you." Sneaky took two steps toward them and into Erik's hands. Sitting on Erik's knee Sneaky took the meat from Glory. She clapped her two front paws as if to say thanks after she had eaten it.

Erik handed the chips to Glory. One at a time Glory handed them to Sneaky. By the time last chip was handed out, the raccoon was in front of Glory wanting more.

Erik told Glory in the pantry there was some dog food. "Put a half cup into the small bowl sitting on the pantry floor under the shelf." Glory came back several minutes later with the bowl full of dog food. Erik thought it was more than half a cup, but for tonight that was good. Sneaky will know she can trust her new friend. Glory placed the bowl over to the back side of the porch, so the company would not scare Sneaky and she could eat.

Uncle Spence came out on the porch. "See you tomorrow Glory, Cliff and Erik. You look like you have your hands full."

"See you tomorrow, Spence. Thanks for helping to unload the van," Erik replied.

Glory was so happy with her new friend. Mary came to the door to say, "Come on in, Glory. Cliff and Erik will need to go soon, too." Erik knew this was his cue for them to pack up for the night.

"Okay, guys – let's call it a night!" Erik replied, ordering the two teens inside, laughing as they stepped inside and closed the door.

Glory helped clean up the kitchen counter. Her mom said, "You need to get yourself ready for bed."

"Bed, Mom?"

"Off with you now - it's late and tomorrow will be another day."

Erik was looking at his watch, "After 12 midnight. Where did the day go?" It was just several short hours ago he and Mary were sitting on the front porch having their morning coffee. Erik looked at his son and said, "Let's get you home, Son. It's late. You have practice in a few hours."

"What time is practice? Where?" Glory asked.

"Three o'clock at the school gym," said Cliff as he moved out the door.

"Good night."

Chapter 6

DAY 3...THE NEXT MORNING...

Mary woke up to the sound of the same rooster. 'Like clockwork same as yesterday,' she thought before opening her eyes. 'I won't need an alarm clock.' The sunshine wasn't coming in the window between the blinds this morning. She could tell it was going to be a damp cloudy morning. Remembering that Maggie had told her that it was going to rain, she had a little better feeling about the rain today. At least, now the van was unloaded so let it rain. She would check out the rest of the house today thinking there's no need for her to still sleep in the twin bed. Although she did like being close to Glory. She recalled the wonderful times that her sister, Jenny and she had when they slept over. They were just little girls each fighting over which bed they would have.

She rolled out of bed, went to the bathroom, brushed her teeth, combed her hair and washed her face. She leaned over the tub turning on the water. She let the water run, checking every few seconds for the temperature of the water. Mary thought, 'Still just luke warm? Warm...hmm - maybe a cup of coffee first' as she turned the water off.

Downstairs, she started the coffee in the new pot Erik was nice enough to bring with him yesterday. It's like he had ESP that she would break the old one. Still she thought how good to see him and have him spend the day with her and Glory.

Today she needed some time to herself she thought as she poured that first cup of coffee. Still in her nightgown she started for the door. Thinking it was so nice on the porch yesterday, she opened the door to dark clouds with a bite in the air. The wind had picked up and the clouds were roaring across the sky. She stepped back inside with a shiver thinking, 'maybe if I get my jacket, I could sit outside!' She sat down at the kitchen table looking out the window across the large open yard. In a daze she could see the kids from her past playing in the yard and the fun she had here. She wondered why had she left?"

Remembering, 'Oh, yes. I thought life was better on the other side of the fence. Little did I know! If only we could turn back the clock to reclaim time and a chance to start again.' She was embarrassed and ashamed of things she had let happen in her life. She sipped the last drop from the cup.

She got up to make another cup of coffee hoping she could make things better for Glory here. She knew it would be very different from the way things were done in the city. Maybe with new friends and family Glory could just be a kid. She shook her head embarrassed by what she had let happen to her little girl.

The city had taken the little girl from Glory. Who was she fooling? The kid, the little girl, she was looking for was the one she had lost inside herself as well.

Leaning over the kitchen counter, she drew a picture of the inside of the house in her mind. Was she ready today to explore the rest of house with so many little memories adding to her thoughts? The house needs flowers. Grandmother always had green plants. Next time she's in town, she'll get some from Erik's shop.

'Erik,' she thought reminding herself of him standing at the doorway yesterday morning. There was a rough look about him (a touch of gray to his dark black hair, flannel shirt with the sleeves rolled half way up, and shirt just tight enough the show off the muscles in his arms). She laughed thinking about the bib overalls like grandfather would wear. She laughed again picturing her dear friend, Erik! He has been through a lot himself. He got married several years after Mary had moved away. Her name was Nora and somewhat older than Erik. Nora was an undercover cop which put her into extremely dangerous spots in the line of duty. They met when Erik was training to be a cop. She remembered how upset his dad was to find out he didn't want to run the family business. Nora and Erik dated just a short time before announcing their marriage. Seven months later Cliff's sister was born. Mary never questioned his love for her – she was just happy he had someone. Cliff was from Nora's first marriage. She went back to work about two months after the new one was born. Grandmother told her Nora had been shot while driving down Lake Belmont Road causing her car to go over an embankment. Their daughter, Amy, was in the car with her at the time and died at the scene. Nora was in the hospital. Weeks went by with Erik at his wife's side before she passed. Having a son to take care of Erik quit the force and returned home hoping his parents would help out with Cliff. Later Erik adopted Cliff to give him his name. Erik is the only father Cliff has ever known. His parents were very proud of him. He went back to work with his dad and took over the business of the nursery and flower shop when his parents passed away. Now look at his son - almost a grown man she thought. Where have the years gone?

Glory was standing in the kitchen doorway. "Mom, are you okay?"

"Sure, Honey. Why do you ask?"

"You just seem to be far away."

"No, Child – I'm right here in our beautiful old house. Can I get you something?"

"I'm okay," she said as she opened the refrigerator door, took out the OJ and turned the carton up for a drink.

"No ma'am! Get yourself a glass!"

"MOM!!" Stopped short as the phone rang and Glory ran to the wall phone. "Hello." It was Cliff.

"Hi, is Ms. Barnes there?" Glory handed the phone to her mom not realizing it was Cliff.

"Hello," Mary said.

"Hi, Ms. Barnes. I was wondering if it would be okay for Glory to go with me today. She seemed to have an interest in the basketball game practice."

Mary laughed to herself. She knew her daughter's interest and it wasn't the game. "I'll check with Glory. Can I call you back in a few minutes? What time would this take place? Okay - I'll give you a call." She hung up the phone.

Glory (thinking it had been Erik) went about checking out the refrigerator.

"Cliff wants to know if you would like to go to the practice game with him."

"SURE!" Glory's eyes lit up like lights on a Christmas tree. "He's cute! Don't you think so, Mom?" as she poured the OJ into a glass.

"Why don't you call him back and let him know you'd like to go? But Glory, first tune down 'the excitement' before calling," Mary said.

Good - this would give Mary some time to check out the house and get some of their things put away. She thought about the beautiful rooster collection that Glory had given her over the years. The set of four paintings proudly displayed the birds in magnificent full colors on a crackle finished canvas. Each 8" by 10" picture was attractively finished with a raised textured border. Mary looked around the kitchen trying to decide where she would hang them to best show them off.

Glory ran to the phone not waiting one more minute for Cliff to change his mind about taking her along. She hung up the phone saying, "Erik will pick us up."

"No, no, I am not going to the practice game! I need to get things done around here! Maybe I will take in a Friday night game or two, but not today."

"Should I call back and let them know Mom?"

"No, I will call Erik" thinking it gave her a reason to talk to her friend.

"Want to check out the house with me, Glory?"

"Sure, Mom. What were the guys laughing about last night when they were carrying our things in and putting them in the other room? I didn't even know there were other rooms back there."

"Glory, I did but we got in late and yesterday went by so fast. I really do need to show you the whole house. Come on! Let's do it." Not wasting another minute, they walked around the corner of the kitchen toward the living room. The hall door was closed. It looked like another closet from the view of the living room. Mary opened the door revealing a hallway that ran to the far back end of house. It led to the other back door going outside to the back of house where the maple tree swing hung. Standing at the back door looking at the swing, they turned around. There were two doors to the left of it. One had a little wooden plaque hung on it with the words 'my playroom.' The other had a knitted plaque with the words 'Things that go in must go out.' Which one would they dare to open first? "Great Grandmother always had a way with words and loved to do crafts," said Mary.

Opening the door with the knitted plaque, they found a large bathroom done in three shades of blues. The wallpaper had large fluffy clouds with colors of blues and white. An old white bathtub big enough for three people stood on four claw foot legs with a shower curtain wrapped around it like a blanket. A large dressing table with shelves was built into wall like a cabinet. A small wall maybe 4 feet in height divided the room to give someone their private moment with another knitted sign hanging eye level of an outhouse with the words 'Goodbye things' written under it. Mary with a smile on her face walked toward the door to see the next room.

"Mom, we have two bathrooms. That's cool."

Glory beat her mom to the next door now excited about seeing the rest of house. They opened the door where the guys had put their things last night and no one said a word about the room. It took both ladies by complete surprise. They entered the large room which was supposed to be a bedroom. There was the most beautiful carousel they had ever seen - a full-size carousel with hand painted horses and two seated carts! It was breath taking. Mary remembered there had been one in the back yard when they were kids, but over the years she thought it had been destroyed. What she didn't know was her Grandmother's love for her husband's work encouraged her to have moved it indoors. There she could enjoy it when the weather was bad or her sickness worsened. What a sight for sore eyes. Mary went over and turned on the wall light to get a closer look at the details of the hand painted horses. The lights came on and the carousel came to life. It turned around in the room like the room had been made for it. Up and down the horses went. The music played a calm tune to their ears. Both were laughing as they placed themselves on horses and went around and round, up and down.

"Happy Birthday, Grandmother," Mary said. She was thankful the guys had not said a word when they placed their things carefully around to one side not to disturb anything. Neither of them wanted to leave the room when someone was at the back door knocking.

Chapter 7

MARY WENT OUT TO see who it could be? It was Spence. She opened the door with a smile.

"Just checking to see if you would like to go to church with us today. If so, the service starts at 10 o'clock."

Mary asked him in – she was full of questions about their new found surprise.

"Well," Spence replied, "a cup of coffee would be nice."

"Sure, come to the kitchen. They passed the open door.

He said, "I see you found your Grandma's weakness."

"Spence, I had no idea she had kept the carousel. When I didn't see it in the back yard, I thought…"

"I know we were so taken aback when she hired two men to carefully take it apart and had them put it back together inside the house. Once it was inside, she started repainting it. With each stroke of her brush she had a story to tell us and we thought it gave her something to do.

"It's beautiful," Mary said admiringly.

Spence continued, "She would spend most of her time in there. She would say that your grandfather was there enjoying the day with her."

"How I wish I could have been here," Mary said with a sadness overcoming her. Grandmother seemed alone when they would talk on the phone. Even with the miles between them, Mary could always talk to both of her grandparents about anything – school, boys, the birds and bees - you know anything. She couldn't do that with her mom or dad. They were too different and too quick to judge before listening to the whole truth. When things got bad with her marriage, she wished she had her grandmother around to just give a listening ear.

Spence interrupted her thought, "Well, what will you do with the carousel now?"

"Oh, it will stay right where it is. It's so pretty and has too many family ties to move it."

"Old Lady Barnes had the electrician rewire that room. They had to put another panel in just for that room so it didn't trip the breakers. I think they marked the panel box for you."

"Thanks, I'll check it out later. How's the coffee?"

"Fine, thanks. There was a chill in the air this morning. You can tell the rain is on its way. Clouds are setting in. Don't think we will see the sun at all today. Well, I need to get home and clean up for church. I was out checking on the horses and thought I'd stop since I was coming right past here."

"Are you using some of the land, Spence?"

"The far south side pasture fields were tall and I thought no one would mind."

"That's fine. I haven't thought much about how I am going to use it yet."

"You are lucky the Barnes left the farm to you. Jenny and I were afraid they'd sell it and possibly even to a developer who would tear down the house and barn. We're glad you're here."

"Thanks, Spence. I wasn't sure how Jenny would feel."

"She'll be okay. She wanted to buy it, but the attorney said it wasn't for sale. That upset her at first, but she'll be fine."

"Good! You and the family are welcome anytime. We can work

out something with the pasture fields if you need more."

"Sounds good, Mary. Thanks! Well, sure you wouldn't like to go to church?"

"I'm sure. I want to get unpacked. Next week I need to get Glory in school and find work. Playtime is about over." She walked Spence to the back door. "Tell Jenny to stop by real soon. Bye." She closed the door as Spence left the porch by the rear stairs and down the brick path towards his truck parked at the barn.

Back inside Glory had found a box of china dishes. In one corner of the room was a card table set up with four place settings and dolls dressed up with beautiful handmade dresses, knitted hats, and gloves all starched. "Look, Mom, I think their faces and fingernails are hand painted."

Mary walked closer - yes, she remembered the dolls. These were her mom's when she was a little girl. I remember Mom telling me how each one had been purchased over the years from where ever her father had been stationed in the Army. Each visit home he would bring her another doll and Grandmother would make outfits for each one of them to have a change of clothes.

"Mom, this room - it's so special. I bet I'll be the only one at school with a carousel inside their house. I bet people thought Great Grandmother was a little nutty."

"She was in her own sweet way, Glory. I wish you could have known her!" Mary could see the little girl in Glory that she thought was lost forever.

Chapter 8

AGAIN, THERE WAS A knock at the door. This time it was Erik and Cliff. Both ladies still were not dressed.

"Erik, I wasn't expecting you until later."

"I know. I need to go into Winchester and I was wondering if you wanted to ride along to keep me company. I spoke with Frank, so we can leave the teens with him until it's time for the game and he will make sure they stay with them until we get back."

"Oh, Erik. I was going to…"

"That's okay - the unpacking will still be here. Winchester may have some newspapers with job classifieds. You said you would be needing work. Plus, I need the new issue of Home & Gardens. Everywhere around here that sells it, has sold out. This month's ad is about installing a new water system for nurseries to reuse pot water and the filtering system. Come on. It will give us a chance to eat out. Maybe we can take in a show or something."

"How late do you think we'll be?"

"Not late I promise."

"Okay - how long do I have to get ready?"

"You get one hour, Missy!" He tapped his hand on his watch and then on his legs as he went to the door saying, "I'll be back!"

Cliff threw his hand in the air, too and said, "See ya!"

Upstairs the two ladies just did not know what to do - excited to get out, but knowing there was a lot around the house that needed to be done. They both needed to take baths, wash their hair, put on make-up, choose what clothes to wear, etc.

Mary told Glory to use the upstairs bath and she would get their clothes together and use the downstairs bath. That way both could be ready about the same time.

The hour went by faster than the ladies would have liked, but both were ready when Erik and Cliff returned.

Cliff came to the door. "Ready? Dad's in a hurry." Both ladies went out closing the door behind them.

Erik standing by the open door of truck said, "Ladies." Glory got in the backseat with Cliff. Mary was standing in front of Erik noticing his blue eyes had a sparkle in them.

"Get in!" he said. "Please! I have something to do." Closing the door, he went around, got in the truck, fastened his seat belt and started the engine. They could hear the train in the distance coming down the track. When they got to the crossing, the four-way flasher was on and the crossing gate was down across the road. Erik sat tapping his foot on the floorboard. He didn't have too much to say at this moment. But he was bouncing in his seat like he had ants in his pants.

"Erik, won't you talk me? What's going on?"

"What do you mean?"

"Erik, you're acting like a boy waiting for the Christmas box to be opened to see the surprise."

"No - I'm fine."

"I know you're fine, but what's going on?"

He remained successfully mysterious as they drove toward town. Entering Main Street, he turned into the parking lot of the only fire station for fifteen miles.

"I need to check on something. Come with me, Mary?" Talking as he jumped out and opened her door, he reached for her hand.

"Erik, you are making me crazy. Why don't we just wait for you?"

"No! Come on - it will only take a minute. Come on, kids. I'm sure you want to see the new fire truck mascot 'Lucky.'

"Who's Lucky?" Glory asked.

"He is the fire station dog. He was found last year in a burning house and the fire station adopted him."

"Really!"

"Glory, we don't need a dog." The teens ran off toward the front door. Mary found it easier to go in rather than trying to stay in the truck. She jumped down and said, "I don't see the big deal."

Inside Lucky, a shaggy haired black and white sheep dog, was sitting by the door. Cliff and Glory were standing beside him when Erik and Mary entered. The room came to life with balloons falling from the ceiling, lights and music. A banner hung across one end of the large hall said "Welcome Home Blondie." She started to cry. No one had given any good positive attention to her in a very long time. Not since Kenny, she thought. She had to shake this feeling. She couldn't believe how many people were here and no cars, trucks, or vehicles out on the parking lot to give it away.

"Erik! I knew something was up!"

He laughed. "I never was one to keep a successful secret… until now," he replied.

"You!" as she hit him on the shoulder.

"Come on - let's join the party," Erik said as he reached for her arm. She walked past the seated people saying 'thank you' as she went down the aisle toward tables set up on both sides - one side with homemade foods of all kinds and the other with gifts for a new home with name tags saying, "Welcome back". A large certificate said **"We owe you one repaired barn."** Mary looked up trying to hold back the tears. She knew the repairs to the barn were going to be more than she could afford and now Frank from The General Store is donating all the materials. The guys and their wives have agreed to put the needed man hours into fixing the barn.

"You guys are so great! What a wonderful welcome home gift! Thanks to all of you!" Mary said aloud.

The teens were not that enthused with the gifts because it meant only work to them. So, they ate and both looked at the clock. "Dad we need to get to the school for practice."

"Okay son, do you need me to take you or you want to walk since it's not raining?" questioned Erik.

Glory was about to ask if they could walk when Cliff said, "We'll walk, Dad. It will give me time to stretch my legs."

"Okay - then Frank will take the two of you back to his house after practice until Mary Ann and I return from Winchester."

"Okay Dad. See ya! Bye, Mary."

"Bye, Mom!" and out the door ran the teens.

Several of the parents needed to leave the party to take their children to the practice game. So, the party was coming to an end.

Erik told Mary their day was not over yet. She wasn't sure what would happen next. She couldn't eat another thing so it wasn't going to be dinner out.

They helped clean up and again continued to thank all the friends. Erik loaded the truck with the gifts and out the door they went.

Chapter 9

ERIK TOOK A DIRT road that led out of town. She didn't remember the road. "Erik, where are we going?"

"You will see."

Not another surprise, she thought. Erik took more care in driving slower this time. They came to a sign saying "Perryville's Octoberfest." Erik turned in the direction of the arrow and continued driving.

"We're going to the Octoberfest?"

"Sure, why not." It's about 10 minutes from here."

"I thought you needed to go to Winchester?"

"Oh, maybe tomorrow!"

The clouds were setting in again for another rain. "Let's hope the rain will hold off just a little longer. Come, My Lady," he whispered as he parked the truck, got out and opened her door. The backseat was full of gifts. "Better lock the truck," he replied. He also grabbed a hip-length rain jacket from behind the seat.

The Octoberfest was in full swing when they arrived. The activities placed them right at the base of the mountain. You could see the twisting road from the base climbing to the top and disappearing to the other side. There were small one room buildings with different activities going on in each. There were hand blown glass items and jewelry stands with things made from leather, silver, beads and even something they called gold. Another building held handmade quilted blankets and knitted items. Another with a wooden stand covered by plastic to protect from the weather was selling items made from leather: jackets, boots, and lots of riding equipment, like saddles, etc. Mary's random looks caught Erik's eye as she pointed at some young girls with runny noses making sand angels in the sand boxes and covering themselves with the sand. She was thinking where are their mother? There was a small spring-fed creek running freely out of the side of the mountain flowing down over the smooth limestone rock wall to a small foot bridge, being used as a crossing for a walkway. At the end of the walkway was a stand set up with cups being used to get a drink of the cold spring water running out of a pipe about waist high from the side of the rock wall. A wishing well was to one side of the creek with lots of quarters in the bottom of the fountain. Lots of wishes had been made today as the wishers tried to make the center holder. Erik stopped, handed Mary a quarter and said, "Go ahead. Make a wish." He held his hand out with another quarter and aimed for the center holder as he let loose, dropping it into the well. "Your turn," he said. She threw the coin and it landed in the center of the fountain. A bell rang notifying the keeper who yelled "We have a winner!" The group chapped and made a big deal. They saw a young couple sculpting a pumpkin. A mother was snapping her fingers at a young girl who was kissing a boy. Erik turned to Mary giving her a light kiss on the chin and moving on without saying a word and smiling to himself.

There was a breeze that had picked up. The fall winds blew the mountain trees making them play a majestic tune with the help of the whispering leaves. They wandered from display to display, stopping at the different event stands and the one-room cabins to take a look at the items. Erik bought two coffees at the food stand and put his jacket around Mary's shoulders as the rain started to come down. They found cover under one of the building's overhangs where the roof-over had made a small porch area. Standing out of the rain they watched a judge take a tape measure to a fish while a small boy watched hoping that he had the winner for "The Fishing Trophy."

Erik asked, "Are you getting cold or wet? Do you want to go?"

She replied honestly, "It's been fun," then braved a look into his eyes, adding, "and I've had a wonderful day."

"Me too," he replied.

For a moment she thought he was going to kiss her. Her heart already fluttering greedily in her throat, she suddenly didn't trust her own common sense. So, she put on a painful expression and informed him, "It's so damn cold there's no feeling left in my feet and hands." She was right, the rain had added a colder chill in the air not to mention the wind.

In a teasing secretive way he leaned over and asked "How 'bout the nipples? They cold too?"

"None of your business, you dirty old letch."

He leaned over giving her a suggestive head to toe scan and grinned. "Like hell it isn't! Doesn't hurt to wish!" he replied.

She was surprised. Erik had never ever come on strong before. He stroked her temple with the tips of his fingers. Her heart missed a beat. Nevertheless, he only wished to remove a piece of her hair from her eyes so he could see them better. Then he kissed the end of her cold nose and bundled her under his arms. "Come on - let's get you home."

She listened to the crunch of his footsteps across the gravels in the parking area as they came around the back of the truck. A moment later the truck door opened and she climbed in. The truck was very silent on the way back to Mary's house. How was the evening going to end? She had a wonderful day. She didn't want it to end, but how could she invite him in after... she stopped herself... her thoughts were running out of control.

To her surprise that was not what Erik had in mind. He liked and enjoyed having fun with Mary but he was not going to lose control of their friendship. He would not let that happen.

When they got to Mary's house, Erik didn't turn off the engine to the truck. Instead he parked, got out, and came around to open her door. She was already out before he could get there. She told him she needed to get Glory's bedroom in order so she was not going to invite him in.

Erik looked into her eyes and said, "I wasn't coming in. I'm going to pick up the kids and we will be back, if that's okay."

"Fine!" She walked toward the house wondering if he was mad?

Chapter 10

MARY CLIMBED THE STEPS up to the porch to find Sneaky ready to greet her standing on her back legs clapping her front paws. "Oh, I see. You want me to feed you, do you?" She went into the house. Several minutes later she came out with two bowls - one of dog food and a piece of lunch meat. In the other bowl was water. She sat it down on the porch saying, "Come on. I don't mind. If Grandmother could do it, so can I."

Going back inside she took off Erik's jacket and laid it across the kitchen chair. Thinking she had made him mad but knowing she could not get involved with someone else and definitely not ERIK. They were too... (her thoughts were interrupted by the phone ringing). It was Erik. Frank had taken the teens for pizza so it would be a while before they would be back.

She said, "Fine. See you later then" and hung up the phone.

She went to the living room, turned on the TV and sat down in the rocker. Not really looking at the TV she was daydreaming. Something came on the news that caught her eye. It was about a man turning state's evidence in a drug case. She stared at the picture. It made her turn green, cold, weak in the knees and sick to her stomach - it was her ex-husband Jack! She tried to stand, knees weak, she sat back down in the chair. Her thoughts were what was he thinking? She and the state attorney's office wanted him to turn state's evidence for a shorter sentence or even the witness protection program when he was on trial. He refused. He took the heat for others that should have also fallen. He let the big shots place all responsibility of the events on him. Her emotions ran wild for the man she loved, her soul mate, friend, and the hate for deserting her when she had stood beside him. The hell they put her and the family through time after time during the months of trial that left her husbandless and her children fatherless. She ran to the sink sick to her stomach. She bent her head into the sink crying at the same time. She couldn't control the anger she was feeling. "I hate you!" she screamed remembering all the terrible visits to the hell holes they called jails. Recalling how with each visit she saw the man she loved become weak and wrinkle faced. Once in the prime of his life, her teddy bear was the guy that others were afraid of because of his size with big muscles, broad shoulders, standing 6'4" with brown short curls and a well-groomed mustache to match. "I did love you so!" she cried. "How will I ever get over you?" She tried to control her feelings, the love of life and the hate that grew inside her all at the same time. It had been hard - the lonely nights giving all the energy to Glory, trying to keep them safe after the trouble she had been through, maintaining their household, and teaching Glory not too hate anymore. Now look at her - she couldn't control herself. She finally made her way into Grandmother's room. She turned on the wall light and the room came to life as she was still wiping the tears. She sat down in one of the carriages and drifted into another world just like when she was a child. Her thoughts drifted to being in the yard with Grandfather working on the carousel carving on the horse designs and her sitting in the maple tree swing. She felt free like she was swinging higher and higher, until she thought she could touch the clouds. She saw Grandfather turn toward her and say, "It will be okay."

Mary came back to reality when she heard a sound at the back door. Someone was trying to get into the house. They knocked again. "Mary Ann" she heard. She got up and ran to the door. The teens and Erik were standing there with wet hair and clothes. She hurried to let them in and went to the bathroom for towels for each to dry off.

"Coming down pretty hard now" Erik said.

She nodded. Erik was thinking she was still mad at him. "Well, Son, we should go."

Mary looked up saying, "Please, not yet!" She looked at the teens and told Glory to go in their bags in the other room find some dry clothes for the three of them. She would make some tea. Everyone looked at her and at the same time said, "Coffee, please!" She agreed with them and went to the kitchen.

Glory found two flannel shirts that she knew weren't her mother's. Yet, she remembered seeing them before. She handed one shirt to Erik and one to Cliff with another dry towel. Glory had put on a sweatshirt and they all started toward the kitchen.

Erik said, "Tell Mom I'll be in shortly."

The teens told Mary and Glory asked, "Mom, can Cliff go upstairs? We can play with the game boy."

"Sure, Honey, go ahead." Any other time she would have said No Way! (not two teens left alone in the bedroom). However, tonight she needed her friend.

By the time Erik came to the kitchen the pot of coffee was ready. She had placed two cups by the pot knowing when the teens went upstairs, they did not want coffee.

"Erik," she said, "I want to apologize for earlier."

"No need" he said, "I was out of line. I am sorry." She gave him a warm smile that melted his heart. He placed his hand on hers and said, "I'm here when you're ready to talk about it!" A tear ran down her chin. She quickly brushed it off with the hair hanging in her face.

"I think," he said, "this would be a good night for a fire in the fireplace. What do you think?"

"Well, I don't want you back out in the rain."

"No problem," he said. "I see you still haven't checked out the entire house."

"No, not yet" she replied.

He opened the basement door taking her hand to follow him and went down the stairs. Mary saw in triple stacks against one wall from floor to ceiling cut firewood for the fireplace.

"Erik, did you do this?"

"Cliff and I did the day before you got here. We knew the rain and cold weather were setting in and thought you might want to use the fireplace."

"Yes," she said. "I'll help carry some to the living room." They both loaded their arms and up the stairs they went. They closed the basement door and moved toward the living room. There was a wood box beside the fireplace. Both dropped the cut logs into the box. Erik took a match from his pocket and lit the papers that Mary had brought from the kitchen. Erik placed the logs just right to give off the draft needed for the fire to burn. He sat back against the back of the sofa on the floor with his legs crossed.

"I never could understand why someone would have the sofas not facing the fireplace."

Mary sat back against the sofa and said, "Erik, we can turn it around."

"No, I'm comfortable" as he placed his arm around her.

"Me too," she said.

The crackling of the wood and the smell brought the teens from the bedroom to see what was going on. They came halfway down the stairs to find their parents nestled together by the fire. Cliff nodded to Glory as they went back upstairs. Cliff was happy his dad seemed to have a friend. He was hoping she would become a girlfriend since his dad had been alone for a long time.

Chapter 11

ERIK WOKE UP TO the fire still having a few light warm coals simmering and still giving off a few crackles and pops. He had not planned to stay all night, but it seems that's what happened. Mary's head was lying on his chest and her arm wrapped around him. He was afraid to move. He was worried it may wake her.

"Miss Beauty," he thought as he was watching her sleep, which he did enjoy, remembering the turn of events from yesterday. He thought it seemed she had a lot on her mind. Puzzled - he knew she had it tough the last few years, but he hadn't really spoken to her about it. He only knew just pieces from what her sister Jenny and her close friend Maggie had told him. To his knowledge since her return home, Maggie had not been out to visit Mary. Maybe she had been busy with working at the general store. He wanted to help Mary get back on her feet again. Growing up she was always the strong one and determined she would go places. He had not seen that in her the last few days. "The willingness" he thought, "you will come around" not realizing he was saying the words aloud. "Mary Ann, you are strong and you will be okay!"

"What?!" she replied.

"Good morning, Sleepy Head."

"What!" She jumped to her feet. "The kids?!" Mary ran up the stairs. Both teens were lying in separate beds in the twin bedroom still asleep each with a pair of headsets on and the music still playing. She could hear it from the doorway. She let out a big sigh and smiled at the same time. She thought 'how can they sleep with that much noise blasting in their ears?'

Erik had gone to the bathroom downstairs and by now was in the kitchen placing the coffee pot under the dripper.

Mary came down the stairs and into the kitchen.

"Everything alright upstairs?"

"Yes" she replied.

"Good," he said. "Sorry, I did not mean for us to spend the night."

"That's okay. I needed to have someone with me last night. It was a rough evening."

"Want to talk about it?"

"Not really."

"Okay, when you are ready, I will be there to listen. Deal?"

She looked at Erik and said, "Thanks."

Erik smiled at her saying, "Coffee, Sleepy Head?" He poured them both a cup of coffee and sat down at the table. "Still raining - the day will be a slow, wet one at the shop."

"Do you need to go and open the store?"

"No, every Monday morning Vivian opens and I close."

"Oh," said Mary. "Well, that's good for this morning. What about Cliff and school?"

"Cliff's first class isn't until 10 o'clock on Mondays. The rest of the week he needs to be there by 8 o'clock."

"Well, this week I need to get Glory there for enrollment. I hope, with any luck I will receive her transcripts from the Jersey City School. I don't want her to get behind. It will be hard enough for her."

"If she needs help, I'm sure Cliff wouldn't mind. He's a straight 'A' student. I was lucky. It just seems to be easy for him. It must have come from his mom!"

"I'm sure over the years you have helped."

"Okay, I used the whip," Erik replied. "No sincerely, if I or Cliff can help, please we will be glad to do it."

"Well, I'll need to know who to talk to at the school? Since I don't have her records yet, I need to know if she will have to wait until we receive them."

"Well, Mary, my thoughts would be to wait for them. How will they know what classes are best for Glory?"

"That's true," Mary replied.

"Well, I need to get Cliff up and get on the road."

"You said you close the shop?"

"Yes, on Monday's."

"How late?"

"The shipment from Morris doesn't get here until three o'clock so it's usually seven or later. Why?"

"Just asking - what do you order from Morris?"

"The mulch - the saw yards there ship to me every week. I get a better price from them. They ship bagged mulch to the store. Then I meet the trucks at the farm for delivery of loose mulch."

"I thought there was a sawmill in Winchester?"

"There used to be. They closed it when Mr. Harry passed. His son said there wasn't any money in it anymore. When the Lowes in Sperry opened, it took a lot of his business. So he closed and moved away selling the land to a developer."

"Do you still grow all your flowers?"

"Oh yes, Ma'am and proud of it!"

"You should be. The shop and farm have been around for years. I'm glad. The small shops are special to me because they're so nice and personal. In the city there just was no personal touch to anything and the pace was too fast."

"Will you miss the fast pace, Mary?"

"I don't know... maybe... haven't thought about it. Glory and I needed the change."

"She has grown into a pretty young lady," said Erik.

"I love her so. It has been hard on her. You know she tells people her father is dead."

"Mary… I'm sorry."

She was trying to hold back another tear. She didn't want another experience like last night.

Changing the subject Erik stated, "I need to get out of here. The morning is quickly disappearing." He got up and headed toward the steps.

"Can I make breakfast before you leave?"

"No, we will catch it later… but thanks." Up the steps he went. Mary walked into the living room with her refilled cup of coffee thinking Erik was right - the sofas need to be facing the fireplace. How could she rearrange the room and still keep all of her grandparent's things? She thought, that would be today's project. Erik and Cliff came down the steps.

"Cliff, would you like a glass of juice or a cup of coffee?"

"Yes, please. OJ to go maybe, if you have it?"

"Sure." She went to the kitchen asking as he put on his shoes and jacket, "Erik, coffee to go? You can borrow my travel cup."

"No, I'm fine."

'Yes, you are,' she thought with a grin on her face.

"Okay, guys, have a good day!" She handed Cliff his juice as she walked them to the back door. The rain was cold and the wind was still blowing. The temperature had to be in the 30's as she stood holding the door open. "Stay dry!" she yelled with a smile on her face, closing the door behind them to keep the heat inside. She was glad the heat had been set to come on when needed. With the temperature dropping during the nights, yesterday being cold and damp, then today even cooler they'd need the heat during the day on days like this.

Chapter 12

WALKING BACK INTO THE living room Mary stood there for minute thinking…then it came to her. She started moving the sofas placing one facing the TV and turning the other sofa to face the fireplace. She pushed both sofas forward so there was a walkway behind them around to the windows. This way she was able to keep from blocking the beautiful outdoor view coming through the picture window. Today, no one would want to see that rainy view. She thought some tall plants in different spots around the windows would help give a warm atmosphere. They should grow well with the morning sunlight. She pushed the rocker from the window over near the piano and facing the fireplace. "Yes," she said, "I'll use it more here" not realizing she was talking out loud.

"Yes, Mom. I like it, too," Glory said standing on the bottom step watching her mom.

"Glory, you're up?"

"Yes, mom. I could hear you upstairs."

"Don't know how, Glory, your music from the headset was sooo loud. I came up to check on you. It could have woken the dead."

"Sorry, Mom," she replied. "What time did Erik and Cliff leave?"

"This morning," Mary said singing a tune playing in her head.

"Really?" Glory went to the kitchen.

"Glory, juice goes in a glass!"

"Okay, Mom!" the teen replied.

Mary arranged some pictures to match the new look of the room. She pulled some of her things out of the boxes from the carousel room. She finished moving the furniture around. She stood back to look at the new layout. She took a picture from one of her bags packed in the box and placed it on the mantel. The picture was of her mom, dad and grandparents with the words on the frame "The Barnes". She had another picture in her hand. It was of Glory, her dad, and Mary taken on a fishing trip. Mary rewrapped the picture in its tissue paper and tucked it back into the bag. "NO! Glory and I don't need the reminders."

"Of what, Mom?" asked Glory coming back into the room.

"Nothing, Honey," Mary replied. She was packing the bag into the box and closing the lid.

"Well, what do you think?"

Glory walked around the room. "I think we will use it more this way."

"Good because I like it too." Mary smiling picked up the box taking it back to the carousel room. She was thinking about the TV News and worrying if she should tell Glory, before she finds out like she did or some teen from school says something about it. She was not sure what to do!

"Mom, can we check upstairs for the other bedrooms or are we going to only use the twin beds?"

Mary laughed. "I think it is time to finish exploring and today seems good to me. The weather's not going to be fit to be outside today."

Glory walked over to the window to see the rain coming down in sheets and blowing across the porch with such force that it was running down the windows. "Gracious!" Glory replied.

"Breakfast first, before exploring?" Mary asked.

"No, Mom, not yet. I need to be up for a little while."

"Okay, then let's head upstairs." Together (filled with excitement and not knowing what they would find behind each door) they started their investigation.

"Mom, how many rooms does the house have?"

Mary started to question her memory. "Well, let me see. I remember the twin room, my grandparents', my mom's, and Uncle Dan's," counting on her fingers as they reached the top stair.

"Mom, I don't remember Uncle Dan."

"No, Glory. He passed away very early with a heart attack. I was only 11. Shortly afterwards, maybe two years, Granddad passed away from cancer. I was 13, just turning into a teenager. Oh, but your great grandmother - she was the strongest of all, besides mom, of course. Grandmother died of old age. She was a strong old soul. She would say Erik's not ready for me yet."

"Erik?" Glory questioned.

"Yes, Honey. Grandfather's name was honored by his best friend an Army buddy. When their first son was born, they named him Erik."

"Your Erik?"

"Yes, Cliff's dad. Your Uncle Dan was also Erik Daniel named after your great grandfather."

"Too many Eriks! How did you keep them apart?"

Mary just laughed.

Upstairs, they walked around the railing and opened the door to the first bedroom next to the bathroom. "Uncle Dan was an early riser with Grandfather. He helped take care of the busy farm. So, Grandmother made sure he didn't have to walk far and make a lot of noise that would wake the rest of the house. I remember your Aunt Jenny and I would stay over in the twin room. We could always hear Uncle Dan when he got up even before he came out to go into the bathroom."

Looking around the room she saw his trophies from winning the horse-riding contest at the yearly rodeos still sitting on the dresser. "I was only nine or ten. But I remember how good he could ride." Mary was holding one of the pictures in her hand. There were pictures of him with cowboys, horses, trucks and farm tractors hanging on the walls. Glory was thinking the room needed updating. Mary said, "I think for now we will leave this room alone."

Rounding the corner to the next room, Mary said, "This was Mom's room." On the door was another one of grandmother's knitted plaques with two girls playing in a sand box. The words knitted under them were *"There's always time to play"*. There's Grandma's little crafty sense of humor again Mary thought. Glory didn't get it, shaking her head. They opened the door. The room was covered with light lavender wallpaper with ladies having sun umbrellas across one shoulder, dressed in long French style dresses, walking down the sidewalk past houses under the green leaf maple trees. The bed had a canopy with a satin lace looking bedspread with matching pillows. A see-through lace fabric draped over and around the poles with purple ribbon tied to hold the lace in place around the poles.

"Mom, can I have this room? I like it. This bedroom is so great." Glory's eyes were as big as quarters and a smile was on the teen's face.

"You can have your pick, Glory. But this house is too big for one person to keep up with so you must help out with the cleaning."

"Sure, Mom. I like this house. It's cool with lots of surprises!"

"Good, then I guess you don't want to see the rest of the rooms?"

"Guess again!" She ran to the next to the last room.

"Glory, this was Grandma and Granddad's bedroom. She opened the door. Mary walked over to the side window. "Granddad liked this room because he could keep an eye on the barn and the front entrance all at the same time until he couldn't climb the steps anymore. He liked the window views," she thought as she sat down in another rocker. "He also could see from the front window just who may come into the driveway and the side view he could keep an eye on the barn and the horses. Farmers back then always had problems with the farms. There would be someone stealing hay or trying to burn down the barns out of anger. It made no sense to me." Mary was shaking her head on why. "I think I will take this room, Glory. Of course," Mary added, "I will make some changes."

Glory laughed, "What kind of changes, Mom?"

"You'll see."

"Like the one room in the city?" Glory replied.

"Maybe."

"That's cool. I'll help if you need me."

"Glory, I will always need you," her mom replied.

They walked around the room. Another old wooden trunk with leather handles was sitting by one wall and a rocker by the window. The bed was an old black cast iron one. Mary sat down on it and the springs told their old age. Mary smiled, "I think I will need a new bed - springs and mattress."

"You think, MOM?" both laughing.

"But I like the cast iron," commenting with a puzzled look on her face. "I don't know if you can buy just a box spring and mattress to fit it. I will need to find out. I like the room - it is large." Mary opened a door she thought would be a closet and it was another full bathroom.

"Great!" she said, "I love it - my own bathroom! I can do great things with this room."

"I bet you will, Mom," Glory replied.

"Well, there's one more room across the hall. Let's finish so we can get started putting things away."

Chapter 13

THEY WANDERED OUT OF what now is 'Mary's Room' and walked across the hall. Surprised there was no sign on the door and it was locked. Mary looked for a key maybe up over the door edge or under the empty flowerpot sitting in the corner by the window.

"Nothing?" questioned Glory.

"Okay, I will see if there are any keys lying around the house and try them before breaking the lock," said Mary.

"Well, Glory, this is your new home. The only thing you still have to check out is the basement, which by the way Erik and I were down there last night to get firewood."

"Firewood in the basement?" Glory questioned.

"Yes, Cliff and Erik cut the wood themselves and stacked it in the basement to keep it dry for the fireplace."

"Cool," Glory replied. "What's next mom, the attic?"

"No, I think for now it will stay unexplored along with the barn."

"The barn? I'm not going out there until the guys get it rebuilt," said Glory.

"That's right. I do not want you going around it. It is too danger-ous. The roof looks like it will fall in at anytime and with this wind it could be today," she said as she looked out the window and saw the pieces of the roof flapping.

"Mom, I haven't seen a washer and dryer. Do we have one? We

can't go the laundromat. Please, say we have one."

Mary did not remember seeing one in the basement. "Glory, I don't know. There has to be one somewhere." Mary didn't remember seeing a hook-up anywhere in the house. This would be one of the first things they would need to purchase - even before her new mattress and box springs.

"Well, I think it's time you go through the boxes downstairs and bring your things to your new room. Along with the things you have put in the twin room. I think I saw your TV downstairs. We'll bring it up and I'll help get it set up for you."

"Great!" Glory said. They started down the stairs. The phone rang. "I'll get it, Mom." Glory answered the phone. "Hello?" she listened then said, "there's no one here by that name. Sorry." Glory hung up the phone. "Some guy asking for Maggie."

"Maggie?" Mary wondered if Maggie maybe coming out here to see us. That would be why someone would be calling for her. "Glory, get your clothes changed."

"But Mom."

"And comb your hair. Please, just change. I will get some different clothes for myself out of the twin room. I need to comb my hair too."

"Why? Mom."

"Sounds like we may get company and it would look better if we quit answering the door in our night clothes or the clothes we have slept in from the night before, don't you think?"

"You have a point, Mom." Glory ran into the twin bedroom and out again, dashing into the bathroom. "Be done in a flash," she replied.

Mary was right. She was standing at the bedroom window when she saw Maggie's car turn into the driveway. No wonder Granddad liked this room, she thought. She went downstairs to meet Maggie at the front door. Maggie was trying to hold on to the umbrella which the wind was about to take away from her as she ran into the house.

"Sorry, I should have come in through the kitchen since it is so messy out there."

"That's okay. It is a nasty day to be out," said Mary.

Maggie looked upset. Giving her friend a hug, she said, "Mary, I saw the news last night. Are you alright?"

"Yes, I'm fine!"

"No, you aren't! Don't you try to fool me."

"Please, Maggie, Glory does not know yet."

"Well, you need to tell her before she finds out the wrong way."

"Find out what, Mom?" Glory came into the room from the backstairs.

"Where did you come from young lady?"

"The backstairs - I found them in Uncle Dan's room."

"You did?"

"Just look at you, Child - all grown up," said Maggie. "I meant to tell you the last few days but we've been hopping in the store when I've seen you. Come here, Girl and give me a hug." Glory gave Maggie a hug and disappeared again up the backstairs.

"We were hopping last night, weren't we, Girl?" The ladies were talking about the party and glad Glory had gone back upstairs.

"Mary, you and Erik look good together."

"Maggie, please, don't start."

"Start what? You know, I like to keep things interesting."

"I know so don't start anything with me. I need to keep a low profile, please, Maggie."

"Okay, okay. Don't get the temper going. I'm just saying if you can land that man, you do it, Girl! That would be a big accomplishment. No one here has been able to do it. If you're lucky enough to catch that, you got something to boast about, Girl."

"Maggie, please!!"

"Okay, okay. You think I could get some hot tea?"

"Sure, I'm sorry! Come on into the kitchen."

Glory came back down the stairs. Maggie asked, "you going to join the ladies?"

"No, ma'am. I have a room to clean!"

"What did you say? What teenager wants to clean her room?"

Mary turned saying, "One that hasn't had a room of her own for a while, Maggie!"

"I'm sorry. I guess things got pretty bad in the city."

"Yes, for a while," Mary admitted. "But we will pick up the pieces and move forward."

"Putting Glory into school soon?"

"We're just waiting on her transcript. I couldn't get them before we left, so I told them to mail them here. I didn't want to start her and then they might need to move her around. She has had enough of that for a lifetime."

"Do you think that was a good idea?"

"What?"

"Having them mailed? Here? That gives anyone the forwarding address."

"Who's there to be afraid of now, my locked-up ex-husband?" Mary questioned gritting her teeth.

"Maybe," replied Maggie, "or maybe the company he kept!"

"Please, Maggie."

"I bet you didn't think of that, did you?" questioned Maggie.

"No, I didn't. I just want to forget."

"And you know you can't do that Mary. I'm your friend - not the enemy."

"Oh, Maggie, I'm tired of the fight!"

"I know, Honey," putting her arm around Mary for comfort. "What can I do to help?"

"Just be my friend," tears in her eyes again. "Glory and I just need our friends to be there for us."

"You got it, Lady! Now dry the eyes and where's that tea?"

Finally, after two cups of tea the girls were laughing about some childhood crazy things that they had done. Glory could hear them upstairs. Glory smiled. Her mom has been so unhappy, she was glad to hear her laugh. Until now the only other person that made her mom laugh was Erik. She knew the two had been friends since they were kids. Somehow, Glory thinking and remembering the promise to her mom, she was going to like him as long as he did not hurt her mom. If that happened, then things would change. But for now, Erik was a good thing and there was Cliff. What a break having Cliff around. It gave Glory a friend too, she thought. Maybe he will learn to like me more. When she finished dusting her new room, she was ready to go through the boxes downstairs and bring them upstairs. She had been waiting for her mom since she knew her mom had plans for some of the boxes as to where they were to go. For now, it gave her a break to sit on the window seat watching the rain.

Chapter 14

A TRACTOR TRAILER PULLED over between the drive-way and the road. It sat there for about fifteen minutes and then pulled away. Glory thought the driver was probably checking his map. Maybe he was lost - easy to do that around here. She still didn't know if she could find her way back to the farm from town. Too many turns and they never go the same way back as they left the farm - she gets all turned around. 'Soon' she thought, 'I will know how to find my way.' Walking around the room she thought that maybe her mom would let her paint later on. She knew for now until mom found a job, things will be a little tight. But we have a roof over our heads that <u>no one</u> can take from us. She had a million thoughts running through her head - all the terrible things she had put her mom through after her dad, Jack, had been arrested and went to jail. Jack was the only father she had really known. Glory had lost her biological father to liver disease when she was very young. She only remembered a few things about her real father - none of them good. He was an alcoholic, she remembered. He always had a glass in his hand and was also abusing her mom. Glory remembered sitting in the middle of a floor, crying in her mom's arms with her father holding a gun pointed at them and the boys. Thinking how did mom still keep trying to do the right things? When she thought about the boys, a tear rolled down her chin. She missed Ben, Craig and Mike.

Then Jack came into their lives. He took Glory and her brothers under his wing. They became a real family and went to softball games, soccer games, basketball and football. He took her to Brownie meetings, helped with Girl Scout cookouts, and cheerleading practice. Jack and mom went to all the school activities. How she missed him and her brothers.

It was hard to think about what Jack had put them through and her mom losing the boys – she lost her brothers. Then he convinced her mom to divorce him. He was our father, our friend. Life is just not fair! She threw the pillow on the floor. Then picked it up again, hugging it, burying her face into the pillow so her mom would not hear her crying. Glory thought about the time she had to spend in the rehab center after trying to take own her life. Her mom must have been going through hell - losing all of us just months apart. How could she make it up to her mom? Would they ever see the boys again?

The phone rang. Glory ran to pick it up, but Mary had gotten it downstairs. It was Erik. He was going to be out of town for a few days. He just heard about a meeting in Upperville. It would be too far to drive home each day. The meeting was going to take maybe a week. Erik asked were there any last-minute things that she may need before his trip.

"No," she said. "Can you leave the gifts at the shop with Vivian? I'll stop by and pick them up later this week. I want to get some plants for the kitchen, the living room and the upstairs hallway anyway."

"Sure." He was sorry he had forgotten them so he told her, "Pick out the flowers and have Vivian do a statement sheet. The flowers will be Cliff's and my gift to you."

"No problem on the gifts, it was raining too hard to unload them anyway. Okay, thanks for calling. Have a safe trip." When she got off the phone, she had a smile from ear to ear.

Of course, Maggie picked up on it right away. "See what I mean. He likes you, Mary and you've got that glow."

"We're just old friends. He's trying to help get us settled. Please, stop making something out of nothing."

"If - you say so, Mary."

"Well, I do. Please, let it go!"

"Okay, Mary. How about going to the club with me one night this week?"

"No, I'm not at all ready for that."

"Well, the girls are having lunch this week - you want to come?"

"No, too much around here to do and I need to find work."

"What line of work?"

"Well, I worked for a trucking company in the city. I was manager of operations - maybe if I went to Morris."

"Why would you want to make that drive every day?"

"What's around here?"

"I don't know but there's got to be something. I have the newspaper in the car. I'll leave it with you. I can get another on the way home."

"Sure Maggie, that would be nice. Thanks."

"No problem. Please, use me as a reference. I want to help and I am glad to see you back. The guys down at the general store were talking about starting the barn maybe on Saturday."

"Really, they hadn't told me anything yet. I was so surprised with the party and the gifts."

"Everybody is happy to see you and Glory get the farm. How about Jenny? Is she okay with it?"

"Jenny hasn't been to see us yet. Spence says, "She was mad at first, but has gotten over it. She didn't have much to say at the party and no phone calls from her since. I don't know - I hope we'll get through this."

"You know she was on your parents' side about your marriage

to Jack."

"I know, but things were good. He loved being a family man and it showed with everything he did for us. Nevertheless, when things turned really bad, my parents were there for me. Until that night..."

"Mary, you can't go back. It won't bring your parents back. Their spirits are looking down on you now and thankfully, you're back home where you belong and away from Jack. Thank God."

"Maggie, if they just hadn't left angry with me. Dad had no business behind the wheel that night. He hadn't been feeling well anyway. They should have spent the night."

"Mary, you can't control other people. There's nothing you could have said that night to keep them from that car accident. So, stop punishing yourself."

"I just feel badly that our last words were out of anger instead of love."

"They did love you and Glory, Mary." Maggie leaned over giving her friend a well needed hug. "Look at the love. It's in this house. It's everywhere and your life goes on. Well, I need to be going," said Maggie. "Give Glory a hug for me. Is she doing better now?"

"Much - thanks for the support."

"Anytime, Girlfriend! Now, let's see if we can get that newspaper."

"Wait - I'll get my jacket and come out with you. At least I can come back in and dry out."

"Okay then." Mary went for her jacket and Maggie wrote a little note:

SMILE - They Love You!
They're looking down singing
with the angels, How proud
they are of you.

She put the note by the refrigator for Mary to find later.

Maggie was at the door when Mary came back downstairs. Mary followed Maggie out to the car. She returned very wet and cold with the newspaper from Maggie's car tucked under the coat. She took off the wet coat hanging it across the rocker by the fireplace and leaned over to relight the fire. It struck her that she should get more firewood first. She went to the basement and walked around before loading her arms with the firewood. "Yes!" she said, seeing the washer and dryer tucked under the stairway. She went back, loaded her arms, and started back up the stairs when she heard a scream. Mary dropped the wood and went running up the stairs. Two flights of stairs later, Glory was sitting in the hall bathroom sink.

"Mom! It's a rat!"

Mary looked around and could not find it. She laughed, "Who scared who?"

"Mom, it's not funny - it was BIG!!"

"Okay, Glory. When I see it, I'll kill it. Okay?" Still laughing she helped Glory down.

She started back down the stairs looking around for the rat with each step. She had no idea what she would do if she saw it. However, that was the only time it was seen. Mary later joked, "They scared each other so bad, either it died or left the house completely. No sign of that rat since!"

The week went by fast. Mary and Glory had gone into town and didn't get lost. The papers from Glory's city school had arrived, so Mary enrolled Glory into school for her to start the following week. They stopped by the flower shop to pick up the gifts and a few plants for the house. They went to the general store for paint. Both Mary and Glory wanted to paint their rooms.

Glory wanted her mom's room to be done first and for her to get a new bed. Then her mom could start using her own bedroom instead of sleeping in the twin beds. She had done without for long enough.

Mary was so proud of her daughter. For the first time in years she heard her daughter thinking of someone else first. It put a warm fuzzy feeling deep in Mary's heart. "My girl just may be coming around," she thought.

They saw Frank who confirmed that a few workers would start on the barn Saturday if that was okay with her.

"Sure. Sounds great and thanks again, Frank. I'm looking for a new bed. Just the mattress and box spring if I can find a set that fits the bed. If not, then I will need the whole thing. Would you know where I might find one? Or will I need to go into Morris?"

Frank said, "Let me look around town. I'm sure someone has one they want to get rid of and is still in good shape."

"Frank, I will pay for it - no more gifts."

"Okay, let me check before you go buying a new one." They went to the counter to pay for the paint and brushes.

"Will that be all?" the clerk was about to say when someone behind her said, "Excuse me. You looking for a mattress and box springs, my dear?"

"Yes…Ma'am!"

"Well, Child, you come with me." The lady was in her maybe 70's, but full of life pushing a walker in front of her. Mary gave Glory the money for the paint and brushes. She told her she would meet her at the car.

When Mary returned, she had just purchased a new bed with mattress and box springs for $50.00 and had a job offer. Mary's eyes were lit up. She had no idea there was a gift shop with furniture and little gift items all for sale here in the town.

"Glory, you will not believe this lady's shop" pointing to the building as they drove past what looked like a house that had been built and survived the Civil War. A sign was hanging out front which said "Robins' Gifts & Interior Designs" but inside was still kind of a mystery of course since Mary had only been in the basement. However, the lady said all four floors of the house were filled with items and designs for sale. "Glory, you must see it."

Looking at her mom she exclaimed, "Mom, slow down, please!"

"Yes, Glory. I'm watching where I'm going" as she was pointing toward the house.

"NO! MOM! You're not!" as Mary was passing a truck which was blowing their horn at them! "Mom, please!"

They finally made it out of town and home safe, but Glory went running into the house.

"Glory, wait!" But, Glory had no time. She didn't want her mom to see her crying. She dashed up the stairs and closed the door. About an hour later Glory came down.

Mary was sitting at the table. "Glory, I'm sorry."

Glory changed the subject. "What's for dinner? I'm starved?"

They had dinner and watched some TV together then off to bed. Mary slept on the sofa that night. She was thinking about Erik as she watched the flames of fire dance across the logs in the fireplace before falling asleep.

Chapter 15

SEVERAL DAYS WENT BY as they worked on painting Mary's new bedroom walls. They found some wall border in the basement she thought would work, but unsure if there was enough to hang it yet or if more would be available to order. She questioned herself on where to get more.

The doorbell rang followed by an impatient knock. Mary went downstairs. It was the new bed.

"Hi, guys."

"Ms. Barnes, where would you like the new bed?" A silver haired gentleman asked.

"Upstairs, please."

"Sure, let us partly unwrap it and we will bring it right in."

She watched the guys - one gentleman was in his late seventy's, the other two were just boys maybe a few years older than Glory.

She had already moved the old bed into Uncle Dan's room for the time being. It had become the storage room for now. It possibly would be the last room that they worked on for any updates and repairs. She wanted to get the rooms being used done first.

Mary was glad to see the bed being delivered. She had almost finished painting the room. There maybe a few touch-ups left to do. However, the wall where the bed is going was complete. Whether or not to use the wall border was still undecided. Maggie and Jenny were making the new curtains and window cushions. Mary and Glory had put a second coat of white finish on the dresser covering the faded yellow color of age. It was a romantic collection - so pretty with white raised scroll detailing around the top and down the legs done in a distressed white finish with a matching mirror. It had a matching clothes-hamper with carved scalloped rim and delicate molding on the hamper hinged door. Maggie called it a "Cottington Collection."

Mary couldn't wait to get the wicker bed up thinking all the pieces would tie in beautifully with her picture still boxed from the move. She hasn't had it out of the box in four years. Now, it finally has a home.

They carried the king size headboard to the top of the stairs.

"Ms. Barnes, where would you like this?"

"Over here will be fine," she pointed toward the larger wall. The older gentleman was coming up the stairs with the mattress. Mary came over helping with one end.

"Thanks," he said. "There's more stairs than I thought. Well, boys go get the box springs."

"Alright Paps," one young man replied.

"Mr. Hall, would you like some ice tea?"

"That would be nice, Child!"

Mary asked, "Glory, would you go downstairs and make three glasses of ice tea."

Glory went down the back stairs since the box springs was coming up the front stairs. Mr. Hall took out his tools from his back pocket. "Boys I will hold this if you go back down and get the rails. Then we can start putting the bed together." Soon it was sitting against the wall facing the window so the morning sun would wake this sleeping beauty.

The men thanked Mary and Glory for the tea and went back toward the front porch.

Mr. Hall turned asking, "By the way the Mrs. says you're coming to work for us?"

Mary was surprised. She thought he just worked for the Robins'.

"Maybe," Mary replied. "I'm sorry. I thought your name was Hall."

"Good! You're a good worker! See ya tomorrow," he said as he was leaving the porch. "Oh, the name is Hall Robins, Missy."

Mary hadn't decided about the job, but she did need to have some money coming in soon. Mr. Robins is a funny character. I bet the days would fly by she thought. Of course, she would feel better if Glory was in school. Good thing the school records from the city had arrived this week and she was now enrolled to start. Both seemed excited about her room. Now that the bed was up and placed in the best location in the room, she continued to think, 'I'll take the picture up and hang it over the bed.' She went to the carousel room but the box was gone. Mary hoped it didn't get thrown out. "Glory May," she called.

"Yes, Mom?"

"Have you seen my picture?"

"Yes, Mom, I took it upstairs for you. It is sitting in the hallway. I need your help to hang it."

Mary took the back stairs and was walking out of Uncle Dan's room with a smile on her face. Glory almost had the picture out of the 3' x 4' box for her mom.

"Glory, I hope there's enough room for it." Mary stood back looking at the details in the picture of an ocean with the sun setting in the background of soft colors of orange, purple, and blues and the reflection of the sun bouncing off the water. A small wood boat was lying upside down on the sandy beach. Two ladies near the water were dressed in long white and pink dresses with matching hats and ribbons. Both ladies were picking bouquets of wild daisies and cattails. The seagulls were flying over their heads and out over the water with tiny white cap waves bouncing against the sandy hill.

Mary and Glory each carried an end of the picture making their way toward the bed. They laid the picture across it face down. They moved themselves around one on each side on the bed. They lifted the picture over the headboard and placed it on a strong nail already in the wall.

"Mom, it's like it belonged there all this time."

"It fits perfectly, looks good, and the colors match," the ladies agreed.

"Well, Glory, Maggie and Jenny should have the curtains done tomorrow and then they can work on the new cushion covers for the window seats. The room is almost done," Mary said. "Do you want to go to town with me tomorrow? I think I will check out the job offer. At least it would be close to home. Maybe when you get into school, you could stop there instead of coming home and we could ride home together? And, I think it would be fun working around Mr. Robins."

"Sounds good, Mom!" Glory replied with a smile. "He is silly. I loved his jokes."

Early the next morning Erik called asking Mary if she would like to go out with him Saturday night? The Club was having a western band. He would be ready to kick his heels up a little after this past week.

Mary was excited and said, "Yes, that would be great! If I…"

"If what?" Erik asked.

Mary Ann replied, "Glory - I need to have someone with her. Let me see if Maggie's doing anything or…"

"Could she stay with Jenny and Spence?" Erik questioned.

"Let me see. When will you be back?"

"Saturday morning," Erik answered.

"Okay, call me when you're back and I will try to work out something for Glory."

She was excited about seeing her friend and getting out a little with adults would be nice. She called Jenny, but no answer. "That's okay. I will see someone in town before tomorrow night," she thought.

Mary and Glory went into town the next day. They stopped by the Gift and Design Shop to talk with Mrs. Robins. Mary was excited. Mrs. Robins wanted her to start on Monday and was okay with Glory coming to the shop after school. She would give her dusting detail until time for Mary to clock out each day. Great, they both have jobs.

Bright and early Saturday morning the guys and Frank were there to work on the barn. There was a lot of clean up to do before the rebuilding could start. They worked most of the morning pulling down broken boards and piling them into divided piles - good ones for reuse, by different sizes and bad ones for trash. Frank told Mary he would have a trash truck stop and pick up the trash pile and haul it away. The other piles they would reuse the wood as they started to rebuild the barn and shed. Mary and Glory helped pull nails out from the wood in the reuse piles. The guys had also roped off the area so no one drove their vehicles near the piles and picked up a nail in their tires.

Spence and Jenny stopped by to see how the project was going. That gave Mary a chance to talk with Jenny. Jenny seemed to be working through the issues of the differences of opinions that the sisters have had over the years, which made Mary feel at ease. She was glad to see her sister stop by. She also hoped for the chance to ask about Glory staying over at their house tonight.

Spence told Mary about a trip the church was taking on Sunday morning with the youth group. The more he talked about it the more Glory was interested. Glory then asked if she could go on the trip with the youth group? Mary told Spence and Jenny she had been invited to The Club with friends for the Saturday night dinner and dance.

"Well, then Mary, you would need someone with Glory while you're gone right? So that works for everyone."

Mary said, she wasn't sure she was going to the club.

"Hog wash," Jenny said. "Let Glory stay with us. You can get out of the house and Glory can go to the youth camp on Sunday."

"Are you sure you wouldn't mind taking her?"

"No, it will do both of you some good."

Mary was even more excited about getting out now. The Club sounded nice. She tried to get Erik on his phone, but just got his answering machine. She left a message. "Yes, Erik, I would like to go with you tonight. Glory will be with Spence and Jenny. They are going to a youth camp on Sunday and are taking Glory with them. Call me!" Hanging up the phone she danced around the room before going back out to the barn where the guys had decided to finish up for the day. She helped pick up their tools and told Glory to go get cleaned up and pack an overnight bag.

"Jenny, what will the youth members be wearing tomorrow?" asked Mary.

"Oh, tomorrow will be a dress down day. Glory can bring jeans. I'm sure they will want to go riding later."

"Okay!" Glory was really excited now. She had wanted to go riding since they got here but it hadn't been the right time to do so. "Great" she replied and up the drive to the house she went, kicking her heels all the way.

Jenny said, "I think she may be just a little excited. That's good!"

Spence told Mary, "We need to check on the horses in the south field. We will do that while Glory is getting ready and packed. Then we will stop by to get her."

"Okay, Spence and Jenny. Thanks, I owe you one." They got into the truck and started down the driveway.

Mary said good-bye to the workers and thanked everyone for the help! Starting toward the house, she could hear the phone. She ran up the stairs toward the kitchen for the phone sure it was Erik. Glory had picked up the phone saying, "Mom, its Erik for you," as she stood at the door.

"Hi, are you back?"

Erik said, "Yes - just got back. Vivian and Cliff weren't home. They must still be in town. I needed to call them so they don't worry about me since I didn't stop at the shop. But I called you first to see if you were going tonight."

"Yes, I left a message."

"Well, I hadn't checked messages yet. Called you first."

"Oh," Mary said.

"Well, then - I will get cleaned up and see you about 7ish?"

"Okay, see you then." She hung up the phone like a teenage girl, with a smile from ear to ear, thinking, "What am I going to wear?"

First, she needed to get Glory out the door and then she could think about herself. Spence and Jenny were back in the driveway.

Mary called out, "Glory, Uncle Spence and Aunt Jenny are back for you."

"Mom, what will you do?"

"I'll be alright here, Honey." Mary went to the door to let Spence and Jenny into the house. "Make yourselves at home. I will check on Glory and see if she needs any help." Mary hopped up the steps as she went by the back stairs.

Glory picked out a silk blouse and blue jeans with a matching jacket for youth camp and jeans with a pullover sweatshirt for riding. "Mom, what will you do tonight?"

"Glory, I am going out with Erik."

"Good, Mom - that's good to hear. Make sure you show him all the hard work we did while he has been away."

"I will, Glory. You have a good time."

Downstairs she went with her coat in her hand. "I'm ready," Glory replied.

"Well then, let's hit the road ladies," Spence replied.

On that note Glory was out of the house. Mary closed the door behind them and she went upstairs to her new bedroom and private bathroom. She decided to take a long hot bath and get ready for a nice time out with Erik. Mary was looking forward to seeing him. She didn't realize how much she had missed him as she was trying to stay busy this week with his absence. Now she would get to spend the whole evening with him.

Mary got out of the bathtub thinking it's only been maybe 30 minutes. She found she had been there a lot longer. Looking at the watch on the dresser thinking she's always late getting dressed. She ran to the closet thinking jeans or a dress? Well, we're going to a western dance so it only made sense to wear jeans. She pulled out her best blue jeans, brown suede boots, red silk blouse and a cowboy hat that matched her boots and started to get dressed. The phone rang. She ran to the phone and it was Erik.

"I will be there in about 30 minutes. Is that okay?"

"Of course," she replied knowing she may not be ready. Hanging up the phone, panic stricken, talking to herself, hair to do she was thinking 'what about her nails?' No time! So, she pulled back her hair and tucked it up under the cowboy hat. She put on her makeup and down the stairs she went. Just in time as Erik was pulling into the driveway.

Chapter 16

HE STARTED UP THE stairs and of course, Sneaky was there to greet him. "Hi Pal, have you been fed? Well, I will need to check on that," he said. He knocked on the door.

Mary opened the door and to her surprise, no bib overalls tonight! Standing in front of her was this tall, well-built, mid-aged man, with a touch of gray in his hair, and well-groomed mustache. He was wearing blue jeans tightly fitted to show off his firm legs, a red cowboy shirt with blue, green and red designs, a western pair of cowboy boots with little horses dancing across the tops of the toes and they looked like new ones.

"Hi, care if I feed Sneaky?"

"No, please do. Glory and I both forgot. I'm sure when we started out the door, she would have reminded me."

"Yes, she would have as she did when she saw me coming up the stairs." Erik went out the door with the bag of dog food thinking her dish must be outside and it was.

Erik came back inside to see Mary dressed with her coat on, ready to go. "Well I guess I don't need to ask if you are ready?" he said laughing.

"Erik, tell me about your week?" Mary asked.

"All in due time," he replied.

On the way to The Club they talked about their week, who they had seen, and the work that was done. Mary was excited about the town friends working on the barn and finally she told him about finishing her bedroom. "Best of all I found a job and I start on Monday."

"Really you painted all by yourself?"

"No, Glory helped. We had a lot of fun with it."

"Good," Erik said. "Then that is all that counts."

"What does that mean?" she replied.

"Nothing. I just can see you both covered with more paint than the walls," Erik was laughing.

"Erik, now be nice," replied Mary, hitting him on the arm.

Entering The Club, they saw several of Erik's friends were there. They were invited to sit down with them. Erik says, "Mary, you okay with that?"

"Sure."

They got a round of drinks and the band began to play. Several songs went by without Erik and Mary dancing. They were laughing and talking to the crowd sitting around their table. Even the tables behind them and beside them were in on their party. Several drinks later...

A fast two step started playing. "Come on guys - our ladies need some exercise." Taking Mary by the hand they started to dance rocking the floor. The others disappeared from the table as well. Two songs later they were still dancing.

They finished the song and sat down for a drink. Mary could feel the emotions running through her veins. Warm and tingly she was thinking she wanted more and how good it was to be out with people her age.

Then another song started to play. "Come on," Erik took Mary's hand and they were out on the floor again. *"Must be doing something right"* the singer was singing. Mary could feel herself melt in his arms. They danced slow and close. Erik whispered, "I must be doing something right."

She drew closer and he felt her body giving into the beat and sound of the music. It seemed when the song ended, they were still moving to the music. Their bodies were close and so tight she felt the energy from the heat of his body.

The band started another song. This time it was an Alabama song. *"It's so right"* the words continued, *"Hold me close"*. They danced. He whispered, "I will, will you?"

She closed her eyes and listened to the song. *"It feels so right"* she could feel herself losing herself in his strong arms and so sure of what he wanted. The music continued, *"It feels so right."* Erik started to kiss her and she backed away saying, "Please, Erik, please stop. It's too soon - too sudden."

"So, you'd turn a guy away hungry?" He danced them back toward the table with the song ending.

They sat down at the table, but Mary half standing, excused herself to find the ladies' room before another song started. Luckily no one was in the ladies' room. She was alone, looking into the mirror, viewing this frightened little girl saying to herself, "What are you doing? You can't, you mustn't let your guard down. You can't." She couldn't be feeling the sexual attraction between the two of them - not her and Erik. "No," she told herself, "I can't. I'm playing with fire," as she pulled a paper towel from the wall unit, wetting it and wiping her face. She pulled a piece of paper from her purse and began to write a note. *"I had to go. Thanks,"* MA. She folded the note and walked out the bathroom door toward the bar. She asked the waitress to deliver the note to Erik after she had left, giving the waitress a twenty-dollar bill for her tip. Mary left the club. She started walking across the parking lot when Frank was pulling in. He stopped his truck to ask, "Leaving?"

"Yes, I just need to find a ride home."

"Hop in," he said, "I'll take you home."

"Do you mind? You're just coming in."

"No. Not at all. I didn't need a drink anyway!"

She climbed into his truck.

"You're place or mine?" he replied laughing.

But Mary was not in any mood for that kind of joking. Her thoughts showed loud and clear on her face.

Frank apologized to her.

She said, "That's okay, it's just me tonight." The rest of the ride back to her place she didn't have much to say. Staring out the truck window, she was thinking about Erik and their hot bodies close together on the dance floor.

Frank asking no questions knew something was troubling Mary. He pulled into her driveway.

"Sure, you are okay?"

"Yes, I'm fine. Thanks for the ride. Sorry, I wasn't much company."

"No problem - I've had nights like that. Don't worry about it. Glad I came along when I did. It would have been a long walk. See you tomorrow. Good night."

"Thanks again Frank," closing the truck door she ran toward the house.

Chapter 17

SHIVERING WITH A NERVOUS chill and the cold damp weather as she ran up the stairs and onto the porch, remembering her jacket was left on the chair beside Erik at the club. She turned the key opening the door to the kitchen. She didn't turn on any lights. She went to the refrigerator got a beer, twisted the cap, and left it on the counter. She walked into Grandmother's carousel room turning on the wall switch. The room came to life. She pulled down the blinds and sat down on one of the folding chairs that matched the card table. She drifted into thought watching the carousel going round and round with the calm tune playing. She thought she was hearing voices coming from the horses that she had focused on.

"Mary? Mary Ann? Why? Why did you leave?" Erik was standing in the doorway. "Sorry, I would have knocked, but you left the door open."

He walked over and placed his hand on her chin. "It's okay, Blondie."

"I'm…" she hesitated as he stopped her. A tear was running down her cheek.

"I can't, I'm not ready. It's too soon." He took her by the arm, turning out the wall light. Hand in hand they went into the living room.

He took the lighter from the mantle and started a fire in the fireplace. Mary was still standing silently watching Erik. He turned toward her, drew her close kissing her forehead and down the side of her temples, then onto her neck. He thought "finally" after several long minutes she moved responding to his kiss as he moved from her ears toward her mouth.

She longed to be touched like this again. The warm taste of his mouth was pulling her in but her reaction was "Don't! I can't."

Erik dipped, taking her off her feet. Kissing her as he lowered her onto the sofa with her lips pressed firmly against his as she mumbled, "Don't." Erik gently forced her arms above her head over his shoulders while their bodies strained and tingled with each movement. Mary did not resist their movements so her words went unrecognized.

His tongue pressed flat against hers. "Don't…waste…so much…time." Devouring her mouth, his hands slid down to her buttocks holding her firm. His thighs pushed against her and wedged her between the sofa arm and his warm flesh. Mary's breath became silent as she pressed her body upward to meet his hips and thighs, moving in responsive circles until she was no longer fighting the moment. Her movements were inviting to his body. His hands moved to the zipper of her jeans, as he slipped his hands inside tightly pressing her warm trim body closer to his. He moved his hands to easily unbutton her blouse. The open blouse displayed her silky see-through bra holding her small, firm, and inviting tips of her breasts that had come to attention. Erik sensed what Mary was doing as she kissed him. He leaned on his forearms on the back of the sofa beside her head allowing her hands to undo his shirt. Mary ran her hands down his magnificent chest through the slightly gray mix of hairs to the smooth six pack abs to open the zipper of his jeans. Her voice only a whisper as the words were spoken, "Jac… I." She heard herself before the whole word was spoken. She hoped Erik had not caught her mistake.

Erik stood to his feet. "All of this and you don't know who you are with? What did this man to do you?" Erik was outraged. He wanted to give to her and receive from her what he had dreamed of for years. But he never tried, never ever letting his real feelings for Mary show through until now.

Mary crying tried to explain she wasn't ready. "I tried to tell you I needed time. I'm not ready. Please, forgive me?" Mary curled up in a ball on the sofa, tears running down her face, knees to her chest, and embarrassed that she let it go this far. How could he ever forgive her?

He walked to the kitchen opening the refrigerator door. Needing something to cool himself down he knew a beer was not the answer. He took a soda, popped the top and stood there. Outraged - what was he thinking? This childhood friend of his was the one for years he had wished he could say what he felt. "Now, oh now, what now?" he said aloud. Closing the door to the refrigerator he came back into the room. Erik offered her a drink.

Mary was still curled up on the sofa, tears still running down her cheeks, trying to say, "I'm sorry...I"

Erik stopped her. "Get dressed," he said, as he looked around the room for any loose items that belonged to him. He took her by the hand and said, "Someday you will tell me the whole story, not just pieces of the story, not just what you think I need to hear, but the whole wretched story."

Mary could sense the anger in his voice and she couldn't bear to look him in the eye. She was ashamed - ashamed of what she had been through, ashamed of what she had turned to, ashamed of what she had just let happen between her and Erik, and ashamed of hurting the one person who was always there for her. How could he ever forgive her? Still she uttered not one word to tell Erik the story he needed to hear.

He stood there. "Do you hear me Mary? I need to know!"

She cried, "I can't Erik…I can't relive it over again."

"Relive? What are you doing to yourself? You can't come back here and not try to move on. You can't go through life not trusting people who really care about you. It doesn't work that way, girl!"

"I…I'm not ready," Mary cried.

"Well, then our different lives continue to go on…don't they? You in your world, afraid to trust and I in mine, needing to know." He went to the door, opened it and said, "Mary, you are not the only one in this life that has been hurt. Until you face it, you'll be alone in this big world." He stood there waiting for her to stop him from walking out the door. "Well, call me if you want to talk." He continued to stand in the doorway, waiting for a reply, but nothing came from Mary. The door closed behind him and Mary sat alone.

Chapter 18

SEVERAL WEEKS WENT BY with no connection with Erik. He had not called. Mary had her mind made up that she was not calling him although, she did miss his smiling face. She missed his laugh as she told her terrible jokes and just having the male sexy body around to remind her, she was still human.

Mary had been in town every day. Her mind made up she was not stopping at the flower shop. Each time she drove by his shop, she would think of reasons to stop like more plants she wanted to buy for around the house. Still she was not going to stop. 'He would call or stop by the house when he was ready to see her,' she kept telling herself. He had always told her, "The man was to do the pursuing." So, she waited to hear from him but the days had turned to weeks and now a month had gone by.

After the past month it seemed Mary's working at Robins' Gifts & Interior Designs Shop turned out to be a great choice for both Mary and Mrs. Robins. Mary's interview informed Mrs. Robins of her knowledge of shipping, deliveries, and tracking supplies. She also was the store manager so Mrs. Robins had someone in charge when she needed to be away from the store. Mary also did the bookkeeping and helped organize the purchasing and delivery areas of the store. All three areas needed a responsible person attending to the purchases and delivery to keep up the book records and make the deliveries run smoother. Mary's background working as Manager of Operations for a trucking company sure paid off. Mrs. Robins thought this could be helpful with her Interior Design areas for shipping the materials directly to the customers' home instead of the materials coming to the store where she would need to set up a second delivery to the customers' home when they were ready to start the jobs. The store was limited in storage space and shipments were not being received as fast as Mrs. Robins had hoped they would be. Then, the turn-around cost to ship or deliver to the customer's home was costing Mrs. Robins double shipping. This alone could pay for Mary hours. Mary was surprised to find Mrs. Robins traveled to New York, New Jersey, Pennsylvania, different areas of Virginia, West Virginia, and Maryland. Mrs. Robins told her she was originally from Nantucket. She loved to design and decorate with the Nantucket style, although her shop was so gorgeous with every room having a different theme. Mrs. Robins also loved candles. No matter what the theme of the room every room all day would have scented candles lit in country shade pottery sitting throughout the house. The house/shop was four stories high. The basement with its ground level open to the parking area was used for a design shop with a few country gift ideas. It had the look of a little country gift shop and her office was in the back. Mrs. Robins' customers would come in looking through design books for their choice of wallpaper and fabrics for the new designs that Mrs. Robins would be creating for their home. Or they would meet with her at the drafting board to create just the right look they had in mind. She always had pots of tea and hot coffee ready for her customers with fresh French Country Biscuits. If they would see a small gift or something in the shop that caught their eye, she would give them a 20% discount just for coming into the shop. Mary first thought when she heard about the discount that it was a bad idea. Mary thought she had to be losing money. But after the first two weeks Mary saw this was a great inspiration. The customers who came in the shop to place orders for wallpaper, drapes, blinds, or other design ideas that Mrs. Robins had created on her drafting board came back just to shop for gifts to mail or ship around the world. Mary was impressed with Mrs. Robins' talents and living arrangements since she and her husband also lived in the house that was always open for the public to buy things. Customers would stop to place orders with Mr. Robins who made neat furniture pieces since he was good at the wood sawing and hand craving. All this kept Mr. and Mrs. Robins with a good turnover of furniture, wood items, etc. for a remarkable business. Just give Mr. Robins a drawing or a picture and he didn't need a pattern, he could just create it.

Mary was glad she had not yet put up the wall border she had found in the basement for her bedroom because she a found a design at the Robins' shop that was just right for her new room. The border would match the painting hanging over her bed. She had decided with her first paycheck she would buy it. So, one day she asked Mrs. Robins to hold it for her so she could buy it on payday afraid a customer may come into the shop and also like it. Mrs. Robins looked at her and said, "My Dear, it isn't for sale to my employees." Mary looked puzzled, but did not pursue the issue. She liked this job and it was important being close to Glory instead of traveling an hour one way to and from work if she had to go to the next nearest city for work. If Mrs. Robins says, "Not for sale" she was not going to question it. She just walked away somewhat disappointed.

Mary's birthday was several days later. Mary had filled out a job application when Mrs. Robins hired her. Mrs. Robins remembered seeing the date of birth. Mary was scheduled to work half a day on her birthday. Around 11:30am Mrs. Robins called Mary to her office. When she walked in, all of Mr. and Mrs. Robins' employees were there and Mrs. Robins handed Mary a brightly wrapped package.

Mr. Robins like a kid said excitedly, "Hurry up, open it! Let's see what you got!" To Mary's surprise it was the wall border she had picked out. Mary was overwhelmed by the lady having only known her for a short period and doing this for her. There was a birthday cake that Mr. Robins baked. He laughed hoping it didn't taste burnt, but it was covered with the best homemade peanut butter icing.

Later that day Mary picked up Glory from school. They drove past Erik's Flower Shop as they had made the same trip day after day to and from school or work with the same thoughts of stopping. But today Mary wanted to stop even more than before, but kept driving. She met her friend Maggie. They took Glory out for dinner and on the way home stopped for ice cream. While at the ice cream parlor, they ran into Cliff. He sat down with them. Surprised to see them he commented, "I haven't seen you in awhile. How's school? Why haven't you been to any of the games?"

Both ladies replied, "Been busy" and both ladies laughed together. Mary drifted into her ice cream thinking of Erik. Her heartbeat became so heavy it seemed to be threatening to choke her and her hands became sweaty. She sat back in her chair and took a deep breath.

Glory said, "Mom, you okay?"

Mary replied, "I'm fine but we need to go."

"Okay, Mom."

"Ms. Barnes, should I call Dad?"

"No, I'm fine. Don't say anything to your dad, please. Come, Glory, let's go home!"

On the way home Glory kept asking her mom if she was alright. Mary told her, "Yes, I'm fine."

Driving home they noticed the corn fields were ready for harvest and off in the distance they could see a John Deere tractor with a wagon behind it catching the grain from cutting the field. They turned the corner following the creek running along beside the road which had orange, yellow, and red leaves drifting down the stream off the crabapple, wild cherry and poplar trees. The frosty nights had changed their colors. How they enjoyed the drive home when with each day the colors of the season were different. They turned into the driveway over the cattle crossing and headed up the drive toward the house. Of course, Sneaky was waiting for her evening meal sitting on the porch leaning on her back legs, clapping her front paws. The leaves from the maples and walnut trees were blowing across the porch. Glory ran up the stairs to find a box by the kitchen door with the tag made out to Mary Barnes. Mary took the package into the house and put it down on the kitchen table.

Glory was excited, "Come on, Mom! Open it."

Mary went to the counter for a knife to cut the tape. Wrapped in balloon designs tissue paper was a hand painted picture of field daisies in a pitcher with a bright rooster on the base.

The card read,

"I haven't forgotten. Erik."

Mary stood with her hand over her mouth repeatedly swallowing with a sudden surge of emotion. She could feel a lump in her throat. His face came back in full view, appealing, his eyes begging and entreating. She spoke out loud, "No, I haven't forgotten either!" Ashamed of how she had treated him for her downfalls. She now wanted to pick up the phone and call him, but with the memory of his voice saying, 'The guys want to do the pursuing' she stopped. She glanced at the telephone and told herself he wants to do the pursuing - he will call when he's ready.

Again, the days turned to weeks and another month would soon be gone. No Erik at Halloween due to her childlike behavior and now Thanksgiving was less than two weeks away. Mary's heart would beat rapidly with a dry taste in her mouth and her palms sweaty when she would hear his name. This emotional feeling she was having was different. It was nothing like the feelings she would have when thinking of Jack. This feeling was more upbeat with a warm wonderful sensation. Each time she would say, "I should call him to say thank you," but each time she would go the phone and while reaching for it she would change her mind. She was fighting this feeling deep inside her soul.

Preparing for the Thanksgiving holiday was beautiful. There were a lot of activities going on at the gift shop. They all were busy preparing orders that were coming in from everywhere and knowing this was the beginning of the Christmas holiday season. Mary enjoyed the fellowship with the towns' neighbors and friends as they came into the shop looking for that just right gift. Mary liked the challenge. Today she was working on the delivery arrangements for an order that Mrs. Robins wanted delivered to Old Town, Maine before Thanksgiving. Her old friend and college roommate had placed an order for a dining room table and four chairs being made by Mr. Robins. He had been carving small birds into the backs of the chairs for days now. Mrs. Robins had asked Mary this morning to make sure the delivery made it there in time. It needed to be delivered at least five days before Thanksgiving. Today was Monday, she thought. Thanksgiving was a week from Thursday and that gave her 9 total days and it had to be there 5 days before. She only had a day to make the arrangements for pick-up and allow the driver driving time for the delivery. Mary sat back in her chair, drumming her pen on the table as she thought, 'Old Town, Maine. The last time she had heard of that place, she was with Kenny. Did she dare see if he was still working for the same trucking company?' She called information asking, "Heyman Trucking, please." She wrote down the number and started tapping the pen again on the table, thinking 'If anyone could get the delivery done on time it would be him. He knew right where to go. His turn around time was wonderful. He never wanted to stay in one spot for long. Should she call him? Does she dare? Thinking 'Do I really want him to know where we are living?' Her knowing Kenny had caused her divorce to be worse than it may have been. That's crazy! She jumped to her feet! Her feelings ran wild. (My divorce was bad because of a husband that didn't take care of his family. Instead he took care of his friends! Leaving us to take care of ourselves. Why shouldn't I call him?) In the frustration of her feelings she picked up the phone and dialed the number to Heyman Trucking. "Yes. Hello. I'm looking for one of your drivers - Kenny Morris. Yes, that's right. So, he does still work there? Good. I have a delivery job for him. Would he be available? Great." She continued to give the information to the lady on the other end of the phone. "Of course. Tuesday afternoon? That would be just fine. Thanks! Have a great Thanksgiving yourself, Dear. Good bye."

That afternoon several hours later the office phone rang. Mrs. Robins had answered it. "Mary, there is a call for you from Heyman Trucking," she said.

Mary answered the phone, "Yes, that's great. Thanks. Good bye."

When Mary got off the phone, she told Mrs. Robins the delivery was scheduled. The truck would be here tomorrow morning.

The next day a tractor and trailer truck pulled into the small town of Edinburg. Glory was at the ground floor of the gift shop when the truck pulled into the parking lot. A tall slim man with dark shoulder length hair got out of the truck. Glory thought she had seen this truck before, but wasn't sure. Tractors and trailers all look the same she thought. When he reached for the shop doorknob, Glory opened the door saying, "Hi. I bet you are here for the Old Town order. I will get mom." She disappeared up the stairs.

Mrs. Robins came from the back room. "Hi," she said. "Can I help you?"

"Hello Ma'am. My name is Kenny. I was told you requested me to make a delivery."

"Oh, yes, Mary will be right down. My husband is finishing the wrapping and boxing now. It should be ready within the hour. Can you wait?" Before he had a chance to say anything Mary came down the stairs. His eyes lit up.

"Mary!"

"Kenny, how are you?" she replied before he could ask too many questions in front of everyone. "I'm glad we could find you. If anyone can get this delivery done on time, it's you!"

"Well," Kenny replied, "haven't found a place yet that I can't find. Where's it going?"

Mrs. Robins asked Mary if she would be okay. She needed to finish her drawing before her clients got there.

"Sure, Mrs. Robins, we will be fine!" Glory by this time was back to her job of dusting. "Come up to my office," Mary told Kenny and they started up the stairs. "Glory, could you make another pot of coffee for us?" They disappeared around the corner at the top of the stairs. Mary was full of questions about where he had been traveling and who was still working with the trucking company. She stopped herself from asking too many questions since she didn't want to know about the rumors of her husband. She went around her desk and sat down with Kenny still standing in the doorway as she took a long look at this 6'2" slim man. He still had his curls down to his shoulders just as she had remembered. Today he's wearing faded blue jeans, long sleeve shirt and well-worn cowboy boots. He was dressed just like most truck drivers. She thought after they were alone, he would have asked more questions about Glory and herself, but he didn't. In a way this made Mary more comfortable. "Have a seat. I will get the information for you. I know you will not have any problem finding the town." Mary laughed and handed him the directions saying, "We need it there by Saturday." She smiled at him knowing he could read her mind.

"No problem" he replied with a sneaky grin. "If I make the delivery on time, do I get Thanksgiving dinner?"

"What?" Mary asked.

"I was just wondering if I could come back here for Thanksgiving or do you have plans?"

"No plans, just Glory and I unless my sister and her husband have us over," she replied.

"Good," Kenny said, "I'll be back in time."

"You will?"

"Sure - wouldn't miss it. I know I've missed you, Missy. Haven't had a riding partner quite like you before or after."

"Kenny, please!" (her face turning beet red).

"Sorry, I didn't mean to embarrass you," Kenny replied. "Well… where's this shipment's Bill of Lading? Oh, yes, and the cup of coffee?"

Mary had the strong urge to hug him. She was fighting her feelings of fear, sorrow, joy for seeing him, and hate of her husband who had put them through the worst times of her life. The reminders were like a sour taste that stays in your mouth.

"Mary, you okay?"

"Sure," she replied, "Let's get that coffee for you. You have a long trip and a short time to get there."

Mr. Robins and the boys helped load the truck (the boys did most of the work). Kenny was the driver so he let others do the loading and unloading. He asked, "Will anyone be at the delivery address on Friday?"

"Well, that's only two days," Mr. Robins said.

"Yes, I can make it but, will someone be there to unload," Kenny asked.

"Are you sure, Kid? That's a long ride. The Misses and I have done that trip several times over the years."

"Oh, yes, I will make it just fine. I know the town well."

"Okay, I will make sure Mary has called the customer to let them know to be home for the delivery. Good luck, Kid and thanks." Mr. Robins went back to his little carving shop to finish working on another gift request.

Kenny started back inside when Mary met him at the door. "The delivery end knows I'm coming?" he asked.

"Yes. What day do you think you will be there?"

"I'll be there by Friday."

"I knew you would," Mary replied. "I told them Friday. If there were any changes, I would call them back." She was laughing while saying, "You haven't changed a bit, have you?"

"Missed me, did ya?" Kenny, smiling as he walked toward the truck, reached for the handle to pull himself up onto his seat before closing the door. "Sure, ya don't want to ride along?" He closed the truck door. "I'll see ya next week!"

Mary just waved to her friend saying nothing and at the same time hoping he didn't come back. She didn't want her mistakes from the past to come driving back into her life.

That evening on the way home Glory asked questions about the delivery truck driver. Mary wasn't sure why Glory was asking - maybe just to have a conversation going. You know kids. When they got home, Mary had a package. She asked her daughter to take it upstairs to Mary's room. She had finally gotten the pillow covers and curtains from Maggie for her room. Glory walked into her mom's room looking around and thinking it's coming together nicely. She was standing by the window overlooking the driveway when she re- membered...the truck. The truck that was at the gift shop today was the same truck that was parked outside their gate a few months ago. She remembered the side painting. That's strange - why she couldn't get it out of her mind. "Mom!" Glory went running back down the stairs. "Mom!"

Mary was on the phone. Some of the guys wanted to work on the barn on Saturday and Frank had called to confirm that it would be alright with Mary. "Sure, I will see you and the guys then. Have a good evening...bye." By the time Mary was off the phone, Glory was busy with feeding Sneaky and other things so she forgot all about the truck.

On Friday Mary received a call from Mr. Bowman. The shipment with the table and chairs had arrived safely in Old Town. Their voices were bouncing with excitement when they asked to speak with Mr. and Mrs. Robins. Neither was there so Mary took a message for them and spoke with Mrs. Bowman about the delivery. "Oh, yes, the young man was tired," she said. "We told him he shouldn't have driven all day and all night. We gave him the name of a good motel in town to get some rest before driving any further."

Mary told Mrs. Bowman, "That was nice of you. How are the table and chairs?"

"Great, we love them. Hall has always been very talented with his handmade crafts and carvings. We have several items that he has made for us over the years. We knew he was the right person to make the table and chairs. Our daughter will be in from college the night before Thanksgiving. She graduates this year. We were trying to surprise her with a furnished apartment when she gets here. Thanks for helping make this dream come true. Well, My Dear, have the Robins call me."

The phone went silent. Mary was glad to hear she had made the right decision for the delivery. Then wondered would he be back or was he just kidding around with her? "Just kidding," she told herself as she hung up the phone and went back to work.

Mary looked at the calendar counting the days from Friday to Thanksgiving. He won't come. She went about what she was doing.

Chapter 19

JENNY OPENED THE DOOR to the Gift Shop stopping by to see any new items on display. She sat down in one of the wooden rockers just put on the floor today. Mary was surprised to see her two days in a row. "Spence and I would like to invite you and Glory May over to our home for Thanksgiving dinner."

Mary had not been over to their home yet. She had been waiting for an invitation instead of just dropping in on them.

"Oh, Jenny, that would be so nice. Thank you." With a tear forming, she quickly turned away from Jenny pretending to reach for something on the shelf beside her. She was glad to see Jenny finally warming up to her.

Minutes later Jenny was ready to leave. "I like the smell of pumpkin pies in the shop. What is it?"

"It's one of the new candles Mrs. Robins just got in. It's just right for the season.

"Well, I need to go. I still need to do some shopping at the general store before I go home."

Mary opened the door for Jenny to leave the gift shop and to their surprise it was snowing. Mary knew it was cold enough and the weather man had said, "*possible snow flurries,*" but this did not look like just snow flurries. It was coming down pretty good.

Mary told Jenny, if it kept snowing, she would need to get Glory and head home before too long. She knew the van did not have snow tires and would not be very good in the snow.

Jenny told Mary that if it did get bad or if they had any trouble getting home, please call Spence. He could take them home in the truck.

"Thanks, Sis." It gave Mary a positive feeling about her sister coming around finally. Mary had been worried about Jenny. She just had not opened up too well to her and Glory being in town and them having the family house. Maybe in time Mary thought she will come around. Once the barn is done and Jenny sees that Mary is willing to keep her word to Spence about the farm land and having the horses at the barn, things will be better between them. She did want to help them if she could with the pasture for the horses. Mary also knew too well she could not run the family farm by herself and she loved seeing the horses running free through the fields. She looked forward to the day when the farm was up and running. She thought it doesn't hurt to dream big!

Back to reality - the snow was really coming down now. Mary thought she had better get Glory and start cleaning up to close the gift shop before it got too late. "Glory!" she called. Glory was outside playing in the snow. She was dancing around the parking lot area kicking the snow with her feet and her palms turned upward to catch it. Mary smiled as she watched her daughter. She seemed to be adjusting very well here. Mary turned off the coffee pot and then emptied both the teapot and the coffee pot. She left a note for the Robins so they didn't worry when they arrived back from Morris. She started up the stairs making her way to the 4th floor to make sure everything was turned off. Mary blew out the candles on the 2nd floor as she made her way back downstairs. She double checked the back kitchen doors to make sure they were locked. Then she worked her way down to the basement shop areas and out the basement shop door locking it behind her with a broom in her hand.

By this time the snow had covered the ground like a white furry blanket. Mary hoped the van would make it home safely. She brushed off the snow, thinking they had better stop by the general store just in case they could not get out tomorrow.

Frank's General Store was busy with others having the same idea about getting last minute items before heading to their homes. Frank was working behind one of the counters trying to help his workers so they could get on their way before the roads became too bad to travel. The weather forecaster was now calling for blizzard conditions within the next several hours in the mountain areas. Mary told Glory not to dally around. They needed to get milk, bread, cereal, coffee (of course), eggs and peanut butter. They needed to pay and get home. Mary paid for their items and headed toward the door. Frank told Mary to give him a call when she got home to let him know they made it safety. If he hadn't heard from her within one hour, he would come out that way to see if they were alright.

Mary said, "Okay, thanks, Frank" and out the door they went.

At the van the snow had already covered the windshield again. Mary turned on the engine and got back out taking the broom from the backseat of the van and brushed off the snow again. Glory already inside the van turned the radio music up loud and was singing a tune. Mary jumped into the van. "Brrr... it is getting colder and snowing harder. I hope we make it home."

"Mom, we will be fine. Isn't it beautiful?"

The drive home was not as bad as Mary thought it would be. She was surprised to see the same road looking so different this evening. They made their way slowly down the curved road toward the red wooden covered bridge that they had crossed every day, but today it was a little tricky. The van started slipping toward the guardrail just before making the turn into the covered bridge. The van's front wheel caught the dry pavement inside the bridge. Mary took a big deep breath as all four wheels landed on dry pavement.

She stopped the van inside the covered bridge just before the exit into the snow again. "Glory, look out there. Isn't it pretty? No dirty buses or busy taxi cabs could disturb the beauty of this wonderland view. What a magnificent postcard picture this would make." She pointed out across to the pasture fields with the white blanket of new snow. Mary put the van in gear, stepped on the gas and drove out into the snow again. The van made its own tracks through the snow-covered roadway around the curve toward the railroad tracks all covered with the white stuff. The railroad tracks' poles seemed to help guide her down the road when she came around the curve. The snow was blowing across the road in small funnels in different directions. Mary knew they were close to being home as the crossing was in sight. Seeing the tracks, she stepped on the gas to pick up a little speed to make the hill and the turn into their driveway. She did not notice the upward climb to the house until the snow forced the van to come to a spinning stop. Mary put the van in reverse and backed up. She placed the gearshift into low gear and stepped on the gas. The van went about four feet and the tires started spinning again.

"Oh, well, Glory, we made it thru the gate. So, I guess we walk the rest of the way. Come on - load your arms with bags and see if we can get everything in one trip." They both took bags of groceries and were lucky enough to get everything. They started walking up the hill toward the house. Sneaky today was not out to greet them as they came toward the porch. The walk toward the house seemed to take longer than the van ride home. It was hard to walk with both arms loaded down and the wind blowing snow in their eyes. They could hardly see the house. The snow stung their faces as they fought their way toward porch stairs. Mary missed several steps as they tried to climb their way up to the kitchen door. This part of the snow did not make Glory or Mary very happy, but once inside with the kitchen door closed, they sighed with relief.

"Well I'm glad that's over!" Mary replied. "Glory, you okay? Set everything down. When we get dried, I'll put things away."

"Okay, Mom. Wow! I'm glad to be home. That was something," Glory said. "Do you think Sneaky is okay?"

"Sure, Honey, she's curled up in her nest. We'll put some food out later for her. Change your clothes and help bring some wood up from the basement. Tonight will be a good night to have the fireplace lit."

"Sure, Mom," Glory answered. "Just can we have some hot tea first?"

Mary smiled, "Yes, I think it is a great time for chamomile tea." Mary put the pot on the stove. She picked up the phone to call Frank and Jenny to let them know they made it home safe and both went to change clothes.

Glory got back to the kitchen first, since she still had clothes in the carousel room. She took out 2 cups then placed a tea bag in each cup. The water was now hot and the chamomile filled the house as she poured the hot water into the cups. Mary stepped into the kitchen wearing a flannel shirt, sweat pants rolled halfway up to her knees and wool socks.

"Mom, you look...." Glory laughing.

"Don't say a word. I am very comfortable in my... er... our home and you know what, it feels GOOD!"

Glory still laughing, "Mom, we have come a long way, haven't we?"

"Yes, Child, we have! Thanks" as she reached for her cup of tea and the phone at the same time. "I forgot to tell Spence the van is at the bottom of the hill in case he comes in with his big truck. I will call him back now."

"I told Frank about the van. He will call me tomorrow. He was glad to hear we were home safe. He hadn't left the store yet, but had sent his workers home. I hope he doesn't stay too late," Mary found herself rattling.

Glory put the groceries away while Mary finished her tea. They went down to the basement making several trips to fill the wood box beside the fireplace. Mary started the fire and sat back against the sofa watching the blue, purple and orange flames dancing around over the wood chips giving off the smell of cinnamon. It was so nice and peaceful as she almost drifted off to sleep but not for long as Glory turned on the TV. The news forecasted the snow to continue through the night dropping maybe up to a foot or more before ending sometime the next day.

"Well, Glory, I don't think there will be any school tomorrow and maybe no work for me. Are you hungry?"

"No, Mom, I think if I need anything, I'll just pick from the leftovers in the refrigerator tonight. Okay?"

"Sounds good to me! Maybe there will be a good movie on after the news." Mary put another log on the fire now that its flames were really strong. She said, "That should hold for the night," as she curled up on the sofa.

"Aunt Jenny invited us over for Thanksgiving at their house."

"Great, Mom, maybe I can go riding again. That was so much fun. Do you think Erik and Cliff will be there?"

"I don't know, Dear. Aunt Jenny didn't say if she had invited anyone else." Mary laid her head on the pillow thinking about Erik. Would he be there? If so, how would he react around them, since he and Cliff had not been back out to visit? She drifted into the memory of that night the two of them were last together here on the sofa. She got all hot with sweat beading up on her forehead with a warm sensation flooding through her veins. "Well, Glory, I think it's gotten warm in here now. Do you?" Mary pulled off the socks and rolled the pant legs above her knees. Why hadn't she called Erik by now? Why hadn't he come to see her or picked up the phone and called? Why? Maybe he was waiting for her to reply to the nice gift he had sent? Her questions went unanswered.

Chapter 20

THE NEXT MORNING THE house was very silent. Mary rose to the sound of the neighbor's rooster in the background - like clockwork. It just sounded farther off in the distance. She looked out the bedroom window to see the snow was still coming down, but not in the blizzard way of last evening. She put on her robe glancing out toward the barn and thinking soon it will look like new when the repairs are done. She headed toward the stairway stopping at each window to check out the beauty of the snow making her way down the steps. She entered the living room with the warm coals still popping in the burning fireplace. The aroma of cinnamon still lingered from last night's wood chips. She again looked out across the yard. The snow was beautiful. The pine and cedar trees were covered with a blanket of white and the mountains looked peaceful and calm. The walnut tree was leafless, only a blanket of snow covered its branches. No life seemed to be stirring, except of course Sneaky who hadn't gotten any dinner last night. Mary jumped as Sneaky popped her head up to the window. "Okay, Mischief, that's not funny!" She went to the kitchen closet, took out her bowl, filled it with dog food and started to the door. When opening the door, there stood Kenny… ready to knock.

"What? How did you get here?"

Kenny and his duffle bag were covered with wet snow and he

looked like a drowned rat. She was so surprised by him that she almost dropped Sneaky's food. She put the bag of dog food under her arm and helped Kenny inside.

Kenny walked over to the table and plopped down, not bothering to shake his feet off before coming in. "I've been walking most of the night."

"What?! Where is your truck?"

He replied, "In a ditch by Miller's Dairy off Simmer Road."

"What were you doing out there?"

"I thought I could take a short cut, but the map doesn't tell you the road was not wide enough for a tractor and trailer. I broke the radio when I hit the ditch and had no way to call anyone, so I walked."

Mary went for a towel from the bathroom for Kenny to dry off. "Like some coffee?"

"Sure, and a warm bed to sleep all day!"

"Okay," Mary replied. "We can't go anywhere anyway." She made both of them coffee and showed Kenny up the back stairs to her uncle's room. "Sorry, it looks so messy. I wasn't planning on any company and we had been using this as a junk room."

"It's fine. Thanks, I will see you in a few hours" as he started to undress.

"Kenny, please, be a gentleman around my daughter!"

"Sure, you got it Babe." His pants dropped to the floor.

Mary backed out of the room as she turned the lock and slowly closed the door. She stood on the other side of the door thinking 'what do I do now?' She looked in on Glory still asleep and she closed her daughter's door trying not to wake her.

Several hours went by, but it seemed like days to Mary. Glory still hadn't gotten up and now she could not get Kenny off her mind. How did he know where to come? She had not told him where she lived. Mr. and Mrs. Robins wouldn't have told him. He was never alone with Glory so she didn't tell him. What was she going to do?

Mary's mind was running around in circles. She really didn't think he would come back after the delivery. Should she call Jenny and say they wouldn't be there for Thanksgiving? No, he will be gone by then she thought. Around eleven o'clock Glory made her way down stairs.

"Mom, did you look out? It's beautiful!" The snow had finally stopped and everything was still very silent outside. "Mom, can we go out and make a snowman?"

"Sure," said the voice behind her, causing Glory to jump, not knowing there was anyone in the house but her and her mom.

"Where did you come from?" asked Glory with a ghostly look of surprise on her face.

"Sorry, Child, I didn't mean to frighten you. Your mom was nice enough to give me a place to sleep."

"Where's your truck?" Glory asked remembering him from the store.

"In a ditch! It will be there for a while. How do we get some food around here? No diners around for miles."

Mary jumped up and started pulling food out of the refrigerator.

"Mom, I'll get a bowl of cereal."

"No, you won't. Your mom's going to make breakfast, aren't you, Mary?"

"Sure!" Mary replied, "Have a seat, Kenny. It won't take long."

Kenny sat down at the table leaning the chair back on its legs and propping his feet on the corner of the table. "Missy, get me a cup of coffee - black!" Glory looked at her mom.

Mary asked, "Glory, please, make another pot of coffee for Kenny and me."

Glory took the coffee from the cabinet setting it down on the countertop. She was not happy to have their visitor when she realized she had seen his truck outside their driveway gate in the past. She got side tracked the other day and forgot to tell her mom about the truck. She remembered <u>that</u> logo.

He asked, "Have you winterized the house for the season?"

"No, Glory and I haven't been here very long," Mary answered.

"That's not a good answer, Mary. You know there are things that need to be done to get ready for winter."

"Like what?" Mary asked. "The house seems to be just fine."

"Like your barn?" Kenny replied.

Mary was seeing the side of Kenny that she didn't like. He could be a very nice and sweet person, but he could be rough, rugged, and downright temperamental at times. She continued to scramble the eggs as the toast popped up from the toaster.

They were about to sit down to eat when there was a knock at the back door. Who could that be? Glory ran to the door. "Uncle Spence, what you doing out on a day like this? We didn't hear you come in."

"No, I have Zinger. He's pretty quiet."

"You do? Mom, can I go out and see him?"

"Who's Zinger?" asked Kenny.

"My American Quarter Horse...the roads are not in any condition to be out in a vehicle, so I'm riding Zinger to check on the livestock. I can't imagine life without my horses."

Kenny laughed. "I like horsepower too, just not the same kind. Sorry, I don't think we have met. I'm Kenny, Mary's friend. I just got in today."

"Driving in this stuff?" Spence commented.

"Well, I was last night, but my truck made its way into a ditch. So, I'm without horsepower for awhile."

"That's the good thing about Zinger, he goes anywhere. Just give him a little grain, some hay and he's fine."

Glory came back to the kitchen with jeans, boots, coat, gloves and her toboggan. She was dancing with excitement, ready to go out and see Zinger.

"Mary, okay with you if she goes to the south pasture with me? I will make sure she's safe and she could ride one of the other horses back. I will need another at the farm for a few days to help out with things."

"Sure, the snow has stopped and it would be good for Glory." Mary was really thinking it would give her time to talk to Kenny. He was not going to stay with them for long. But, little did she know Kenny's plans were very much different than hers.

Spence and Glory left the house, laughing and talking as they stepped carefully down the steps.

Kenny commented that after he ate, he would clean the snow off the steps. He wouldn't want someone to get hurt.

Spence climbed into the saddle then leaned over with his arm out to help Glory up behind him.

"Horses" he said, "are a very important part of our lives around here. We need to make sure you know how to care for them, help manage the farm and maybe have your own horse."

"Really, Uncle Spence, you think I could own one? Besides, having a horse around the house in the pasture, I could go out to the yard to see it every day. That would be awesome!"

Spence told Glory, "We use them as our business partners to make money to pay our bills. Each horse has its own unique talent and personality. We have breeders from all over the country willing to use their stock with ours. Last year they came from Montana and Colorado."

Zinger climbed the mountain trail toward the pasture field just to the south end of the farm. Glory had been to the pasture field with Spence from the road, but this was her first time to travel the mountain trail. It was heavenly. The snow-covered trees dipped to the ground from the weight of the snow. They reached the top of the hilly trail overlooking the town below. It was a winter wonderland. She could see rows of townhouses, the shops of the town, and the school. She could hear the chimes from the church tower ringing. Glory could see the smoke coming out of the chimneys. She could smell the wood burning like the first day they had arrived in town.

Zinger started jumping around as he saw the other horses by the bright red painted barn. The roof had held up. Spence was worried about it. He had been meaning to replace it, but just repaired it instead for lack of the materials. When they approached the barnyard, Spence helped Glory down off Zinger and tied him to a post.

"I hope mom's okay! Uncle Spence, do you know Kenny?"

"No, Glory, I hadn't met him until today. Why?"

"I'm not sure but I think I've seen his truck parked outside our driveway before." Glory replied.

"You sure?"

"I think so, Uncle Spence. I met him this week when he came into the shop for a delivery. Mrs. Robins needed an order delivered to Maine. I remembered the sign on the side of the truck when we got home. I was going tell mom, but when I came downstairs to tell her, she was on the phone. Then I forgot about it until he showed up at our house today."

"Well, we'll keep an eye out, okay?" Spence placed his arm on his niece's shoulder to calm her.

"I need to go into the loft and bring down some hay. Want to help?"

"Sure." They made their way through the snow to a small door. Inside the barn there was a stairway up to the loft. They climbed to the top and Glory stepped carefully into the loft filled with baled hay.

"Watch your step." Spence went to an opening in the floor and started pitching the bales of hay through the opening to the floor below after untying the strings. The horses were waiting with their hair covered in snowy blankets. "They will need a few extra bales in case I don't get out here again today. I like to check on them twice a day, but the weather may not let me come back until tomorrow."

Glory saw a sign hanging in the corner. The words read: **"Long Tail Ranch."** "What's this, Uncle Spence?"

"That's the name of the farm."

"Why isn't it posted somewhere down by the main gates?"

"The original signs fell down and this one was hanging out on the side of this barn. When I painted the barn, I hung it there so it didn't blow away. The nails had come loose and I didn't have new nails or the correct hammer with me to put it back up."

"Why are the horses swinging their tails like that?"

Spence laughed, "That's how the ranch got its name. Your great grandfather built this farm here in the foothills raising horses with beautiful floor-length tails. Their long tails not only make noble horses look more graceful and beautiful, but the tails are efficient fly swatters as well."

"But there's no flies out today."

"That's right, Glory, but they are so used to swatting they do it all the time. I just can't imagine life without horses. That's why when it's meal time, they get fed first. When it's cold outside, the horses need shelter to get in from the weather. I'm hoping when the main barn is finished, we can bring the horses to the main pasture fields."

"Oh, Uncle Spence, that would be wonderful to have them close to the house where I could visit them each day!"

Spence told Glory, "The whole town is hoping your mom gets the farm up and running again. Your great grandfather made a lot of money off horses and they brought lots of people into the town for business."

"Uncle Spence, did you bring any grain?"

"There is grain in the drum by the doorway where we came in, but I'm not going to give them a lot of grain."

"Why?" Glory asked.

"It's best to increase the roughage (hay) rather than grain in cold weather because grain digests faster and the heat leaves the body quicker. Hay is digested more slowly, making the heat last longer and keeping the horse warm from the inside out."

They climbed back on the step and made their way down the ladder. Spence took a tin cup made out of a quart size can from the drum. He dipped out 3 full cans and put them into a bucket. "Here, this is all the grain we are going to give them today. They will feed on the hay more so than the grain."

"Which one are we taking back with us?"

Spence looked around the fifteen or so horses. "Sherlock has shoes and will do better in the snow. He loves kids so you will not have any trouble with him."

"Good." Glory was a little nervous about the ride back, since she would be riding her own horse. She was having a good time in the barnyard helping Uncle Spence comb each one of the horses getting the snow off their backs so they would dry off in the sun.

Chapter 21

WITH SPENCE AND GLORY gone to check on the horses in the south pasture, Mary tried to talk to Kenny. She had seen him once before in this kind of mood. She wasn't sure why he gets this way, but she didn't like it.

"Kenny, it was nice seeing you drive into town last week. What is troubling you so much today?"

Kenny looked up saying, "My truck, I'll feel better when I have control of my truck."

"Sure, I can understand that and as soon as we can get someone out there, they can get your truck out of that ditch and you on your way. Do you want to call someone to let them know you are safe in case the road crews find your truck?"

"Sure, I need to do that."

"Okay, here's the phone. I will be in the living room when you're done."

Kenny dialed the number to Heyman Trucking. "Yes, Karen, I will be out for a few days. Don't schedule any work for me until I get back to you. Sure, I'll call you." He hung up the phone.

Mary heard the conversation since she left the kitchen door open for the heat from the fireplace to help warm the kitchen. She thought, "He didn't say anything about the truck. Why?" She heard him dialing the phone again…this time it was to the fire department.

"Yes, I want to let the county police department know my truck is in a ditch off Simmer Road. That's right… no…no one is hurt and I'm safe at a friend's house, but it may be several days before we can get the truck out due to the weather. Thanks…hold please…Mary, what's the number here?"

Mary came back into the kitchen and gave him the number 557-2363. He repeated the number over the phone. "That's good… sure will… bye."

He walked over to Mary, grabbed her arm and began to kiss her. She tried to pull away, but his grip was more than she wanted to fight. He picked her up in his arms and started up the back stairs.

"Don't, Kenny," Mary was trying to say but Kenny wasn't paying any attention to her words.

"Why, Mary, has it been that long? Did you forget what we had together? I didn't! And now there's no husband to play head games with you."

His words flooded her head with the powerful times that the two of them had together. With each step he took, his tongue stroked her neck, caressed her ears, and teased across her lips. His warm breath tickled her neck as they moved up the back steps. In the bedroom he placed her on the unmade bed. He pulled off his t-shirt and one hand started unbuttoning her blouse. While at the same time, he ran the other hand over her breasts making the nipples stand to attention. His tongue was back on her neck again, moving in circles around her ears and down her chest.

"Kenny…" she said breathlessly.

"What? You want me to stop? No way, my dear… I have been waiting for this day. Now you are mine." He continued to run his tongue over her body as he came to the last button. He popped the button on her jeans and the zipper tore from the seam as he ripped the threads in his excitement to finally have her. He pulled the jeans from her body as his tongue continued to circle around her navel.

Mary just laid there not fighting his touch. She remembered how rough he could get and how gentle as well. How determined was he to have his way with her? What if she refused him? She would be better off to let him have his way. He continued with his tongue down to her panties. "Nice," he said as his hands gripped her hips and she felt his teeth as he used them to pull her panties down. Her underwear dropped around her knees. He worked on his jeans. The belt buckle hitting against her leg as his jeans fell to the floor. He stepped out of the jeans and moved his attention back on the bed placing his body beside her. She felt him as he blew warm gentle circles on her belly and up across her nipples while he pressed his firmly built body against hers.

Mary again said, "Kennnyy."

He put his hand over her mouth as he pressed firmly to keep her from saying No! He moved his other hand between her legs fingering her most private area. "What? Not excited enough my dear? Well, I need to do something about that." He started blowing around her nipples then nibbling them with his teeth as he moved down between her legs. The touch of his rough hands made it clear he wanted her and he was going to get what he wanted. He stopped for a second and leaned over the bed for the belt. His hand moved from her mouth as he reached for the belt. She knew if she didn't give him what he wanted he would get rougher with her. She did not want bondage with the belt. He had done that before.

"No… Kenny…you don't need that. Come, Baby… I'll give you what you want" she said softly. She started moving between his legs and her tongue started caressing his chest, his neck and his ears. She needed to satisfy his sexual fantasy and get back downstairs before Glory got home.

He liked feeling dominant and liked restraining his partner while he slowly teased them into an orgasm. She knew she needed to play the game and make him think she too wanted this as much as he did. She forced her leg up between his to caress his firm tool. He wanted more and his movement became more intense. Mary moved her leg inviting him inside her. His sweat was dripping off his face and down on her chest. His movements became even more intense.

Mary grabbed his hips and started moving with more force in an up and down motion. "Come on, Baby, what are you waiting on? You wanted it…now you have it…ride it baby."

Forcefully, he screamed out, "My God, Girl! You still got it!" He pumped her harder and harder until she thought she was going to die. Finally, he ejaculated. She had to maintain herself until she could be sure he was satisfied. She needed to make him think she enjoyed herself. She let her body respond to his touch - now gentle, lightly caressing her legs, and arms out to her finger tips. Kissing her lightly on the lips he whispered, "I've waited a long time for that, Girl," smiling at her.

Whispering Mary said, "Kenny, I need to get dressed before Glory gets back."

He replied, "Sure, Girl. What's stopping you?" He laid over to one side to let Mary move off the bed and toward the floor as she picked up her things. She opened the bedroom door to the hallway making sure she relocked it as she left the room.

"I need to wash up. I'll be in my bathroom. You rest now." She went down the hallway to her room. Closing her bedroom door behind her, she began to cry holding her hand over her mouth because she did not want to let Kenny hear her. She moved to her sink and quickly washed off. She ran out to the closet and grabbed another shirt and a pair of jeans that looked a lot like the ones she was wearing before Kenny tore off her clothes. She quickly went back to the bathroom, brushed her hair, fixed her face, and went downstairs. She hoped he had gone back to sleep, but to her surprise he was in the living room by the TV when she came down the stairs.

"Well, now don't you look good enough to eat?"

"Kenny, please, Glory will be home anytime now. Please, be nice and a gentleman around her."

"Sure, Girl, you keep up the good job and I'll be so nice to you."

Mary was sitting at the kitchen table when Spence and Glory got back. She saw the horses coming around the backyard from the mountain trail. She remembered Sherlock from pictures that her mom had of the farm from their last visit. Spence tied the horses down by the barn and they walked toward the house. Mary met them by the back door and asked, "Ready for that coffee now?"

Spence wasn't going to turn down something warm this time. He noticed Mary seemed very nervous. "Everything okay, Mary?"

"Sure, Spence, just wanted to have coffee with a friend."

"Sure, why not warm up for a minute before making my way home. Can I use the phone?"

"Help yourself."

Spence called Jenny to let her know he would be home soon. "Yes, I stopped to check on Mary. Glory went with me to check on the horses. She had a great time and I'm bringing Sherlock home with me. Sure...we'll see...okay, Dear...bye now."

Jenny says, "Hello. She wanted to know if you will bring the pies for Thanksgiving dinner?"

"About dinner, Spence...since I have company, maybe we should just stay home this year."

"That's crazy. Bring Kenny along. He can eat with us."

"But..."

"No buts about it...he needs to eat, doesn't he?"

Mary replied, "There's no way the roads are going to be open."

"Well, then I will just need to get out the horse sleigh."

"You still have the sleigh?"

"Sure do."

"Oh, Spence, that's great!" with a big smile on Mary's face.

"So, you make the pies and I will pick you guys up around ten o'clock tomorrow. Deal?"

Mary looked somewhat puzzled, but told Spence they would be ready. Looking forward to the sleigh ride - she hadn't taken a ride like that since Jack went away. They had sleighs in the city for hire, but out here in the country with the winter's first snowfall there were sleighs everywhere. What a blessing that could be.

"Kenny," Spence said, as he walked into the living room, "Would you like to join us for Thanksgiving dinner tomorrow? Dinner's at my place."

Kenny still watching TV replied, "Maybe."

"Well, let me know. I need to get the horses home and take care of them so I can have something to eat myself. It's been a long morning."

"Spence, I'm sorry. Can I make you a sandwich?"

"No, Mary, thanks but until I get the horses done you know I don't eat."

"Some things just don't change, do they?" Mary questioned with a smile. She walked Spence to the back door.

"You sure you're okay, Mary?"

"Yes, Spence, I'm fine. Please, call when you get home."

"You call if you need anything!" Spence replied. Out the door he went down the steps toward the barn. He climbed on Zinger and with one hand holding the reins to Sherlock he headed toward the road.

Mary went back in the kitchen, picked up the phone to let Jenny know Spence was on his way, and to tell her she would make the pies. Mary asked as she hung up the phone, "Glory, want to help?"

The two ladies pulled out the apples from the closet and the canned pumpkin from the shelf. Mary got down from the top shelf a large mixing bowl. "Glory, can you cut up the apples? I will mix up the first batch of pumpkin." She had purchased the pie shells and pulled them from the freezer. Soon the kitchen was filled with the country cooking smells of fresh pumpkin and apple pies.

Kenny sat motionless in the living room watching TV. Mary thought about what he had said concerning the snow on the porch stairs. He said he would clear the steps. But the snow's still there. She shook her head.

Several times Glory wanted to say something to her mom about Kenny, but didn't want him to overhear. She didn't understand him being there and he had taken over the living room.

Just then, Kenny came into the kitchen checking the refrigerator for a beer. **"What - no beer!** Mary, I'm going to need to teach you when I'm around, there's beer chilling!" He smacked her on the backside as he was passing her.

Mary looked up saying, "I didn't know you were going to be here, remember?"

Later in the evening the phone rang. It was the County Police looking for Kenny Morris. "Sure, just a moment…Kenny, the phone is for you."

The officer told Kenny the county snow crew was going to be out on Simmer Road. Did he need a ride to his truck? They would see if they could pull him out of the ditch.

"About an hour… that would be just fine. Thanks. I'll be watching for you. Yes… that's the address. Thanks again." Kenny hung up the phone. He told Mary the State snow truck was going to pick him up. They were going to help get the truck from the ditch.

"That's great," Mary replied thinking to herself maybe he will go on his way.

Fifty-five minutes later they heard the snow plow out front. They were opening Mary's driveway as they made their way toward the house. "Well, that's service," she said.

When he left the house, Mary knew he would be back. He didn't take his bag with him. But she was glad to get a break for both her and Glory to watch some TV. They went into the living room with the TV still on boxing. Mary quickly turned the station. She hated boxing! The news was on. She stopped the channel to see what's going on in the area. A lot of accidents reported. One interview showed a tractor trailer truck in a ditch on Simmer Road.

"Look, Mom, isn't that Kenny's truck?"

"Sure is, Glory." They listened to the report and Mary knew by the pictures if they got the truck out of the ditch, it would be a few days before Kenny would be leaving.

"It looks like there is damage to the truck, Mom."

"I think so, Glory. He was lucky."

"Mom, will he be here for very long?"

"Why, Glory?"

"I just don't know…I don't like him," she said shaking her head. "He looks at you different than Jack or Erik."

"Glory!!!"

"I'm sorry, Mom. He just makes me uncomfortable."

"Well, you make sure to tell me if he does anything to harm you. You hear me. He'll be gone soon." After the news, they both watched a movie. Kenny hadn't returned yet.

Glory said, "Goodnight" and went up to bed.

Mary did not want to leave the door unlocked so she wrapped herself up on the sofa waiting. She replayed what had happened earlier in the day and what Glory had said about Kenny making her uncomfortable. He wouldn't. He better never do anything to Glory.

She tried to shake the feeling and at the same time remembered the tenderness from the last night she and Erik were together. 'How I was such a fool. Erik is a good man. A good father! Why did I feel I needed to act like that?' She laid back on the sofa comparing the three men - how different all three were in their own ways.

Jack was a 100 % gentleman when it came to their sexual activities with his tender hands and sexy voice whispering in her ear. They would cuddle as his hand would caress her body softly like a feather dancing across her body enhancing the pleasure.

Erik's hands were so tender, caressing her body, giving her goose bumps of pleasure as she wanted more with each touch and each kiss. As their relationship had started developing and bringing them closer, she wanted more of his French kisses. The touch of their mouths exchanging saliva had her hot and excited. With each stroke that night she wanted to eagerly respond to him. Instead she wouldn't talk to him. She should have explained her feelings that night to Erik. 'Why won't you call me?' she thought.

Now she was alone. Again, she had sex with Kenny knowing she didn't care for him that way. Why did she do that again? Didn't she know nothing good was going to come out of this? Why had she called for Kenny to make that delivery in the first place? Did she like bringing the problems to her doorstep? Tears were running down her face when she went to the back bathroom to dry her face.

On the way back down the hall she stopped by Granny's room. She opened the door and turned on the light. The room came to life. "Oh, Granny, why do I do these really brainless things? You'd think I really was a blonde."

Chapter 22

MARY THOUGHT SHE HEARD a truck by the barn. She turned out the light in Granny's room and went to the back door to turn on the outside light. The snow plow was clearing the driveway between the house and barn making extra parking for the guys if they still wanted to work on the barn on Saturday - weather permitting. "Great," Mary thought but as cold as it was, she didn't know when the snow would be gone and when the guys would get to work on the barn again. Mary looked at the clock. It was 2am. She knew Kenny had been gone a long time, but didn't realize she had been daydreaming for that long.

Kenny came to the back door waving to the guys as the truck left. "Hey, Girl." He tracked snow in with him as he closed the door and turned out the porch light. "Well, my truck will need some work before driving it."

"We saw it on the news tonight. How much damage was done?"

"I'm not sure," Kenny replied. "We had to leave the trailer beside the road. The tow-truck took the tractor into town. The owner of the station will call me Friday. Everything would be closed tomorrow for Thanksgiving."

"Too bad, Kenny!"

"Well…that just gives me more time with you, my dear." He backed Mary up against the wall, pulling her wrists above her head and pressing his wet cold clothes against her warm body.

"Kenny, please!"

"Don't want to play, Honey? Maybe I do!" The bathroom door was open and he took her by the hair to the tub. "DRAW US A WARM BATH! You look as wet as I am." He took off his coat and dropped it to the floor.

Mary turned on the water to the tub. She got towels from the closet and looked for some bubble bath oil. She found some Milk & Honey Foam bath essentials, opened the bottle and started pouring it into the tub water. She remembered Kenny like the bubbles.

"That's my girl! Make lots of bubbles so we can have some fun. No daughter to stop us now!"

Kenny moved closer to her while she sat on the edge of the tub still checking the water with one hand to make sure it didn't get too hot. "Nice smell, what is it?" asked Kenny.

"It's Milk & Honey. It is supposed to smooth and soften your skin as you enjoy the luxurious fragrances. Here - indulge yourself" as she put a bubble on his nose.

"Girl, you are crazy! Get those clothes off and get in there?"

"Me? Getting in? I thought the bath was for you."

"Yes, it is, Mary. It's for us. I need some tender lovin'! It was cold out there."

Mary turned her back to him as she started to unbutton her blouse. She didn't want another blouse missing any of the buttons. She undid her jeans and stepped out of them before he had a chance to tear another pair. She felt Kenny's hands undoing her bra then his hands moved to her hips and down came her panties. His hands moved to her shoulders as he turned her to face him and her bra dropped. He stood there with his most private parts hanging long and limp. "Mary, do you know how much I enjoy you?"

Mary stood there not knowing what to say. She needed to be very careful with her words. She tried to change the subject by saying,

"The water will get cold. Get in." Kenny didn't reply with words, just stepped into the tub and sat down.

"The water feels great after being out in the cold for so long."

"I'm sure it does." Mary took the extra towel and placed it on the floor by the tub as she bent over. Kenny kissed her breast circling the nipple with his thumb. Mary stepped into the tub and sat down facing him.

The tub was great. Mary knew from the first time she saw the tub there would be lots of room for two people. She leaned back, placed her head on the edge of the tub, and closed her eyes enjoying the warmth of the water. Of course, Kenny had other things on his mind. He poured water down over Mary's chest with his hands as he watched her breasts stand to attention from the hot water. She opened her eyes with a smile to see him smiling back at her. She took her foot moving it between his legs using her toes to feather across his stomach and up his chest. He caressed her breasts teasing from one to the other as he whispered, "Let it go, Mary."

She moved her foot between his legs to find his obsession for her body had raised his passion to stand at attention. "When the mood takes you, Girl, you always could get creative. Do it, Girl. Do your thing! Allow your erotic fantasies to come out!"

Mary climbed on top of him, straddled across his lap, kissed him, and brought her whole body down in contact with his. The bathwater soothed the motion as she used the tub rail for leverage to move her body up and down while he kissed and caressed her breasts, across her shoulders, around her neck and ears, then back to her nipples. The scented water was heavenly. Its silky texture made it easier to do the things Kenny requested. Mary lost herself in the overwhelming physical workout. Most of us would have become exhausted but it made Kenny want more. He grabbed her firmly now pushing her down on him harder and harder. Those momentary fine lines between passion and lust made Kenny bite hard into her nipple causing it to bleed. But that didn't stop him. He continued to push her hard against his tool. He was wild and hot with lustful sexy ideas as he continued. He forced her to her knees with her back toward him. "Don't worry about a thing, My Dear" as he entered from the rear pushing her into the water hard against the surface of the tub wall.

Again, she thought, "Why does he get so rough?" She cried as he forced himself in and out again and again. He stopped long enough to force her back on her knees for a better grab.

She begged, "Kenny, please! Please, let me turn and let me satisfy you. Slow down and let me do the work for a while."

"In time," he said. Still on his knees he turned Mary to face him. Mary grabbed his shoulders afraid she was going to fall. He grabbed her as he forced her on his tool again from the front and started to pump as his passion pressed her knees hard against the sides of the tub. Kenny grabbed her ass and stood up quickly. Not bothering to dry off he moved across the room placing Mary on the dressing table. Pushing her hard on her back, he forced her feet over his shoulders and continued to pull in and out, time after time finally coming to a climax. The emotion with his expression came hard, showing Mary his true essence of fulfillment. "Yes! Oh, God, Yesss," he yelled.

Mary faking the enjoyment led Kenny to believe her final climax as she thought, "Finally?"

But Kenny was not done with her. He dropped her legs bending them downward forcing her knees toward the floor and her feet under the table. Kenny leaned down and started kissing around her belly as his lips moved down her body. He worked slowly to her pubic area. He stroked and rubbed her mons with his fingers tugging gently on the pubic hair enticing Mary to want more. Kissing along the sides of her legs and caressing with his finger inside her as he spoke, "No matter how hard I came now it's your time. Lie there and enjoy!"

Mary moaned encouraging him for more of his tenderness. He nuzzled into her mons gently caressing and kissing. His tongue playfully stroked, even thrust a little into it. He changed the rhythm and action of his tongue as he licked from side to side. Kenny thought how sexy she looked moving for more of his touch. He became hard again watching her enjoy his stroking as she again became so very moist and slowly building to that sensational climax. At that he climbed on the table and placed himself on top in the sixty-nine position. He experienced the wet, hot body one more time. Mary grabbed him pulling him close wanting more. They both experienced the licking, kissing, and caressing, and the willingness of each other's body. They enjoyed the touch and the overwhelming excitement of one another until orgasm was no longer a fake. Mary laid on the table lifeless completely spent by the force Kenny has used to make sure she was pleased.

Chapter 23

MARY WOKE UP TO a banging sound outside. She rolled over to get out of bed (oh, her body ached). She laid there wondering what in the world is the banging? She finally sat up. She edged her knees over the side of the bed sitting there for a moment before standing. She hadn't felt like this since the last time she and Kenny had been together nearly two years ago. Mary forced herself to walk to the window to see Kenny crushing the icy snow which covered the back steps down below her bedroom window. She reached for her robe as Glory came into the room.

"What's with the noise, Mom?" Glory was eyeing her mother for a reply, "Mom, you okay?"

"Yes, Glory. Why?"

"You don't look so good."

"Oh, Glory, I'm fine. Now go get on your robe."

Mary walked into her bathroom looking at herself in the mirror. Glory was right. She didn't look too good with tired dark circles around her eyes. "Well, I guess that's what I get for playing around last night," she told herself not knowing she looked worse under her robe. She pulled her hair back in a ponytail, brushed her teeth, and washed her face. Leaning over the sink, she braced herself with her arms. She decided to go ahead with her shower before going down stairs. She turned on the water, adjusted the temperature and turned toward the mirror as she undid her robe and gown. To her surprise, she had bruises and bite marks covered all her body. The bite on her breast she remembered. The others bites were not as deep or as big, but they were still there. She quickly covered herself as Glory came thru the door. "Glory, please, give me some alone time this morning, would you?" she screamed in a tough tone.

"Sorry, Mom. I needed…"

Her tone continued. "Your needs can wait - see you downstairs!"

Glory closed the bathroom door saying, "Sorry, Mom" confused, but walked back to her room. She was going to wait for her mom before going downstairs. She just did not want to be alone with Kenny. She felt that he was BAD NEWS and thought he had something to do with mom's bad mood. Why did he show up here? Why had she seen his truck here long before the snow came? Too many questions but she didn't dare ask her mom now.

Mary took her time in the bathroom. She showered looking at the bruises around her waist and knees. There were three serious bite marks, one on her breast and two down where her panties would cover them. Thinking to herself, "Kenny you just don't realize how rough you are." Little had Mary realized this was the way Kenny liked it. The rougher the better - it made him feel in control. She could hear him still banging on the hard-snow-covered steps. 'That should have been done yesterday when the snow was still fresh.' She laughed to herself.

She got dressed, finished her make-up, and moved slowly into the bedroom to make the bed. She pulled the sheets to fluff them and found a spot of blood on one sheet. "Oh, no, where did that come from?" She quickly moved the comforter up over the bed before Glory came back into the room. Nauseous she went back into the bathroom checking the medicine cabinet for a bandage. She wanted to make sure her bra did not make the bite on her breast bleed again today. She covered the bite mark checking her shirt to make sure the bandage couldn't be seen.

Finally, she made her way to the hallway passing Glory's open bedroom door. Glory didn't see her mom for the teen was into the music she had playing and not paying attention.

"Glory," Mary shouted." Have you been downstairs?"

"No, Mom. I was waiting for you."

"Okay, come on. Let's get our day started and Happy Thanksgiving" as she gave her daughter a hug. They walked arm and arm to the stairs.

"Kenny should have cleared the snow yesterday, Mom. It wouldn't have been as hard."

"I know, Glory. Sometimes men just don't use their heads. You know? But at least he is trying to clear it today."

Mary tried not to let Glory know how rough she really was feeling. Her knees ached as she walked down the stairs.

The coffee was on. It looked like Kenny had also eaten breakfast with the dishes still on the counter.

"Mom, he doesn't clean up after himself. Does he?"

Mary smiled at Glory saying, "I'll talk to him, okay?"

Glory got her mom and herself a glass of OJ and told her mom she was going back upstairs to get her shower. "What time will Uncle Spence be here?"

"Around ten, Glory. Please, be ready!"

"No worries," Glory said as she ran up the stairs. She would be ready. She was looking forward to the sleigh ride and she liked being around Uncle Spence. "He does treat me like a kid yet I learn a lot from him," she thought as she entered her room and closed the door.

Kenny came through the back door and of course, brought snow in with him. Mary asked him to clean his feet before tracking through the house as she was coming out of the bathroom by the back door. He looked at her. She pulled him into the bathroom. Kenny asked if she wanted more of last night with a big smile.

"NO! Look what you did!" Mary pulled up her top and opened her jeans showing him the teeth marks and bruises. He shrugged his shoulders.

"Girl, you just need to toughen up."

"Kenny, I have bruises on my hips and knees from you."

"Well, you've been without too long, I'd guess! Keep me around. I'll toughen you up," he said - laughing.

"It's not funny, Kenny. What will I tell Glory if she sees the bruises?"

"Well, tell her you fell last night on the porch stairs and that's why I was trying to clear them. Okay, Mary. I don't want to hear your whining." Out the door he went slamming it behind him as he headed toward the barn.

Mary didn't like the feeling she was having. He's been here two days and already taking over. Why did it have to snow? Why did he come back and how long was his truck going to be out of commission? He needed to go!

Mary went back to the kitchen to get her pies ready for the ride with Spence. She was looking forward to the sleigh ride. Glory came back downstairs ready and jumping with excitement. You would have thought the two girls were getting ready to go on their first date.

"Mom, the horses and sleigh will be so much fun, don't you think? Uncle Spence was saying when the barn gets completed, maybe we can bring the horses from the back pasture to this barn and let them in the front pasture fields. It would be closer for him to check them and I could help keep an eye on them as well."

"Sounds good, Glory. But with the snow it will take longer to get the barn ready. There's still a lot of work to be done out there. Plus, the fence line needs to be checked as well before bringing the livestock to this side of the farm."

"I know, Mom. I'm just excited about it. Maybe I could even

have my own horse. You think we could, Mom?"

Mary thought, "Maybe, we'll see."

They could hear the jingle of the sleigh off in the distance. Both of them went to the living room windows to see Spence making the turn toward the railroad crossing before turning into the driveway.

"Oh! Mom, look! Do we have a camera? I want some pictures."

"Glory, on my dresser there is a camera. Will you get it?"

Up the stairs Glory ran and was back before Spence could get the horses up the driveway. She went running out the back door (coat, hat and gloves in her hand). "Uncle Spence!" she hollered snapping the camera as she ran.

"Good morning," he called, as he pulled closer to the barn.

"The horses are beautiful." She yelled, "Good morning, Sherlock and Zinger." Glory was ready to pat Sherlock's head when Kenny interrupted.

"Glory, put on your coat and tell your mom to come on," with a rough tone to his voice as he yelled.

"It's okay, Kenny, we still have time. I'm sure Mary will be right out. She was looking forward to this ride," Spence remarked.

"Sure, she was," Kenny snapped.

Glory was snapping pictures with Uncle Spence at the reins. She turned to go back to the house when her mom came out wearing her high brown leather boots, a brown toboggan, a long wool coat and gray gloves carrying a box with the pies neatly wrapped inside.

Spence asked Glory to take the reins. She took the reins and continued to talk to her new friends as he stepped down from the sleigh to help Mary with the box of pies.

Kenny interrupted again, telling Glory one more time, to put on the coat, and this time pushing Spence out of the way to take the box from Mary.

Spence turned back to the horses and sleigh. "Mary, good morning. Ready for your ride?" he asked.

Mary was full of smiles at Spence, standing tall with his black cowboy hat, oversize riding coat almost dragging the ground and his winter knee high boots.

"Oh, yes, Spence. Good morning to you and Happy Thanksgiving! I have been looking forward to this!" She took her time climbing into the sleigh with Kenny at her side as he climbed in behind her and both sat on the back seat.

Spence noticed Mary was having a little trouble getting into the sleigh. "Good thing the sleigh has two seats," he said. "Glory, you can ride up front with me and help with the reins." Glory was glad to do so and she was full of chatter and questions about their ride as she finally pulled her coat over her shoulders and buttoned it. Mary and Kenny sat in the back with Kenny's arm across Mary shoulders.

"You okay, Mary?" Spence questioned.

"Oh, yes, Spence. Thanks for coming to pick us up."

"Glad to..." he replied. Spence turned the horses and sleigh around heading down the driveway and back out onto the road. Mary asked if there had been any traffic.

"No, I didn't see anyone on the way over. I see the snowplow came through."

"Yes, last night when they came to pick up Kenny. They helped him get the truck out of the ditch. It was nice of them to plow the driveway too."

"Yes, that will help, but the snow isn't going anywhere as long as it stays this cold. There's a blanket by your feet. Put it around your legs or over your shoulders if needed. Glory, there's another one under your seat if you need it. Kenny, did you get the truck out?"

"The tractor - but they had to pull it into town. It needs some repairs before I can drive it. I need for someone from Heyman to come pick up the trailer. I'll call them tomorrow."

The ride was lovely. Both girls were smiling from ear to ear. The beauty of the mountains covered with snow was calming and relaxing. They came to the covered wooden bridge that Mary and Glory crossed when they went to and from town, but Spence took another side road that followed the creek instead of crossing the bridge. It was an unplowed road which had only a single pair of tracks running down the center of it from the sleigh. Mary had noticed the road before when they had gone to town, but had never taken the narrow dirt road which followed the creek on the opposite side. They could see and hear the creek water running over its rocky bed with just a touch of snow covering some of the rocks that were sticking out above the water. The snow was clinging to the branches of the crabapple, wild cherry and poplar trees pulling their branches out over the creek bed. Two birds passed by fighting over some berries they had found. Mary thought how beautiful the view, how calm and how silent with no noise from the big city buses, cars and busy people. She realized she had not taken the time to enjoy the small things of life. Mary was glad to be here enjoying her ride through the countryside in the horse drawn sleigh as it turned the corner onto another road. This time there were tracks from other vehicles going around another turn into a private driveway. The horses made their way through the snow, climbing the hill and around the S turns toward a little A-framed house with two built-out one-story attachments on each side. The house was nestled on the top of the hill overlooking the valley below with fields and fields of countryside and mountains creating a picture-perfect view of the valley. Spence stopped the horses and sleigh next to a small red barn on one side of the house. In front of them was a wooden handmade swing glider and a roof covered gazebo placed just perfectly on the top of hill to overlook the remarkable view.

Kenny asked, "Why don't you keep the horse here, Spence?"

Spence answered, "The gentleman who owns the farmland around us will not allow me to use the land. He owns from the road up to the yard fence on both sides and only allows road access to our house and barn...only because that's what the county requires." Our land is the house, barn and 10 acres of trees up the mountain.

"How much land is actually yours?"

"Ten acres, but maybe someday I will talk him into selling. He's never here. Lives in the city and has someone cut the field with a bush-hog. It's sad because we could use the fields for hay and pasture. I have tried to talk him into allowing me to cut the field for use of the pasture, but so far no go!"

Mary had noticed coming up the hill there were several trucks parked near the house. "Who all was coming today?" she asked.

"Well, Vivian and her friend - he has 3 children. That is them running around the swing. Maggie and the guy she is now dating. Erik and Cliff were invited, but I understand they went to Blacksburg for a basketball game and of course, you all."

Kenny being his usual self, asked if the house was going to be big enough for everyone?

"Sure will. It's bigger inside than you think. Go on in. I'm going to give the horses some grain and water." Spence started undoing the reins and unhooking the horses, taking them both toward the barn.

Glory ran to the other teens. She was happy to see other kids her age. They all were making a huge snowman by the swing and gazebo where she joined in. Their laughter echoed as they rolled the snow into large balls that were so big that they couldn't put their arms around them. They worked together placing the second large ball to make the body of the snowman. One of the boys went for sticks to use for the arms. Aunt Jenny came out with its hat and a carrot for the nose. Mary took pictures of the teens for her scrapbook.

Kenny stood by the sleigh looking over the view. Mary took a picture of him when he wasn't looking. She went back to the sleigh to pick up the box of pies and started to the door. Spence once again noticed that Mary had some trouble getting out of the sleigh and making her way through the snow toward the door. Also, he noticed that Kenny seemed a little too overbearing with watching over Mary when she would start to talk. He decided to keep his eyes open. Not sure why, but he too agreed with his niece, he didn't like Kenny.

Chapter 24

THE LADIES WERE ALL inside in the kitchen helping Jenny with the last minutes items. She went over to the oven to feel the heat. Jenny took the pies placing them on a side table filled with food.

"Everything smells great, Jenny. What can I do to help?" asked Mary.

"Nothing - we are about ready, just waiting on the guys to come in and get warm." Jenny knew Spence would be in soon and after he cleaned up, she would have him carve the turkey. By that time everything that was in the oven would be ready to put on the table for their holiday feast.

"We'll call the teens so they can get cleaned up and start getting everybody ready to be seated for their Thanksgiving dinner." Jenny had been cooking all day today and the day before. The turkey was done early this morning and looked wonderful sitting on the corner of the dining room table waiting for the family tradition for the man of the house to carve the bird.

Meanwhile the ladies were catching up on the gossip. You would have thought they had not seen each other in years instead of just a few days with each of them having a snow story to tell.

Kenny walked in from outside. The ladies stopped. Mary introduced him and told them he's staying with her and Glory until his truck is repaired. Jenny, Vivian and Maggie thought 'of course he is.' Jenny and Maggie both knew about Kenny from Mary when things went sour with her marriage, but had not had the "pleasure" of meeting him. What they had heard, they had not cared to ever meet him. Things were bad enough for Mary, but with Kenny in the picture it just made things worse. Now they were having Thanksgiving with him. How did this happen? What was he doing around here anyway? Mary noticed both her sister-in-law and her best friend looking at her with questions.

Vivian did not take her eyes off the tall stranger knowing her brother had been staying away from Mary. Could this be why? If so, Vivian thought, "I'm glad he didn't come today."

Mary sensed that she still was not Vivian's favorite person and possibly couldn't wait to let Erik know she had another man staying at her house. Oh, how she wished it had been Erik last night knowing there wouldn't have been any bruises to her body with his gentle touch. Mary coughed and walked to the window, looking out over the hillside with a tear in her eye. "Jenny, the view is breathtaking."

"Yes, I really love it here. We both wish we could get Mr. Ellsworth to allow us to use the farmland on either side of us. But he just won't talk to us."

"Too bad," Maggie said.

"Well, when we get the barn finished, we'll see about bringing the horses over to the main pasture and using the back for hay," Mary replied. She walked over and gave her sister a big hug. "Happy Thanksgiving, Sis."

"Mary, I'm glad you came. I mean not just today, but to the farm." She gave Mary a big hug giving both a feeling that the family issues between them were getting better.

It wasn't long before Jenny was announcing the meal was ready. Spence had carved the turkey and the other ladies helped carry the food from the small kitchen into the larger dining room area. What a feast Jenny had prepared.

When everyone was seated, Mary took a picture with the curtains open to the beautiful mountain snow-covered picture-perfect view.

Jenny asked, "Kenny, would you take another one, so Mary can be in the picture?" At the same time, she thought he wouldn't be.

Kenny took the camera and quickly snapped the picture not taking the time to focus the camera.

Maggie was asked to say grace. When she was finished, Spence asked, "Who would like a glass of wine?"

The ladies of course, all wanted a glass. The men went for the hard stuff which Vivian's male friend had brought. Spence decided not to drink. He needed to make sure Mary, Glory and Kenny got back home and that he could return with the horses safely.

Kenny was making his jokes about Spence not drinking. However, Mary was glad to see Spence could have a good time without a drink. Mary herself had only the one glass of wine with her meal. The other guys were drinking pretty hard and Vivian was as well. Mary was noticing she was making eyes at Kenny who was sitting across from her at the table.

Mary remembered Maggie's friend, Billy. She had met him when she and Erik were at The Club. They had all sat together and he seemed to be a lot of fun making everyone around the table laugh with his jokes. They talked about getting together to play Set-Back or Pinochle.

Of course, Kenny said the guys needed to get together for a hard game of poker. Mary got quiet quickly when Kenny started making plans for the guys to come by her place and play some cards. She didn't think he would be staying in town that long nor was he staying at her house. She felt it was about time for him to go. But was he thinking the same way?

Finishing dinner, they all moved to the living room.

"Coffee anyone?" Jenny thought maybe the guys would get the hint, but instead Kenny took the three men's glasses to the kitchen for another refill. Mary was pouring a glass of tea with the refrigerator door hanging open. Kenny hit her on the rear as he went for the ice tray above her head.

"Kenny, please."

"Please what, Mary! What's with you today? Miss Fragile, 'don't touch me.' Oh, poor Mary."

Mary thought the drinking was not making his attitude any better. She stopped and moved out of his way.

He poured a very strong drink in one glass and less in the other two. Kenny looked at Mary saying, "Better than a truck stop, hey Girl?" The memories flowed over Mary like it was yesterday. Yes, the night she met Kenny…it was on Thanksgiving. No wonder he was willing to return to see Mary over the Thanksgiving holiday. He tipped his glass to her ice tea and said, "Girl, that was some weekend we had." Mary dropped her head. No smile came to her face. The hurt was much worse and she tried not to show the tears forming in the corners of her eyes. She backed away and took her coat from the hook by the door making her way outside. She walked around the gazebo and across to the barn. Opening the door, she stepped inside and closed the door behind her. She walked over to talk to Sherlock and Zinger when Maggie's friend, Billy stepped into the barn.

"Mary, I thought I saw you come in here."

Mary quickly wiped the tears and turned toward the short, overweight, brown haired guy and said, "Well, I just needed some air."

"Thinking about Erik?

"Why would you ask that?"

"Because you two were an item, weren't you?"

"No, we were just old friends."

"Okay, if you say so. But the look in his eyes when the two of you were together was not just friends."

"Billy," Mary began to cry. "What have I done?" Maggie's friend, Billy took Mary into his arms to comfort her.

"You need to tell him how you feel."

Just then, Kenny walked into the barn and seeing Mary in some-one else's arms did not go over well with Kenny. He grabbed Billy's shoulder and swung a punch at him, just missing Mary, but catching Billy on the chin. "Hey guy, what's your problem?"

"You're my problem," Kenny said, "You leave her alone." Mary was shouting for Kenny to stop!

Kenny's fist was drawn to hit again. "I'll stop… you get YOUR things, it's time for us to go."

Mary replied she wasn't going anywhere. "You need to leave, call a taxi, your new friends from the snow plow service, I don't care! Just get out of here." By this time everyone was out of the house and standing by the barn door.

Spence came inside and asked if Mary was okay?"

"Yes," she replied. "Billy, you okay?"

"I'm fine! I'm sorry everyone! Mary and I were just talking."

"Kenny?" questioned Spence.

Kenny turned toward the door, hot headed, pushing the barn door with all his force against the fence behind it and walked out asking, "Jenny, can I use your phone?"

Kenny made a call and started walking down the snow-covered hill toward the dirt road.

Mary came out of the barn. "Kenny, where are you going?"

"Anywhere, but here," he replied. "I know when I'm not wanted."

Mary apologized to everyone and walked over to Billy asking, if he was okay?

Jenny thought, "Mary why couldn't you have left Kenny at your house."

Spence thought, "Mary's in too deep with this man."

Vivian and her friend said they were ready to leave. They called for the teens, climbed into the double cab 4x4 truck and made their way down the hill. They stopped to pick up Kenny and continued out the snow-covered dirt road, packing the snow as they left.

Mary thought Erik would be sure to hear about this.

Maggie came over and gave Mary a hug. "You okay?"

"Sure" Mary said in a whisper and just nodded her head.

Jenny wishing aloud, "Everyone, please come back inside, there is dessert and coffee for everyone. Mary, your pies look so good." Mary told her sister that Glory helped with the baking and did most of the work.

"Guys?" Jenny questioned.

Spence and Billy said they'd be in, "Just give us a few minutes." Both stood outside making sure Kenny didn't come back to do anything to get even. It also gave them a chance to talk.

Spence asked Billy, after the girls had gone back inside, "What happened?"

Billy explained he saw Mary upset and she went into the barn. "I came into the barn to see if she was okay or if she needed anything. We started talking about Erik and she started crying. I was just giving her a shoulder to cry on. I think she is missing Erik."

"Jenny and I think the same thing. But she won't talk about what happened."

"Do you think Kenny is the problem?" Billy replied.

"Well, he's a problem, but I don't think he was Mary and Erik's problem. We need to keep our eyes open for this character. I don't like or trust him."

Both men agreed to that, each putting their knuckles together before deciding to go inside for dessert and coffee.

The rest of the afternoon went well. Maggie and Billy sat in one large chair by the rock fireplace. Spence was telling the story of how some of his friends helped him find the rocks so they could build the fireplace wall and where the wood came from for the mantle.

Mary and Glory were on the floor in front of the fireplace enjoying the heat and listening to the stories. Spence and Jenny were on the sofa. All of them were getting ready to watch the Redskins/Dallas football game about to start on TV. 'The family Thanksgiving afternoon' Mary thought with a smile. When the game was over, Billy and Maggie asked Mary if she would like for them to take her home.

She said, "That would be fine. That way Spence wouldn't have to take the horses back out again." Although, she was going to miss the ride back in the sleigh she didn't want to worry about Spence coming home after dark on the road with the sleigh and horses.

Spence told Mary that he and Jenny were going into town tomorrow with the sleigh. "There will be room if you and Glory want to go."

Glory was up for another ride. "That's great Uncle Spence, isn't Mom?"

Mary replied, "We'll see tomorrow, Glory. Thanks, Spence. Can I call you in the morning, Okay? Jenny, thanks for a very nice Thanksgiving dinner and I'm sorry again for earlier."

"It's okay, Mary. Don't let that man take over your life… you hear me? You have been doing so well. You and Glory have come a long way in the last several months. Don't turn that to something bad just because that man says so."

"Okay, Jenny…we'll talk tomorrow." She gave her sister a hug as they left the house with Maggie and Billy. They climbed into Billy's truck already warm from him starting the engine and turning on the heater while the girls said their goodbyes.

The ladies laughed going down the hill sliding from one corner to the other around the turns. Not having a four-wheel drive truck, Billy said he had put cinderblocks in the back to give weight for better traction. They did some sliding and spinning, but they made it home safe. Mary could see their house as they crossed the railroad tracks. They spun into the driveway avoiding the van on their way up the hill toward the house. The driveway was like a sheet of ice due to the frozen snow being packed down by the snow plow. Billy told them, "Once the sun comes out and warms things up a little, the snow in the driveways will melt."

"No" Glory replied, "I like the snow."

Chapter 25

ON THE WAY BACK home, Mary couldn't help but wonder if Kenny would be there. Hoping he wasn't, but the reality was he would show up there sooner or later. His suitcase was still at her house.

Mary didn't ask Maggie and Billy in. She wanted to make sure Kenny wasn't there and that the two men would not have another face to face. No one would be there to break it up this time.

Maggie and Billy understood not being invited in without saying anything to each other. They only said, "Good night." Mary and Glory made their way to the stairs with Sneaky waiting for her meal. Billy backed his truck down the driveway sliding out onto the road.

"Mom, do you think Kenny will be back?"

"Yes, Glory, he will. His suitcase with his clothes is still here. He will be back. I hope after he has calmed down!"

They went inside, Glory got Sneaky's food dish ready and Mary started the teapot. Since it was getting dark, both went outside together to feed Sneaky who was glad to see them. She was jumping from one to the other as Mary and Glory bent down to play with her. Sneaky began to act funny - making noises like she was mad.

Mary jumped up to see Kenny standing over her shoulder. "Where did you come from?"

"I have been in the barn waiting for you."

"In the barn? You must be frozen - get inside and warm up." She placed her hand on his shoulder and he forced her away.

"Don't!"

Mary dropped her hand to her side and told Glory to get inside. They walked into the house without saying another word. Kenny went in the living room, of course with snow on his feet and sat down on the sofa. Mary took out the mop and cleaned the trail of water from the kitchen floor through to the living room.

Standing in the doorway to the living room she said "I'm having some tea, like some?"

"No." Kenny replied. "How about a beer?"

"Sorry, I don't have any. Coffee, tea or soda, that's it."

"No, thanks."

He took over the living room watching some kind of sports thing. The ladies in the kitchen talked about the wonderful day they had with the sleigh ride being at the top of the conversation. It wasn't long before they both heard him snoring. With him sleeping Mary told Glory, "Go up to bed. See you in the morning."

Mary turned down the TV, covered Kenny with one of Grandma's knitted blankets and started up the stairs herself.

"Mary, what was going on between you and that guy today?" Mary turned surprised to find Kenny awake.

"Nothing, Billy found me crying and was just trying to comfort me. That's all. You had the wrong idea, Kenny."

"Then, I'm sorry Mary. I didn't mean to mess up your day with your sister."

"You didn't Kenny. Now good night, see you tomorrow." Mary was hoping, praying under her breath that he would just let it go as she started toward the stairs.

He didn't say anything. Mary went up to bed.

The next several days seemed very long. Mary didn't go into town with Jenny and Spence, but she did let Glory go with them.

Glory came back saying she ran into Cliff at the ice cream parlor and again at the general store. He told her about their trip to Blacksburg and the basketball game.

Spence told Mary, "The guys weren't going to work on the barn this weekend. They seem to think there's still too much snow, it's too cold and it's too windy for anyone to be on the roof working."

She agreed.

Monday morning, she got Glory ready and they were going to go to town. She needed to get back to work.

Kenny asked if he could drive them and use the van to go check on the repairs of his truck.

Mary agreed, hoping the truck would be ready. But once more it wasn't. Kenny knew he would need to get the trailer from Simmer Road. He called Heyman Trucking, asking for Mr. Heyman. "Yes Sir, it's out of the road, but they needed to take the tractor into the garage so I haven't been able to get the trailer into town." Mr. Heyman agreed to send a tractor out there and bring the trailer back to their yard. Kenny gave them the directions and asked someone to call him after they had picked up the trailer, that way he would know they had the trailer and not some stranger.

Mr. Heyman told Kenny they would pick him up if he wanted to work until his tractor was ready. They were short drivers or he could ride with someone.

Kenny agreed.

Mary was glad to hear he was leaving and even more so he was going back to work.

Over the next week, the town was starting to look like Christmas. Everyone had been putting up lights and trimming with lots of glitter. The snow still covered the ground. The snow fell several more times to keep the white fluffy winter countryside fresh with its beauty.

The Interior Design Shop was busy with orders. Some customers stopped by the shop just to enjoy the smell of the different new candles that had arrived in the store for the holiday. Busy shoppers were coming and going, enjoying the Christmas scenes all over town and looking for that just right gift.

The small country town knew how to show the jolly side of the Christmas season making Mary think of the old song "Tis the Season to be Jolly!" Mr. and Mrs. Robins were busy with orders. The customers wanted special things made from Mr. Robins' wood shop for gifts. Others were looking for Mrs. Robins' special designs of fabric creations for their gift ideas. Mary had been busy with special deliveries and shipments of materials requested. She had to order more materials than usual for Mr. Robins to have for his creative wood ideas.

The town was filled with new ideas and everywhere the kids had built snowmen throughout the town. Every evergreen tree in town was shining with lights. The warm glow of the season decorated the homes and the shops, inviting you to come in for awhile. The general store with the new arrival of toys had lots of Christmas ideas and gifts throughout the well stocked walls.

The antique church with its graceful nativity scene was filled with lit candles for evening services everyday as Christmas drew closer. The kids were excited about the Christmas play's first performance being held this weekend with the hope of encouraging the families and friends to bring peace and joy into their homes this holiday season.

The Bed & Breakfast Inn was hosting company Christmas parties for the different shops and even the factories around the area. The companies invited their employees to the galas and provided them with rooms so no one would be driving drunk afterwards. The continued overnight snowfalls made it even imperative to help each other get home or better yet get a room. To be able to share the company of friends and family invited more people to come into town to enjoy the holiday season. The town was busy. Mary thought several times about stopping by Erik's flower shop, but just kept passing by, thinking, he will call or stop by. He told me the man is to do the pursuing. But he didn't and as time went on Mary began to believe that Vivian had told him about Thanksgiving Day. She was always ready to give Mary the old knife in the back whenever possible.

Mary stopped by The Bed & Breakfast Inn for lunch just days before Christmas. She had been busy all morning with the deliveries and needed to disappear from the sight of boxes. She walked across the street and stood looking into the windows, dreaming of the gifts of collectible figurines placed around the window box. Mary was impressed with the Christmas wreaths centered above each window and over the doorway of the stonework building. Each one had tiny hand painted lights and signs saying, "Merry Christmas to all."

She entered The Bed & Breakfast Inn and found herself a seat at the counter. With her back toward the crowded tables she placed her order with the waiter and continued to dream about the charming horses and sleighs going down the street. She heard his voice, she froze, and her palms began to sweat. She wanted to jump up and hug him, but as she turned, he was walking out the door. She sat back down, watched him cross the street and walk out of sight toward his shop. Oh, she hadn't forgotten and wanted more. Yes, Kenny had been staying at her house each time he came into town to check on his truck, but she had not allowed him to touch her since the night before Thanksgiving. She told him, he could stay until his truck was ready, but any missteps on his part and he would be staying elsewhere. He had been gone for several days taking Mr. Heyman's offer to work with one of his other trucks while waiting for his repairs to be done. For some reason they were having problems getting the parts needed to get his truck back on the road. In the meantime, while Kenny was in town, he would do small deliveries for Mr. and Mrs. Robins. That helped to keep Mr. Robins in the shop making his wooden toys and other hand carved items.

Mary ate her lunch and went back the gift shop. She continued to unpack the boxes putting the new items on the counter in front of her to be priced. She unwrapped a small 2 ft long by 1 ft high wooden rocking horse with real horse hair mane and tail. She stood there lightly stroking the mane, running her fingers through the real hair, wishing she could have been able to speak to Erik just for a moment - wanting to hear his voice say, "How are you?"

Mrs. Robins came out from her office. "Oh, I see the new items came."

"Yes," Mary replied. I love the horse. What prices are we putting on these new items?"

Mrs. Robins told her to price 50% over the wholesale prices on the invoice. Mary looked at the invoice and the horse was going to be priced at $200.00. "Wow" she thought aloud. "Yes, that's just my taste." She placed the horse on the counter being careful not to drop it. Mrs. Robins was watching Mary eyeing the nicely carved, hand painted horse with its matching saddle nested on its own rocker.

Mrs. Robins asked Mary to make sure all the new items were priced and out on the shelves before she left today.

"Sure," Mary answered.

Tomorrow started another weekend and Mary would not be working. Mrs. Robins knew the new items would be sold over the weekend if they were out.

Mary had half the box to go to unwrap and price each item before 5pm. "Okay," she thought. Glory came in from the back room. She had been upstairs dusting.

"Glory, grab a marker and help price these items while I am unwrapping. I will give you the price to put on each item. Please, be very careful not the drop them."

"Mom, I dust them - remember?"

"Oh, yes, that's right. Please, just be careful!"

Glory moved quickly pricing the items. There were several pieces of the same thing, but only one horse. Mary finished the last of the unwrapping, which was the Hawthorne Village Collections. Each item of his collection (she read on the flyer enclosed) he had hand painted. She unwrapped a tiny antique car, a horse and sleigh, tiny people, small Christmas trees, street lamplights, a general store, a post office, a church, a school, several country cottages, and tiny children for the playground. Others dressed like ice skaters were for the tiny pond. Mary placed the pieces around on the shelf below the glass counter by the cash register. This way when customers walked to the counter to pay, they would see the lovely collections. Mary knew the collection well. She was sure it would sell fast.

Mrs. Robins came back in to see how much more Mary had to do before finishing for the evening. She was taken by the collection. She had seen it when she was in New York and it was a must buy at the time. Mary had a good eye for placing the new items within the store. Mary asked, "Will the stairway be finished by Monday?"

Mrs. Robins said, "If we have some help."

Mary told her if she needed her, she would work tomorrow.

Mrs. Robins said, "Monday we can finish dear. The Grand Christmas Parade from house to house is Tuesday. We will be ready. I think Mr. Robins has requested Kenny to help with the evergreens and holly branches. They should get that done tomorrow, if so, we should be okay. But, thanks Mary"

Mary went to the shop door exiting to the parking lot. She turned the Welcome sign to be seen from outside "Closed, reopening @ 9AM." Mary walked back to the shelf where she had placed the horse and said, "Goodnight" stroking its mane and tail one last time.

Mary was tired. She worked all day yesterday putting up the Christmas wreaths and the Christmas trees on every floor, each decorated in a different theme. Then today she unboxed the new gift items, priced them and placed them around the shop for display. She was glad to be going home for the weekend, but at the same time being in the Christmas decorating mood she wanted to help with the stairway. Mrs. Robins had told her the decorating ideas for the staircase and what it would look like. Mary thought how Mrs. Robins would be sure to win the contest for Best Christmas Decorating Award this year.

Glory and Mary said, "Good evening." With that they walked toward the van. Mary was getting better at driving on the snow-covered roads.

She got behind the wheel as Kenny called to her, "Hold up!" He came across the parking lot to the van. "I'm going to Perryville with the guys tonight. I will see you tomorrow."

Perryville, she thought remembering the last time she had been there was with Erik. "Okay, see you tomorrow." She started the van and made her way out of the parking lot. The memories of the wonderful time she and Erik had that rainy afternoon came rushing as she passed by the flower shop thinking, "I should stop." But she continued to drive.

Chapter 26

THE WEEKEND WENT FAST. Mary was thinking as she drove Glory May to school only two days left before they would be out for Christmas break and Christmas would be here. Driving into town she wondered about Kenny. She hadn't seen him since Friday. She hoped he worked on Saturday. He was to help Mr. Robins finish the stairway for the open house on Tuesday.

Mary dropped Glory by the school and stopped at The Bed & Breakfast Inn for coffee. She ran into Cliff, who sat down with her for a moment talking about how he and his dad had helped Mr. Robins with the staircase on Saturday.

"We thought we would see you," Cliff said.

"No, I wasn't scheduled to work that day," she said. "Sorry, I missed you." She wished she had been there. Maybe she could have spoken with Erik. At the same time thinking, Kenny didn't show up!

When she arrived at work, Mr. Robins was getting ready to leave. He had to make a delivery in Perryville this morning. He would be gone the best part of the day. "Mrs. Robins will need your help with the stairway this morning, Mary."

"Sure, no problem Mr. Robins," Mary answered.

Mary went inside to view the most attractive staircase she had ever seen. The fresh cut evergreens and holly wrapped the staircase. There were carefully placed individual fresh fruits including pears, apples, and oranges throughout the greenery. Fresh holly berries trimmed with deep red handmade bows hung down over the side banister of the staircase. The evergreens wound up and up the stairway and out of sight. Mary stood there with her mouth wide open.

Mrs. Robins came into the room taking her hand to Mary's chin to gently close her mouth. "Good Morning, My Dear!"

"Good Morning, Mrs. Robins. It's beautiful and the aroma from the fresh fruit. Who would have thought?"

"Thanks, we worked all weekend to get it ready. I had to put the 'Closed Sign' out yesterday to be able to finish. Once the word got out everyone wanted to come by to see."

"I see why! You have that talented touch."

"Well, you will need to help finish the top floor. I ran out of holly berries yesterday. We went picking yesterday afternoon. The vines are by the kitchen back door. So, get your coffee and let's get started. I just took more fruit upstairs and I'm going down for more bows from my office. We will leave the 'Closed Sign' out until it's finished."

"What will people think?"

"My dear, the ones who have been around here from year to year know we are getting ready for the grand opening of the Christmas contest. You will see!"

Mary was overwhelmed with excitement. She didn't need any more coffee.

Mrs. Robins and Mary worked together placing the bows and ribbons just right around the stairway from the third floor to the fourth. They placed the finishing touches of fresh fruit in just the right places within the evergreen and holly branches. The smell of fresh citrus filled the house. Once they were finished, Mary freshened the Christmas trees, filling in the holes where ornaments had been bought and checked the evergreens around the fireplaces on each floor. She was lighting the unscented candles on the mantel as she made her way to the basement shop door. Mary's excitement about the Christmas Open House Contest set for Tuesday showed on her face.

"Mary, we will need to change the candles. Use the unscented ones. We want to keep the fresh fruit smell until after Christmas." Mary moved around the shop, checking to make sure she had lit only the unscented candles as Mrs. Robins had requested.

When she re-entered the basement gift shop area, she noticed the rocking horse was gone. "I knew it wouldn't be here long." Thinking how enchanted it was with hand painted detail even the price tag was not going to hold anyone back from buying it.

Finally, Mrs. Robins laughed as she told Mary to open the shop doors and turn the "Open Sign" lights on. She knew within minutes the shop was going to be buzzing with lookers. "Mary, this after-noon can you stay a little longer than usual? I need to be at Miss Cleary's to help decorate her dining room for her Christmas party on Christmas Eve. The shop I know will be busy, but Glory can help you. Anything that gets sold, we are wrapping for the custom-ers. Also, anything that leaves a hole on the shelves or the trees we need to fill in. The photographers will be here tomorrow. We want everything to be just right."

"Sure, no problem, be glad to, Mrs. Robins." Mary continued to work around the cash register getting ready as the "Open Sign" was blinking on and off.

The curiosity of the village soon had the gift shop filled with busy shoppers and lookers. Each one telling a story of past years they had visited the Robins' Gifts & Interior Designs Shop and this year Mrs. Robins had outdone herself.

"Sure to win," one customer stated as she was leaving.

Mary was pleased to hear the good words about her new and treasured friend. Maggie stopped by the shop to ask Mary to join them for Christmas dinner. Mary's first question was wondering about Kenny?

"Haven't you heard?"

"Heard what, Maggie?"

"You won't need to worry about Kenny. He's having Christmas with Vivian."

"What?"

"That's right. She stopped by the general store yesterday and told Frank and I she was going with Kenny to Morristown for Christmas. "Is she nuts?" Maggie questioned.

"No, Maggie, that doesn't surprise me. Remember what she did with Glory's dad?"

"Well, I thought after that mistake, she'd wake up some."

"No, Vivian will be Vivian," Mary answered.

"But, Mary, to be with another man that you have been with just doesn't seem right."

"Maggie, yes, it hurt me at the time, but it also helped me. He was a very abusive alcoholic. I wanted to take Glory and the boys and leave him, but didn't know how. When I walked in and found them together, it helped me to move on with my life. So now, I'm grateful. I'm sorry that I don't have the boys. But maybe someday I can make it right for them."

"What about Kenny?" Maggie questioned.

"Another bad choice on my part, I shouldn't have gotten involved with him. He's bad news and I realized it. Soon his truck repairs will be done and he will be gone."

"I hope you're right. He scares me. He seems possessive with you."

"He's that way with any woman he's with. He's a very controlling person. I don't need that. Not now! I just hope Vivian doesn't get hurt."

"Hurt, what do you mean, Mary?"

"Nothing, Maggie. I need to check on the customers upstairs.

Can you see yourself out?"

"Sure? See you tomorrow. I think this house will win the contest." Maggie bumped into Glory as she came through the door. "Your mom's upstairs with customers," Maggie told her as she was turning to say, "Bye now," as she left the store.

Mary was busy with the shop so she didn't give Kenny and Vivian another thought.

Glory ran up the stairway to top floor checking out the decorations and listening to the comments of the customers about the well-designed layout of each Christmas ornament. Glory came back down the stairs. Mary told her she needed to work by the register today to help wrap gifts that were purchased and fill in any holes she may find from items that were sold. Both Mary and Glory thanked the customers for coming and asked them to please come by tomorrow to cast their votes.

Mary remembered the voting boxes weren't out. She dashed into Mrs. Robins' office looking around for the boxes. When she couldn't find them, she pulled two boxes from the shelf and started wrapping leaving a hole in the top for their vote cards to be placed through. She ran upstairs to her office to get index cards. Back downstairs she had Glory cut the cards in half. She told Glory to place one of the boxes by the front door on the second floor entering the hallway toward living room and dining room. The other box should be placed by the door going to the parking lot. Both boxes had signs saying "Thank you for your vote." She gave Glory a handful of pencils to leave on the table beside the cards and box. Mary was surprised that Mrs. Robins had forgotten them. But Mary remembered from their meeting the voting boxes needed to be out the day before the contest.

The rest of the day as people entered the shop and the home areas, Mary asked, "Please, take a card and place your vote into the box as you leave."

Mary was amazed at the customers who came in from as far as

twenty or thirty miles away to see the Christmas designs. They each had a story of the past years that they had come to view this home and every year the designs were so different. One customer from out of town was from the Washington Post News and asked if he could take pictures for the paper. He handed Mary his card.

Mr. Andy Jensen "AJ" Mary read. Mary didn't think Mrs. Robins would mind so she let him take photos of the Christmas trees, fireplaces and the staircase. They walked out to the front entrance and took pictures of the outside showcasing the large sign "Robins' Gifts & Interior Designs" as well. The evening sun was just ready to set and Mary knew this was going to be a wonderful spot with the winter wonderland background of mountains covered with snow. Mary asked, if he would see that Mrs. Robins received a copy of the pictures.

"Very well," he said. "I will be back tomorrow to see who wins. I'm sure this house by what I have seen so far has a very good chance." He had been driving around the county checking out the perspective homes listed in the contest.

"Tomorrow is Christmas Eve," Mary thought. She realized how different this Christmas will be from the Christmas just one year ago. Thinking of the city and when it would snow there, how dirty it would be the same day the snow stopped. Here the snow has been on the ground for a month and looked as beautiful tonight as it did the first night it snowed. And how the people adjust and go on with their lives, where the city seemed to close down.

The next day Mary was ready to get into town. She wanted to see and hear from people coming into Robins' Gifts & Interior Designs. Both Mary and Glory were excited that Mrs. Robins had a good chance to win this year as they talked during the drive into town. They stopped by The Bed & Breakfast Inn for a bite to eat. Mary parked the car to see Erik getting into his truck.

"Mom, stop him, talk to him," Glory yelled.

Erik waved, but left the parking lot. Mary felt that large lump in her throat again and her palms were wet with sweat. Mary took a deep breath.

"Mom, you should have talked to him."

"Glory he will talk to me when he's ready."

"Mom, the two of you are acting like school kids."

"Maybe we are Glory, but you stay out of it. You hear me?"

"Okay, Mom, I just miss having them around. We had fun together."

Mary did understand what her daughter was saying. She missed them too.

When Mary and Glory entered the parking lot at the shop, the parking area was full of people waiting for the doors to open. Mary and Glory were early so they could help with any last minute things that Mrs. Robins may want to change. They made their way to the door and closed it behind them. The "Closed" sign was still out on the door. "Mrs. Robins, we're here!"

"Great," she said, as she came from her office. "Thanks for remembering the vote boxes, Mary. We work well together. Good morning, Glory. You ready for a busy day?"

"Yes, Ma'am!"

"Good, I will give you ladies about ten minutes and the doors will open for business."

Mr. Robins was coming down the stairs with a cup of hot apple cider. You could smell the aroma.

"Hall, today you and Glory will be in charge of the coffee, tea and hot cider pots. Keep them warm and full."

"Yes, Ma" he replied to his wife winking at Glory.

"Hally, can you also take turns with Mary running the cash register. Glory, can you also handle the wrapping?" This keeps Mary and I free to wait on the customers.

"Sure thing"

"Mary, you and I will keep a close eye on the doors and filling in any empty spots from the items we sell."

Mary placed her hand on Mrs. Robins' shoulder, "Mrs. Robins, everything is magnificent. You will do just fine and stop being so nervous!"

"I couldn't sleep last night, Mary, after you told me about AJ being here and taking pictures for the Washington Post. He's well known in Nantucket for his stories on Country Home Designs from across the country."

"You deserve to win!" Mary answered.

The day was a huge success. The voting was scheduled to stop by 3pm and the total numbers were to be called into the county office by 4pm. Mr. Wellington, the judge for the town of Edinburg, was there at 2:30 ready to close the voting boxes right at 3pm. There was calmness over the shop by 3pm. Everyone had come and gone leaving their votes in the boxes. Mary asked the judge when Mrs. Robins would know who won?

"They are posted the day after Christmas at the courthouse and the winner is given their reward plaque and check the next day by The State Governor at a luncheon in their honor."

"Well, this is a big event isn't it?" Mary replied.

"Oh, yes. Mrs. Robins has won several years, but not last year. She was sick and didn't put her heart into it like she did this year. I think she has a real good chance to win."

"Great" said Mr. Robins as he came around the corner while Judge Wellington was talking.

"The Mrs. needs to win - she has worked really hard on this."

"Yes, Mr. Robins and it shows," said Judge Wellington. "The whole town is hoping she does."

That evening everyone was tired, but also excited it was Christmas Eve. Mary helped clean up and started out the door. "Mary, where are you going?" questioned Mrs. Robins.

"Home… I still have some wrapping to do before midnight and we are going to Maggie's tomorrow."

"Well, My Dear, the two of you come back in here for a moment, please."

Glory found a seat down beside the small Christmas tree in the gift shop area and there she waited. Mary came back in and sat down beside Glory. Mr. Robins had gone upstairs. He was making four cups of hot apple cider to bring back down. Mary and Glory sat waiting. Mrs. Robins brought out two boxes from her office in the back. She handed one to Glory and one to Mary. Mary's had an envelope on top of the box.

"Here ladies… Merry Christmas! Please, open them." Mary waited for Glory to open hers. It was a wooden musical jewelry box with hand carved horses. "Oh, it's beautiful. Thank you." Inside was a pair of earrings she had been complementing Mrs. Robins on each time she would wear them.

"Mary, your turn." Mary opened the box to find the rocking horse she unwrapped the day of the large shipment. Mary looked at Mrs. Robins, "I thought someone had bought this."

"We know, My Dear. I took it off the shelf that evening when you left. Merry Christmas!"

Both Mary and Glory were very happy with their gifts. "Well, we still need to decorate our tree. We had better be going."

Little did they know that someone had been at their house while both were working. Mary parked the van behind the house. Glory jumped out to find Sneaky waiting by the kitchen door. "Well girl, I have an extra treat for you tonight." Glory pulled a small bag from her pocket and opened it. Sneaky - not shy, was trying to help, pulling at the bag. It was Indian corn. "Look, Mom, Sneaky seems to like it."

"Glory, did you leave on a light this morning?"

"I don't think so, Mom."

Mary opened the kitchen door. A warm welcome Christmas scent was in the air. Mary walked across to the living room door to find a small Christmas tree decorated and the fireplace burning.

"Kenny must have been here, Mom?"

Mary went over to a note propped under the tree. The note read;

Merry Christmas,
I haven't forgotten.
Erik

Mary sat down on the sofa and tears ran down her face. No, she had not forgotten either.

"Mom, who's it from?" Mary handed the note to Glory.

"See, Mom, we should have stopped at flower shop. He wanted to see you. Why are you being like this?" Glory ran to her room.

Chapter 27

THE REST OF THE evening was very quiet at Mary's house. Glory only came down to eat and went back to her room. Mary knew she also missed her brothers. It made it harder with the holiday. Mary went to the phone and dialed the number.

"Ms. Pitt, Hi, it's Mary. Can I talk to the boys?"

"No," said the voice, the phone went dead. Mary tried the number again. "Please, if not to me, please let Glory talk to them."

"No, stay away!" The phone again went dead.

Glory had come down for a drink, standing in the living room doorway she overheard the attempt her mom had made. Yes, she missed them. They all would gather by the tree, unwrap at least one gift before bedtime, have hot chocolate with marshmallows and sing Christmas carols. They were a real family. This would be the second year of not being together. Why did Dad desert us? Why do we have to pay for his mistakes? Will we ever be a family again? She came out, placed her arms around her mom and said, "Thanks Mom, you tried."

The two went into the living room. Mary walked over to the piano and said, "Okay, Glory, we will just do this ourselves. "Mary sat down and started to play. The two of them sang together with tears running down their faces. Mary was clearing her face when a truck pulled into the driveway. Glory looked out, "It's Uncle Spence and Aunt Jenny." Glory opened the front door to welcome them.

"Mary, we thought you might need some company tonight."

"Thanks guys." She gave them a big welcome hug and invited them to come in out of the cold.

Glory made hot chocolate. Uncle Spence handed out gifts. Aunt Jenny played the piano and they sang Christmas carols.

Around 11:00 Glory went off to bed. This gave Jenny, Spence and Mary a chance to talk. Spence asked if there was anything he or Jenny could maybe do to get through to Mrs. Pitt.

"I don't know? She really has her mind made up." Mary replied.

"Well, maybe nothing can be done tonight, but we will work on this. Maybe she needs to see how different things are now," Jenny said. "You are really making a good home for Glory. Don't give that up."

"Thanks, Sis"

"Well, we are out of here. See you tomorrow at Maggie's. Good night and Merry Christmas."

Mary was alone again as her sister and brother-in-law drove out of the driveway. She moved to the kitchen, picked up the phone and put it back down again. She was moved by Erik donating his time to decorate the tree and his warm touch of thoughtfulness. She wanted to call as she had tried so many times before, but something kept stopping her. 'I can't do it over the phone. He will stop by to see me.'

She went to her desk drawer, pulled out a Christmas card and wrote a small note:

> *Erik,*
> *Thank you for the lovely tree and your warm thoughts. You are missed. Merry Christmas,*
> > *Signed, Blondie.*

On Christmas morning Mary and Glory were busy getting

things together for Maggie's Christmas dinner gathering. Kenny came into the house with a big smile on his face.

"Where you been?" Mary asked.

"Around."

"Why didn't you at least call Mrs. Robins and let her know you were not going to help with the staircase?"

"No, problem, Vivian called her brother. He went and helped. We were out of town."

"Kenny, please don't do anything stupid to Vivian."

"Come on, you're not jealous, are you? Girlie, if so, I can handle the two of you."

"No, Kenny I'm not jealous. I don't want you to hurt her, you are wild sometimes."

"We'll be just fine!" Kenny disappeared around the back stairway toward the room he had been using. Mary looked out the window. Vivian's car was parked under the walnut tree with her on the passenger side. Mary wanted to run out to the car, shake some sense into her, but knew that would just make her stay with him longer. He was like a bad spell, that takes over your body and you can't say no.

Mary stood by the window thinking of the first day Kenny and she were together; how weak and hurt she was that day, how destroyed she felt by Jack's demand of divorce. She just didn't care and wished she could die. Kenny got off on her weakness and after being with him for several days, she couldn't feel anything. She didn't think she could have feelings for any man again. Mary jumped as Kenny came back into the room breaking the spell she had drifted into.

"What's on that pretty little mind of yours? Thinking about the offer to join us?" He was carrying his bags.

"No, Kenny, that's not my thing."

"Really...I could fix that...if you haven't tried it yet. You'd be good at it!"

"Kenny, stop. Glory could overhear."

"Well, I could teach her too."

Mary jumped in his face screaming, "*DON'T YOU EVER* lay a finger on my daughter! *YOU HEAR ME!*" angry and pointing her finger at him.

"Well, that's a mean streak. I'll need to check that out my dear." Laughing he left, leaving the door open. Mary slammed it shut.

"Merry Christmas to you, too and glad to see you and the bags are leaving!"

Glory came down from upstairs. "Mom, everything okay? Was that Kenny?"

"Yes, Glory, please promise me...you will never be alone with him."

"MOM???"

"GLORY, JUST PROMISE ME!"

"Okay, Mom, I promise."

Mary about jumped out of her skin for the second time when the phone rang breaking the spell Kenny had just put on her. Answering the phone, "*HELLO!*" she yelled.

A voice echoed across the phone, "Mrs. Barnes, please?"

"Yes, how can I help you?"

"Mom, it's Craig."

"Craig?" Mary placed her hand around her throat. She felt like her heart went there cutting off her wind. Trying to catch her breath she questioned, "Where are you?"

"I'm at the bus depot in Morrisville."

"You are where?"

"I'm in Morrisville. Will you come pick me up?"

"How did you get there?"

"Mom, will you come pick me up?"

"Of course, I will. Glory and I will be there. You stay put... you hear me? Please, don't you leave the bus station. It will take me almost 40 to 45 minutes."

"Mom"

"Yes, Craig"

"I've missed you!"

"Oh Craig…I've missed you, too. We will be right there, don't leave with anyone!" Crying Mary hung up the phone. "Glory, get your coat!"

"Mom… What's going on?"

"Glory, now!"

Mary still not saying where they were going, pushed Glory out the door. They got into the van and drove in the opposite direction of Maggie's house. Glory put on her new headset asking no further questions. She listened to the new CD that Uncle Spence and Aunt Jenny had given her for Christmas the night before. Once in Morrisville, Mary stopped at the gas station and asked, "Where's the bus station?"

The gentlemen pointed down the street, saying, "About two blocks on the right."

Mary jumped back into the van, drove two blocks, parked the van and told Glory to come with her as she jumped out of the van.

"Mom"

"Glory, please! Now!"

Glory still did not know why they had come to Morrisville instead of going to Maggie's.

Mary ran to the lobby with Glory on her heels. There sat Craig, waiting as he had been told. Glory saw her brother and began to cry. Screaming, "My Christmas wish! It's been answered."

Both hugged Craig with every bit of strength in their bodies and did not want to let go! Both had missed the boys so much!

Mary took him by the shoulders. "Craig, does anyone know you are here?"

"No, mom. I left two weeks ago."

"Two weeks and no one has called me? What's going on, Craig?"

"Mom, we want to be with you and Glory. Grams is old. She's sick and doesn't understand how we boys need things, attention, and someone to take care of us. We need the kind of attention you always gave us."

"Oh Craig, I'm so sorry for everything."

"We know it's not you...we know you love us...why can't others see, we need you?"

"Someday they will, Craig."

"Someday is not good enough, we need you NOW." Craig seemed angry, hurt, and tired.

Mary put her arms around him again and told him she would see what could be done.

"Merry Christmas, Mom."

"Merry Christmas, Son. Come on." Mary still teary-eyed helped Craig with his things. They walked toward the van. Glory so excited was full of questions wanting to know how did he find us? They got into the van. Craig sat in back with Glory May. The two teens chattered like Magpies as Mary listened to every word while she started the van and pulled away from the station heading back toward Edinburg.

Glory told Craig they were going to spend Christmas day at Maggie's house. Uncle Spence and Aunt Jenny would be there. Craig remembered them. But best of all he remembered Maggie.

"She has always been your closest friend, Mom."

"That's right."

"She's crazy. I mean a lot of fun, crazy" Craig quickly added.

"Yes, she is, Craig. I'm glad you remember her."

A half hour later Mary realized she had forgotten the gifts that needed to go to Maggie's house. Mary thought, "I will go after them later in the day. They're adults, they will understand."

Just about two miles from Perryville, she turned off Zinn Road, went another 100 yards turning again into Maggie's driveway toward a one-story wooden ranch style house, nestled in the woods. Maggie had always liked the mountains and had gotten a great deal on the house when she was working real estate. It's a two-bedroom, two bath, ranch home with a front porch on two acres of land that she mows herself. It has a large yard with lots of trees for shade. Not that you could see the ground for the snow still covered everything, but still it had a very charming appearance for a dark brown log home. Mary was thinking she really did have good taste for the country style living.

When they went inside everyone was glad to see Craig. Yes, everyone had a lot of questions, but Mary tried to put off the questions until after Christmas or at least until evening. "Let's just enjoy the day and I will get answers for all the questions. I promise," she said. Mary was just glad to have him with them, even if it is for one day. She too had been doing a lot of praying for them to be together again, if only for Christmas.

The two teens went outside while the ladies were finishing the dinner preparations. They built a snowman and threw snowballs at each other and at the cars that drove by on the narrow two-lane road. They seemed happy to be together. Mary kept looking out the window, every few minutes with so many questions.

Mary asked what was she going to do? Looking at Spence, Jenny, Billy and Maggie, "I don't want to send him back."

"Mary, you can't keep him. They will arrest you."

"I know… I just need time to think."

"Mary, you must call Mrs. Pitt. She is probably going out of her mind with worry."

"That's what I don't understand. I called last night to talk to the boys, she wouldn't let me talk to them and she didn't tell me Craig wasn't there. Instead she hung up on me. I called twice and both times she hung up. She gave me no idea that Craig wasn't there.

Does that make any sense to you?" she questioned.

"No, but you still need to call her, Mary."

"Okay. Then after dinner we will. Together, we'll call. They can't prevent me from wanting him to be safe and happy, can they?"

Soon everyone was at the Christmas dinner table, which was full of wonderful dishes that everyone had helped cook. Mary apologized again for not bringing her dish and the gifts.

Maggie told her, "Enjoy the day and stop worrying about the dinner dish. There was enough food to go around, and we can always pick up the gifts later."

Spence said grace and thanked God for the opportunity to spend Christmas with Craig. "Please, give us a guiding hand on what to do next and make sure the boys and Mrs. Pitt have a good Christmas as well." They all agreed saying "Yes, please we pray. Amen."

When dinner was over, the teens wanted to go back outside. Mary told Craig, he needed to sit down and tell them what happened and how he got there. She would call them inside when the dishes and dining room table were cleared.

The ladies cleaned up the dining room table and the dishes. They called the teens back inside. Everyone went into the living room and sat around the fireplace where the teens could dry off.

Craig began to tell his story. "Grams likes to hit the bottle like Dad would do. She drinks Jack Daniels and sleeps a lot, a glass in one hand and a cigarette in the other. We mostly took care of her and ourselves. One evening she told Mike he would need to stay out of school the next day. She needed him to do the housework. Mike told Grams about a test he had been studying for and was to take the next day. She told him, "The hell with the test. I've lived a long life and didn't get or need schooling. You need to get out in the world and work, that's where the experience of life comes from, that's your schooling." Mike missed the next three weeks of classes and they took his scholarship away from him. He had worked so hard for it.

He and Grams had an argument over him losing the scholarship and the next day he didn't come home. Two days went by and still we heard nothing. Grams kept little Ben and me out of class the rest of the week. We worked around the house. Doing the cleaning, doing her laundry and cleaning up her mess where she had gotten sick. She wouldn't eat much of anything, just sat in that chair and drank all the time. She would always call us George. George, do this and that or yell at us, because she had burnt a hole in the rug or her bed was dirty, or her food wasn't ready, not eating it when we prepared the food, then it was too cold. It was too much, so I did what Mike did, I left. Mike still had not come back when I left. I tried to get Ben to come with me."

"And no one has heard from Mike?" Mary asked.

"Not that I know of, nothing before I left," Craig said.

"How did you get here?"

"I called the city school asking for Glory. They told me she had been transferred to Edinburg, Va. I looked it up on the map and started hitchhiking. A nice lady picked me up in Gum Springs. She was going to Upperville, so I rode with her. On the road, we laughed a lot and I felt comfortable enough so I told her the story that I was trying to find my mom. She put me on the bus and told the driver not to let me out of his sight until I was in Morrisville."

"Okay," Spence spoke up and said, "Did you get the lady's name? Let's call the local police department. I have a friend there. He can advise us about placing the call to Old Lady Pitt's home or how to check on them. Then we can let them know Craig is here safe and we want Ben to be delivered to us. If we need to go there to get him, we will. Then we will try to find Mike and see what we can do to place the boys in a better home. Who knows maybe they will give them back to Mary? Jack isn't in the picture anymore. The whole town if needed can vouch for Mary. She's trying to get her life back on track."

Everyone agreed. Spence picked up the phone and called the local police department. His friend was working. The local police department agreed to send him out to talk with Mary and Craig. Spence's friend was with another officer who came out to speak with them. They got a statement of what may have happened, spoke to Craig with the family adults present and called the City of Richmond police department to see if anyone had filed a missing person report on the boys. The Richmond police said they would send a car out to check on the address in question. No missing person report had been filed. If Mary was going to report Mike missing, they would need a picture.

It seemed like hours later the police department phoned back, they had found an older lady who was suffering a stroke. There was a teen boy with her. Both have been flown to Charlottesville hospital.

"Are they, is he, okay?"

"Ma'am, can you come to the hospital? There will be two officers there to talk to you? We will be keeping both under guarded protection until they have found out all the facts and both will be admitted into the hospital. We will try to have more details when you arrive at the hospital to confirm your story."

Mary told them she would be there in about three and a half hours. It would take at least that to drive from Edinburg, with the snow-covered roads maybe a little longer. She gave the officer a cell phone number. The officer told Mary to be careful on the roads, said the two would be in good hands at the hospital, and gave her the name of the officer and doctor to ask for when she arrived. They would call her with any changes. The officer asked, "You do give permission to treat the minor?"

"Yes, of course."

Craig didn't want Mary to leave him again. Mary told him, "It will be okay, you are going to stay with Aunt Jenny and Glory May. I will be back and we will be together again." She promised him things would be okay. Spence and Jenny agreed Glory and Craig could stay with them.

Maggie and Billy agreed they would drive Mary Ann to Charlottesville. They loaded into Maggie's car. Both children stood with Spence and Jenny as the car left the driveway and headed toward their long drive. Mary nervously questioning what could have happened? Why didn't they have any details on their condition? Could this be why no one would talk to her last night?

Chapter 28

SPENCE AND JENNY LOADED the teens into their truck. Jenny got behind the wheel. Spence got into Mary's van and followed Jenny toward the farmhouse. Mary had given them a key to check on the house, pick up some clothes for Glory and leave Mary's van at the farmhouse. On the way, Spence had told Jenny to stop at the south pasture. He needed to make sure the horses were okay so he wouldn't have to come back out. He reminded Jenny that Blacky, one of their American Quarter Horses, was due to have her baby colt anytime. Blacky has had several prize stock colts and Spence was like a new dad waiting for the baby to be delivered. They parked out by the road and Spence walked toward the barnyard fence with both teens at his heels. Glory was full of stories to tell Craig about the farm and the fun she has had with Uncle Spence since they had gotten here.

Spence put his finger to his mouth for the teens to be quiet. He whispered, "We don't want to frighten the mare." Spence pointed to the barn stall. Spence was right the mare was due anytime and it looked like it's now. She was down in the barn stall. Spence took off his coat, dropped it on the fence rail as he climbed over, and called Jenny.

"Jenny, I'm going to need your help. Bring me the bag from behind the truck seat." Jenny ran back to the truck getting the bag and some rags, running back toward Spence handing him the items as she too climbed across the fence into the barnyard. Spence told both teens to stand very still, not to frighten the mare. He didn't want her to become frightened or start fretting and hurt herself. Spence could tell something was wrong. He checked out the mare examining her condition. He looked at Jenny and said, "The colt is turned the wrong way. I need to help turn it." Spence and Jenny both worked together trying to turn the colt around for the delivery. "We need the head between the feet for a good delivery," Spence told her. He took his hand pressing up inside the mare trying to turn the colt.

Jenny had moved by the mare's head trying to talk to her and keep her calm. She wiped the mare's head and down across her neck staying in the same movement with each stroke of her hand. "Good girl…we're here to help…come on, Blacky. Let us help, you can do it." Jenny was calmly talking to the mare. But she was very frightened inside as she watched Spence actively working very hard to help Blacky with the delivery. She knew they had a problem if he could not get the colt turned.

After several minutes had gone by Spence finally said, "I think, we can do this… I think it's turned. Let's give this a try girl. Come on Blacky, I'll help you, let's do this do together." He had placed his feet one each side of the mare's butt and begun to pull. "Yes girl… come on…you can do this." He called to Blacky…

Spence pulled with very ounce of strength he had in his body, red faced, as he strained. "Here it comes, girl!" Once the feet got started, Spence could see the head was still between the colt's feet. This was a good sign. Spence placed his hand behind the colt's neck pulling again and quickly the colt popped out. Spence fell backward from the force of his pull, and the release of the colt's birth, with a sigh of relief. Spence worked quickly to clean the colt.

"It's a boy" he yelled. The colt was weak, but Spence finally got him to stand on his feet. "Shaky and weak, but seems to be okay."

Spence was worried about Blacky. The mare didn't seem to be doing as well. He went back to working with the mother. She wasn't passing the afterbirth. Spence finally told Jenny, "She doesn't seem to be doing as well." He told Jenny to go the truck and call the vet. "I think we still have a problem on our hands."

Jenny called for Glory to quickly come across the fence, but calmly come to her. Glory moved across the fence and slowly toward Aunt Jenny and bent down.

"I need you to continue stroking Blacky just like this. Don't be frightened. She's not going to hurt you if she knows you are trying to help." They stroked together several times then Jenny backed away from the mare as Glory continued to stroke in the same way that Jenny had been doing.

Jenny walked out of the barn stall, but ran toward the barnyard fence for the truck, meeting Craig halfway to the truck, who had gone for the phone. Jenny called the vet. It was going to take him about an hour and a half to get there.

Spence frustrated told her, "We don't have that hour and a half."

Jenny quickly placed another call. She yelled, "Help's on the way." Maybe ten minutes later, if that, Erik and Cliff were pulling into the barn. They went into the barn stall and examined the mare. Cliff quickly took out of his carrying bag, a needle and gave the mare shot. Waiting only a few minutes he took out his knife and began to make an incision. Soon he was pulling the afterbirth from the mare. Still Blacky laid very calm eyeing her new colt and the people around them. Cliff took needle and thread from this bag and he continued working with the mare to sew up the incision he had made. The mare still very quiet, breathing long drawn breaths like she was in some pain. She had begun to perspire so much it foamed up as Glory ran her hand down across Blacky's neck. This went on for another half hour, but to everyone there it was like an eternity. All at once, Blacky began to nicker in a low pitch.

"Come on, Blacky stay with us," Erik said. The colt still on his feet was nosing his mom's head and nickering in question for a reply. Glory did not take her eyes off of Blacky…she continued to stroke her neck and head.

"Come on girl…you need to take care of this beautiful baby of yours." Glory replying to Blacky's nicker.

It had now been over an hour and a half since the colt had been born, time was passing. Spence knew the colt needed to feed from his mother in order for him to get the vitamins needed for the colt to make it. Spence was worried. Was he going to lose both his prize mare and the colt? Could they save them?

Cliff finished and said, "We've done all we can at this point, the rest is up to God and the will of this mother." He helped clean up the afterbirth and bagged it for disposal. The colt seems to be strong, but Cliff knew that Spence was right - he needed to nurse his mother soon.

They continued to stroke Blacky. With towels they wiped the mare down to clean her, cool her off and tried at the same time to get the colt to nurse by placing his nose between the mare's legs to show him where to feed. Blacky continued to make slow low nickers and still eyed everyone around her. Glory wasn't sure if Blacky was talking to her new baby or talking to them. But each time Blacky would nicker, Glory would talk back in a slow calm voice, "Come on girl, it's okay. We're here to help."

Two hours and fifteen minutes had passed. Spence nervously watched his watch. He checked the mother and new baby every five minutes getting more nervous with each passing minute. "What do you think?" he said to Erik and Cliff.

"We've done all we can. Now it's a waiting game, but once you start giving different milk to the baby, the mother's not going to let the baby feed even if she does make it."

The guys agreed to wait a little longer. Spence had spoken about placing the new colt with another mare that had lost a colt and her milk had not dried up yet. Erik was right. Once he placed the colt with another mare, usually the horse's instinct would not take the colt back.

"Spence, let's give her a little longer," Jenny said. "I don't think she's given up. She'll get her strength soon. We can't give up on her."

Fifteen more minutes went by. Jenny and Glory stayed by Blacky. Calmly they continued to wipe her head and down her neck in the same movement they had used before the colt was born. Finally, with a burst of energy from who knows where Blacky pressed herself to her feet with a loud nicker. She shook her head several times and then pressed her new born baby with her head toward her stomach. Spence helped the unsteady colt find his spot and he began to nurse. Everyone was excited to see it happen.

"Now that's it, Girl…let him feed." Spence continued to wipe down the mare as she stood there letting her new baby nurse. Blacky stood trembling, shaking her head up and down, as she nickered in lower calm sounds as if to say, "Thank you everybody."

Cliff told his dad and Spence the next several hours would still play a big part in the outcome. The men knew this from years of having horses, but it was good to see Cliff involved. The mare was very weak. Spence told Jenny to take the teens and go to Mary's house. That way the teens could go to bed and he would stay with Blacky and the colt.

"No, Uncle Spence, we want to stay with you," Glory asked.

"Right," said Craig. Craig had never seen anything like this before. He was so taken to be a part of the birth of a new colt he didn't want to leave.

"You're sure? It's going to be a long night."

"Yes, Uncle Spence, please."

"Okay for a while… at least it's not as cold tonight as it has been."

Blacky was trembling, still standing, but the mare was quivering and still giving off the low nicker every once in a while, like she was trying to talk them. Spence asked Jenny, "Is the blanket still behind the seat in the truck?"

She answered, "Yes."

"Craig, go to the truck and get the blanket, please."

Craig ran back to the truck again, soon returning with a wool plaid blanket. Spence and Erik covered the mare. The colt still was nursing and Blacky didn't seem to be frightened by the movement around her and her new baby.

Cliff said, "Maybe we could have a fire, Spence? It would give some heat for us and possibly help the colt dry (still damp from birth and the cold winter night air) and maybe help to get the mare warm." They had been wiping her down with damp cloths. They had taken a bucket of water from the horse's drinking trough to dampen cloths to help clean up Blacky. The fire would feel good at least for an hour or so.

Spence said, "Okay."

Cliff went over the fence and said, "Hi, I'm Cliff, want to help me?"

"Sure, I'm Craig." The two teen boys went for wood beside the barn.

Spence told them, "There is some dry wood just inside the barn door."

The boys came back and placed the wood over some hay they had brought with them from the barn to start the fire easier. Soon they had a bonfire going and the heat felt great. Spence went for a cup of grain for Blacky. "Can you eat something now, Girl?" He placed the feed in his hand and under Blacky's mouth. Blacky began to eat, which made Spence feel a little better. "I think she'll be okay, don't you, Erik?"

They had now been there over four hours. The mare and colt seemed to be doing better. The mare was breathing more normally and with her now up on her feet, it gave the guys a good feeling. "Let's give them until morning. We'll keep them in the stall tonight. I will come back first thing tomorrow and check on them. If they are doing okay then, I'll let them out into the field to get some exercise. Thanks for bringing Cliff. I sure do appreciate the help," Spence said smiling.

"Glad we have a doctor in the house and he could help," Erik answered. They put out the campfire with a bucket of water and handed items across the fence to Craig and Cliff to take to the trucks. I'm glad Cliff and I were nearby when Jenny called. Who's the boy?"

"Mary's son!"

"Oh, which one?"

"Craig, He just got here today."

"Where's Mary?"

"She went to Charlottesville. Seems something happened to Mrs. Pitt and Ben. Don't know too much yet. Mary will call us when she knows more."

"Did she drive herself?"

"No, Maggie and Billy drove her. She was too worked up to drive herself. She was with us at Maggie's for Christmas dinner when she got the information."

"Will you keep me informed?"

"Sure," Spence agreed as they walked toward the trucks together. "Craig, this is Erik, Cliff's dad."

"Yes, sir, Cliff was telling me he's studying to be an animal doctor. That was something out there. I've never seen anything like that." Craig was bouncing with excitement from being part of the experience.

"What are you going to call him?" Jenny asked.

Glory yelled, "Uncle Spence, I have a name!"

"Oh, you do and what might that be?"

"Chance, I think we should call him Chance."

Spence hugged his niece and said, "I think that's a great name. Let's go get warmed up, what do you think?"

Spence told Erik and Cliff he would call them in the morning after he had checked on the horses. They got into their vehicles and Spence followed Jenny over to Mary's house, where they still needed to get Glory some clothes and leave the van.

When they got into Mary's house the phone was ringing. "It's Mary," Jenny said, as she answered. "Yes, are you there and…? Jenny listened before saying anymore. "Okay, no, we were at the barn at the south pasture. Blacky was trying to deliver and needed our help. No, we just got here. Okay, I'll tell them. No, you just don't worry. Take care of things there. We love you too!" She hung up the phone.

The teens had gone upstairs. Jenny sat down and looked at Spence. Mary says, "They're at the hospital. Mrs. Pitt is in critical condition in ICU and Ben is unconscious with six stitches over his eye. He's in the children's ward."

"Does she know what happened?"

"No, doesn't know much of anything yet. She said thanks for taking care of Glory and Craig. She would call tomorrow and we were welcome to stay here if it gives more room for the kids or if you needed to be closer to the south pasture field."

"We'll see," Spence said. "Will you make some coffee?"

"Sure"

"I'm going to check on the kids. And then see if I can wash up some."

"Spence, in the back bathroom Mary has towels in the corner cabinet."

Spence went into the living room and both teens had gone upstairs. He turned the corner at the top of the stairs to find the teens in the twin room, each across a bed and sound asleep.

"Well, that wore them out." He went back downstairs.

"Well, both kids are fast asleep."

"Already?" Jenny questioned. "Well, it has been a busy and exhausting day for them," she said as she set a cup of coffee down for Spence. "I guess we'll stay here tonight or do you want to go home?"

"I think I'm going home to get cleaned up and change clothes. Want me to bring you something back? Maybe a change of clothes?"

"I'm fine. I'll sleep on the sofa until I hear from you."

"Well, let me drink this and I'll go."

"You're going back to the barn, aren't you?" Jenny asked knowing her husband and the pride he took with his horses he wouldn't sleep anyway.

"Maybe," Spence said. "I don't want her to get down. I know I bruised her trying to turn the colt. I will feel better if I keep an eye on her tonight."

"Ok, take this phone with you," as she reached into her pocket. "You can call me here and give me an update or if you need Erik and Cliff again the number's programmed. I'll see what Mary has that I can pack. You need something warm to take with you." Jenny looked around the house and found an old quilt by the basement door. She packed Spence a sandwich and found a thermal coffee pot in the kitchen closet. Jenny filled the pot and handed it to her husband. "We'll be okay, Spence. You go take care of the new mother and her baby."

"Thanks, Jen. I knew you would understand."

"Things will be okay." She gave her husband a big hug and closed the door behind him as he went out and down the steps.

Chapter 29

MARY FINALLY ARRIVED AT the hospital and she was nervous, as she was standing over Ben's bed. The doctor had given him something to help him rest and he was hooked up to several monitors. They were not sure yet what had happened. The police were going back to Mrs. Pitt's house and would talk to Mary in the morning. Mary seated herself beside Ben's hospital bed holding his hand. He had a cut above his eye and bruises on his face. The doctor had repaired the cut with six switches and told her he had been unconscious since they found him. They were going to take him for more x-rays and tests. They would know more possibly tomorrow. He had been unaware of anything around him since they brought him in. The doctor suggested to Mary to keep talking to him through the night. "Even if we don't think he hears us sometimes in this type of injury, they really do hear you."

She sat there thinking it was a good thing she called the police department to check on them. She had so many questions and knew it was going to be a long night.

Hours went by. Maggie came into the room to find Mary with her head lying on the edge of the bed and Ben's hand still enclosed in Mary's. She had not moved from his bedside since they had gotten to the hospital. Maggie had asked the nurse several times about Mrs. Pitt, but was told she was still very critical. She decided to go back in with Mary. Maybe she could talk her into going for a cup of coffee. There was a machine down the hall. Maggie moved quietly to seat herself down on the chair in the far corner of the room since Mary seemed to be sleeping. She noticed the sun starting to come up through the hospital blinds. Hopefully, there would be good news with the start of a new day.

Billy was seated outside in the lobby. He had made good time driving last night with the roads still snowy in spots and the interstate being busy with Christmas travelers. There were lots of others traveling the highways and there had been several accidents that they had passed. He worried what news Mary would hear today. He hoped it would be better than the news she got last night. He sat there not knowing Mrs. Pitt or Mary's son, Ben, but prayed for them to be okay. He hoped Mary would be able to keep the boys with her, but wondered if they would be placed with the state instead. To him Mary had always seemed like something was missing. Now knowing about the boys, he could understand her emptiness. He thought maybe if she and Erik got back together, it would help. They seemed to make a really good couple. Billy saw the doctor that had spoken to them last night coming down the hall. He stood up as the doctor walked into Ben's room, even though he wasn't family he stepped up to the door anyway.

Mary had not been to see Mrs. Pitt yet. She went to see her son first when they got to the hospital. Mary asked, "How is she, is she doing any better?"

The doctor stood shaking his head, "Not good. She had a stroke, has burns on most of her fingers and still not responding to the medicine we are giving her for the stroke. But she has been asking for you."

"For me?"

"She can't move her body since the stroke and her speech is not real good. She drifts in and out. Would you be willing to see her and see if she would respond to your voice? We have her on the fourth floor in ICU."

Mary didn't want to leave Ben's side, but at the same time she needed to speak with Mrs. Pitt if possible. She agreed to do so after the doctor had checked Ben and said there was no change in his condition. They left the room together with Maggie saying she would not leave Ben's side until Mary got back.

Mary walked with Dr. Howard to Mrs. Pitt's hospital room in ICU. She was hooked up to a lot of different machines, which made Mary very nervous. Dr. Howard was standing on one side of the bed and Mary on the other. Mary moved slowly toward Mrs. Pitt, took her hand and began to call her name.

"Frankie, it's Mary. Can you can hear me?"

"Mrs. Pitt, please try to move a finger if you can hear us. Can you move a finger?" Dr. Howard asked.

Mrs. Pitt moved her forefinger slowly.

"Are you in any pain, Frankie?"

"Mrs. Pitt, if you are feeling any pain, let us know by moving your finger one more time." No movement.

"Can you understand me?" Mrs. Pitt's forefinger moved slowly again.

"Frankie, I need to ask you some questions. The doctor is here standing next to me. Do you remember what happened? Frankie?" No movement in the finger.

"Okay," Mary patted Mrs. Pitt's hand. "Do you know where Mike may be?" The finger moved.

"Have you seen him since Craig left?" The finger moved.

"Were the two of you angry with each other?"

The finger moved.

Mrs. Pitt was trying to say something, her voice very low. The doctor leaned over to listen to what she was saying… "I need you to take the boys…they need you…I was wrong." A tear was running down her face, her chin quivering, "I should have never taken them from you." She took a deep breath. The machines behind her began to sound off.

"NO! NO!" Mary yelled. "Frankie…Mrs. Pitt…Don't do this!"

The doctor quickly started working on Mrs. Pitt. The nurses ran in working with the doctor, but they couldn't save her.

Mary stood there in a daze. What just happened? She backed out of their way to give them room to work. The room busy with others, she stood by the doors as the doctor and nurses worked together trying to save her. Finally, Dr. Howard came over to Mary, taking her by the arm, they went out into the hallway and he said, "I'm sorry."

Mary leaned back against the wall looking down the hallway with so many questions unanswered. She saw Billy walking toward her.

Billy knew something wasn't right. Reaching Mary, he took her into his arms for comfort. Mary's tears streamed down her face, automatically she broke away from Billy and ran to the elevator.

"Ben!" she yelled leaving Billy and Dr. Howard standing by the door.

Arriving back in Ben's room, she replaced herself by his side. Tightly holding his hand, she needed to know what happened.

The doctor came back in and said they had notified the police department. They were on the way over to talk with her.

Dr. Howard rechecked Ben's vitals and said, "They are good. Your son seems to be holding his own. We will run more tests and x-rays today. It's not uncommon with a blow to the head to be unconscious. For the next several days we will keep an eye on his condition."

The doctor was injecting something into the tube which was connected by an IV in Ben's forearm. "This is a precaution against infection. We will observe his condition and we will keep you informed. I will talk to the head of the hospital to make a room available with family privileges so you can be near Ben. They have a good family plan with the McDonald House and the hotel across the street for families needing to stay close by their loved ones. I'm sorry for your loss."

Maggie sent a questioning look over to Billy standing by the door.

Mary heard the words of condolence, but her only thoughts were of the boys. Leaning over Ben, she was also worried where Mike could be. What will happen now? What happened at Frankie's house?

The police came back to speak with Mary expressing how sorry they were for her loss and updating her on their current information. They had gone back to Mrs. Pitt's house and posted an officer in case the boy (Mike) did show up there again. Neighbors across the street said they hadn't seen much of the boys - only to see them carrying bags of groceries in about once a week. A neighbor next door said the old lady was always yelling at the boys. She didn't think the kids had been going to school for several weeks. Once she saw Mrs. Pitt chasing one of the boys with a broom.

Mary told the officers Craig's story about Mrs. Pitt being very mean to them. One of the officers confirmed the boys hadn't been in school for several weeks. Did she know this? Mary told them she had tried to call Mrs. Pitt and no one would talk to her.

"I was told I couldn't come to visit them, what was I to do? But I still tried to call. No, I didn't know anything until Craig called for me to pick him up at the bus station."

They told Mary there would be an emergency hearing to possibly place the boys back in her custody. Would she want that responsibility? If not, the hearing would make the boys a ward of the state.

"Yes, O God Yes!" she said. "I would gladly take them back. I never wanted to give them up." Mary was happy to hear someone finally realizing where the boys needed to be.

"It's not going to be easy," the officer told her. "They took the boys from you and now you are going to need to show the judge they were wrong in doing so."

"Sure" Mary told the officer. "What about Mike?"

The officer said, "We will put out a state wide Amber Alert on him." The officer handed Mary three pictures. "Are these the three boys?"

"Yes," Mary told the officer where each picture had been taken as she named the boy in each one. The officer wrote the boys' names on the backs of their pictures with their ages, possible height and weight, eyes and hair color.

"I will notify the news and place his picture around. With any luck he's just with his friends and not into any trouble. Do you have a number where we can reach you?"

Mary gave the officer her cell phone number and informed them she would be staying right here with Ben until she could take him home with her.

"What about the arrangements for Mrs. Pitt?"

Maggie spoke up and said she would help Mary make the plans needed.

Chapter 30

BACK AT THE FARM the sun had come up to start a beautiful new day and Craig was up before anyone else. He went through the house studying objects and pictures looking for familiar things. He remembered the farmhouse. Mary had brought Mike and him here several times when his real dad was still living. He looked out the window across to the barn. He remembered the cigar tree still standing beside the three walled framed shed next to the barn, placed back into the hill, like the ground had grown around the shed. Papa (Glory's great grandfather) would keep his farm tractor in the shed out of the weather. Craig remembered the shed never ever had but three walls. It was still there. He smiled because today its three walls and roof are white and fluffy. The fun we had here, he thought. They climbed the hill beside the shed to step out across onto the roof and into the tree. They used the long slimmer cigar looking vines from the tree to pretend they were smoking cigars. His smile got wider. Then thinking about his brothers, a serious look came over his face. What was going to happen to them now? Would they be able to stay with Mary and Glory or would he have to go back to Mrs. Pitt. "No, I won't go," he said out loud. "I'll run away again."

"You will do no such thing!" Glory yelled. "I tried that it doesn't help. It only makes things worse. We are going to stay together this time. Promise me Craig, you will not leave." Crying she placed her arms around her brother. "Promise me...I have missed you." She's shaking him without realizing it.

Craig didn't have answers for his sister. He knew Mary and Glory loved him, but that didn't stop others from taking him from their family once before. What was going to be different this time?

Jenny woke up after hearing the two teens shouting at each other. She ran upstairs asking "What's going on?"

"Craig's talking about leaving again."

"Craig, please don't break Mary's heart again."

"What if they don't let me stay?"

"Craig, you need to have faith. Mary will be back here as soon as she can and we will help her fight to keep you here, but we need your help as well. Please, promise. We don't have to worry about you disappearing. Please Craig!"

Craig promised he would not leave. He wanted to see Mary, the only mother he remembers and he wanted to be part of the family again. He admitted he was afraid.

Jenny gave him a hug and said, "Things will work out, you will see. We just need to pray about it."

"Aunt Jenny, can we go see Blacky and Chance today?"

Jenny told the teens when she heard from Spence, she would ask him, telling the two teens he had gone to check on the horses. "Meanwhile let's get some breakfast and clean up. Glory, you need to show Craig around the house, and the things you and your mom have done to the place."

The two teens were back to picking on each other, but Jenny knew it was just new brother/sister fun. She went back downstairs.

Mary called to give Jenny the news. She thought Billy and Maggie would be coming back home. She would be staying with Ben until she could bring him home with her. Jenny told her the kids would be fine with them, just get Ben well and bring him home with her. She had no more than hung up the phone when Erik called.

"Jenny, is there any news from Mary?"

"Yes, she just called." Jenny filled Erik in with what she knew so far about Mrs. Pitt and Ben. "Sure, talk soon, bye."

She made coffee and tried to call Spence. She left him a message to call her, letting him know only that she had heard from Mary, but not giving him the details.

When he returned her call, she informed him about Mrs. Pitt and asked how could they help with any of the arrangements?

Spence told her he would talk with Mary.

"The teens want to come to the barn. How are Blacky and the colt doing?"

Spence said, "I will bring the kids over later in the day. Just stay at Mary's with them for now. Erik and Cliff are going to meet me around 10am. We'll let you know after that."

"Everything... okay?"

"Blacky is very weak. The veterinarian from Perryville is coming to meet us at 10am."

"She will be fine, Honey," Jenny told her husband before saying goodbye and hung up the phone. "Please, Dear God" Jenny said. As she sat down at the kitchen table putting her face into her hands, she began to pray about the mare, the colt, Mary, the boys, and Glory - the phone rang again.

"Jenny, Ben still has not woken up. The doctor says he's still running tests. He says sometimes a blow to the head will respond this way. The tests seem to show everything is okay but he's not waking up!"

"Mary, slow down."

Mary still talking, "They will keep him to make sure, continue to run a few more tests, but they think he's okay!"

"Oh, Mary I'm so glad you are with him! What are the chances to bring him home with you?"

Then she slowed down, Jenny could hear the trembling in her

voice. "I'm going to meet with a judge this afternoon through the Richmond Police Department. They have set up the emergency hearing. I'm hoping between the doctor's witnessing Mrs. Pitt's death wish and the witnesses at Mrs. Pitt's residence I have a good chance. The officer thinks the chances maybe good to place the boys back in my care. Keep your fingers crossed Sis… talk soon." the phone went silent.

Erik, Cliff, Spence and the vet from Perryville met at the south barn just before 10am. Cliff was confident he had done everything correctly, but he too was worried about the mare. She seemed to be running a fever and looking very glassy eyed and weak. The colt on the other hand was bouncing around the stall. The vet examined Blacky looking her over real good. He checked the stitches Cliff had done the night before. He listened to what they had done to save the colt.

"I think," said the vet, "She will be fine and Cliff, you young man, did a great job. Keep up the good work. We need more vets around here. I'm going to give you some medicine to give her with her grain and another shot for infection as a precaution. She's a strong mare, but very uncomfortable right now and possibly will be for several days. But as long as she is letting the colt nurse and she is eating it is a good sign. Let's do some precautions to keep the infection and fever down. This shot will help! I think they will be fine. Colt looks fine, good job with the delivery. Spence, you do a good job raising your horses. This one's going to be around for a lot more babies… you just wait and see. She just needs time to heal. Also give her a little longer between colts this time. It may have been just too close from the last delivery and she wasn't strong enough to deliver on her own. Good thing you came by when you did."

With a sigh of relief Spence laughed. His dream was for the farm to become once again what he remembered it to be.

As the vet was loading his things to leave, Spence noticed the small sign hanging inside the door that Glory had brought down from the loft and placed there. "Erik, do you have a hammer in your truck?"

"Sure!"

"Can I borrow it?" Spence thumbing the nails trying to straighten them, walked to the front of the barn, waiting on the hammer. Erik came back with a hammer and Spence started hammering the nails to place the sign firmly against the side of the barn.

"There! It is time we show this valley the farm is back up and running again. Chance, you're going to be the first of the new stock for this farm."

Both guys had smiles on their faces smacking hands together in a high five as they agreed. Spence placed his hand on Erik's shoulder as they walked toward their trucks saying, "It will happen."

The whole town was hoping for this miracle to happen to bring the horse traders and the big western farmers back to Edinburg. These farmers and ranchers from places like Montana and the Dakotas enjoyed coming to this small town for horse trading in the past which helped the businesses around here so much. Yes, they still kept in touch with Spence, but he didn't have the room or pasture to raise as many horses at the time these farmers had been interested - not like the whole farm could produce. If the farm could get back on its feet, what a business it would be. It could be overwhelming for someone who didn't know what they were doing. But Spence had been thinking about this for some time now and was sure if Mary agreed they could do this - they could have the farm running again by late fall. Knowing there would be other farmers willing to help out is why the town's people decided to work on the repairs on the barn. They wanted Mary to restart the farm.

Chapter 31

BACK IN CHARLOTTESVILLE, BILLY and Maggie discussed that they were not leaving Mary's side until they knew if the judge was going to grant her the right to have legal custody of the boys again. They took Mary to the courthouse and they met behind closed doors in the judge's chambers. They had let Maggie and Billy sit in on the judge's hearing for the custody issue, but they weren't allowed to say anything. They sat in the back and tried to be very quiet. Standing by Mary was the officer who had been at the hospital and who had taken the statement from Dr. Howard (the doctor who had heard Mrs. Pitt's dying wishes). The officer also had statements from Mrs. Pitt's neighbors. He stated, "There is no other living family on Old Lady Pitt's side." The judge sat listening to the story of Mary's sons being taken away from her.

The judge questioned had there been any drugs around her home?

"No, Sir. My daughter and I moved back to Edinburg, which is my home town and my grandparents left us the farm. Glory and I have been there since September. I would like the boys to be there with us to run the farm."

The judge said they would take a short break and he would make his decision.

They sat outside the judge's chambers for what seemed to be

hours. Then a young man came and waved them back inside. Billy and Maggie again placed themselves in the back of the room. Mary stood in front of the judge trembling. The judge began to speak and Mary thought she was going to pass out waiting for him to say the final words. The judge granted temporary custody of the boys back to Mary.

"I will be checking into your story Ms. Barnes and I want to see you and the boys back here in ninety days."

Mary asked the judge if it would make a difference since they were living in a different county.

The judge looked at Mary and said, "Temporary ninety day custody granted to Ms. Mary Ann Barnes (naming the three boys). This is the order of the court. A copy of this order will be sent to the Edinburg county courthouse to be on record. I will see you in ninety days, back here." The hammer hit down onto the mantle. "Good Luck Ms. Barnes."

Mary cried tears of joy. She dreamed of the chance to have the boys back and now it's coming true. Only one problem, she still did not know where to find Mike and he had no idea of everything that had happened. What are the chances they will find him? She prayed for him to be okay? They walked out of the courthouse and Mary couldn't wait to get back to Ben. She hoped he was awake because she wanted to take him home as soon as the doctor says it's okay. She called Jenny.

"Jenny...I" tears still running down her face, she finally got the words out... "I have temporary" she paused... "I have temporary *custody* of the boys."

When the call came from Mary, everyone was there (Spence, Erik, Cliff, Glory and Craig) standing in the kitchen together. Jenny said, "Just a minute, you can tell him yourself." Jenny handed the phone to Craig.

"Yes," he said trembling. "Mom, everything okay?" A troubled look was on his face. "You're sure?" A large smile came across his face as he tried to be manly holding back the tears of pure joy.

Glory was full of questions, "What's going on, Aunt Jenny?"

"Craig will tell you, Honey."

Craig got off the phone jumping around the room shouting, "I get to stay! Glory, we can be a family again!" The two teens were jumping up and down, hugging shoulder to shoulder, jumping around the room with excitement.

"When's Mom coming home?" Glory asked.

"She will call us, when she knows about when they will release Ben. He will need to stay a few more days at the hospital. They are still running tests."

The teens invited Cliff to join them and the three went upstairs to Glory's room.

Erik was calmly seated at the table. He looked at Spence and Jenny, as he said, "Guys, tell me everything about how Mary came to lose the boys to begin with."

Spence and Jenny knew how much he cared for Mary. They both agreed it would be good for all of them if they could work out whatever the issues were between Mary and Erik. But without him knowing everything, the two would not be able to work on their issues. Mary had a hard time talking about it and someone needed to tell him.

Jenny began with high school and Mary meeting George.

Erik remembered Mary getting married just out of high school to an older man with two sons. Erik and Mary had always been close through school until this stranger came into her life. He was not sure how they had met. Erik tried to talk her out of getting married, but after dating only a very short time, they married anyway. With a new family and two young boys to take care of he heard Mary was pregnant. Afterwards Erik didn't see much of Mary and they grew apart. He went to the police academy from high school. Erik remembered

Vivian and Jenny talking about Mary's life with the boys' father being very rough. Mary found out he also had been seeing his ex-wife who also was pregnant during the same time as Mary. He was an alcoholic, a war vet and had problems dealing with the real world, and having children didn't help. Soon they had yet another little one bouncing around the house with the ex-wife wanting nothing to do with her new son, making their father drink more and more. Mary took care of the children, while he played with his drinking friends making bottle bombs out of milk jugs. He became real sick to the point of going into the hospital. The doctors told him he had liver disease and needed to stop drinking. When he got out of the hospital, the news just caused him to drink more and get angrier at the world and everyone around him. Mary had left him taking the three boys and Glory with her. Shortly afterwards, within weeks of the doctors saying he needed to stop drinking, he died. Mary was granted legal guardianship of the boys. The only living relative was their grandmother "Mrs. Pitt" who they called Grams. But she didn't want "three runny nosed boys" to take care of. She was in the prime years of her life and wanted to be free because she liked her time with the men. Mrs. Pitt also enjoyed her drinking and was always out with a different man every night acting more like Mary's age than her own. So, Mary had no problems from Mrs. Pitt keeping the boys. Mary devoted her life to taking care of the four children, not leaving much time for herself. But she didn't complain. She loved the children and promised them someday they would have a real family. She would laugh saying their shining knight would come riding into town.

Jenny continued to fill in the blanks: "A couple years went by and Mary met Jack through her friend Maggie, who was dating one of Jack's friends. Jack and Mary hit it off right away. He lit a fire in her that we had never seen before and Jack loved children. He couldn't have children of his own. Mary seemed very lucky to find someone like him. She had so much fun with him and he wanted to be a family man. He took the children under his wings. They went to ballgames. He even helped coach the boys' teams. They went to music lessons and Boy Scouts, took Glory to Junior Brownies and helped coach Girl Scouts. They went on camping trips, family church gatherings, school PTAs, you name it and they did it as a family. Jack and Mary after dating for a year decided to move in together, then after another year they decided to get married. Mary's life had done a ninety degree turn for the better and their life was good."

"Jack and Mary had been together seven years and decided to adopt the boys and at the same time Jack was also going to adopt Glory May to make their family complete. Mary knew she had guardianship of the boys, but in the back of her mind she always wondered if anyone would ever turn up to take her family apart. Mrs. Pitt (Grams) each month would tell Mary how she could use the money that Mary was getting from the state for the boys' care. Mary was more worried about them being a family than the money. They started the paperwork for the adoptions and they were going through the waiting period before the judge signed the final decree. Mary had received a phone call from their attorney stating the judge scheduled to sign the final paperwork in two days. Mary was overwhelmed with excitement. They were finally going to be one complete family."

"The terrible night before the adoption papers were signed, the state took the boys from her ripping her heart apart." Jenny continued to tell the story... "Mary had gotten a phone call from Jack's employer. He was the owner of a very high end car dealership in the city. Jack had been managing the dealership along with several others in nearby towns and two across the state. The police had arrested Jack on drug charges. Mary no more than laid the phone receiver down when she heard a knock on the door. The police were there to take the boys into temporary custody. Mary needed to go the police station for questioning about her husband's arrest and they had a warrant to search Mary and Jack's home."

"No drugs on him, no drugs in his system, no drugs found at the dealership or at their home, but there were witnesses saying, he was the leader of the biggest drug marketing group the city had seen. Mary couldn't believe what she was being told about her husband. She needed to see him right away and without warning the boys were pulled from her custody."

"I remember the case, they said several kids had died from overdoses, bad drugs" Erik said, "It was in all the papers."

"That's right...well... they were able to pin the case on Jack who always said he was innocent. Mary believed him. Several of the witnesses who were true drug dealers and facing jail time themselves turned evidence over to the state lowering their sentencing and some got off without any time served. They used this information saying Jack was the mastermind behind the drug ring and the judge came down hard with Jack's sentencing. When Mrs. Pitt got the ear that Jack had been arrested, she went to the judge that same morning. He was about to sign the papers and she begged for the boys to be given to her instead of letting the adoption go through. She was their only living relation. She had the state attorney's office on her side and the judge granted the guardianship for the boys to be given to Mrs. Pitt."

Erik again remembering the newspaper stories threw his hands up over his head. "I had read the case in the paper. This trial took months. The State turned several witnesses free for testifying against Jack and providing evidence to help guarantee a conviction for the longest term in history for drug marketing. The newspapers had a field day even saying the sentence was more serious than someone facing death charges. I didn't realize that was Mary's husband. They had a lot of conflicting information. The talk around the police academy was the case only made the news and a conviction granted because the judge and the state attorney were up for re-election.

There were too many drug witnesses wanting to be free and being promised a 'get out of jail free card' if they followed the attorney's lead. Jack refused to testify against anyone."

Jenny continued … "This broke Mary's heart. She not only had to sit day after day in the courtroom which turned into weeks of hearing the stories against Jack, but now she had also lost the boys. Mary begged Mrs. Pitt not to break up the family. It didn't do any good. Mrs. Pitt had decided she wanted custody of the boys and it was granted to her. I agreed with Mary it was more because of the money than anything else. But Mary was told she could not have any contact with the boys, not even a good-bye. Mary had to go back into the courtroom and listen to the terrible things she never knew about her husband. This was a side of him she had never seen. For the last seven years she thought she knew this man. There didn't seem to be anything the family could do, but help Mary take care of Glory May. Mom and Dad went into the city to help Mary so she could go visit Jack. Mary stood by her husband. Dad and Mom always said, "She didn't really know him." This caused problems between Dad, Mom and Mary. Mom and Dad would say he was always going away on business trips, transferring vehicles from state to state, and buying them big expensive gifts. Where did the money come from? But Mary loved Jack and he was good to her and the kids giving them the family she had promised the children they would have. She thought his only downfall was keeping her away from the farm and in the dark about this other life. It was like he had two lives. But their attorney told her, she was lucky not to know what was going on or she too could have been arrested."

Jenny told Erik "Yes, I was unhappy that Mary had been awarded the farm. But I was glad when I found out Mary and Glory were coming back to the farm to live and not sell it. She needed a chance to restart their lives."

"I was only afraid she would sell the farm, instead of returning to it. Now I think my grandfather knew he needed to take care of her all along. The farm gives her another chance."

Erik sat listening to the story of Mary's life. He thought he had known her since they were kids playing in the fields together, but he realized now there was a lot he didn't know. Now he sees why that last night they had been together was so hard for her, but if she had just opened up to him about it. Instead, she had pushed him away with no clue, only giving him bad signals.

He knew he needed to do something to make her realize she could take a chance and be happy again. He told Spence and Jenny that he needed to go into town. "Will one more teen in the house be okay for several hours?" he questioned.

"Erik?" replied Jenny.

"Please, if not, I'll understand." Erik asked.

"No, that's fine!" Spence said, "They're upstairs having fun. Go do what you need to do." At the same time, he was curious as to what was on Erik's mind.

"Thanks, you will see." Out the door he went spinning the truck tires as he left the driveway.

Spence told Jenny, "I really hope they work out the problems between them. I think he really cares for your sister and he's a good family man. Plus, this farm could use him."

Chapter 32

ERIK ARRIVED BACK AT his shop. He placed several phone calls. He went into the large walk-in cooler and got three dozen long stem roses then realized that was crazy. She wouldn't be home for several days maybe longer and they would be dead before she could enjoy them. He seated himself in front of the shop window looking out across the busy street. Thinking, should he go to her? Should he wait until she got back? What if she didn't give him the time of day? He went to the phone dialing her cell phone number.

"Hello,"

"Mary?"

"Yes"

"Mary, please don't hang up."

"Erik?"

"Yes"

"Erik, I'm sorry, I should have …"

Erik cutting her off… "Mary, how is Ben?"

"The doctor says his testing doesn't show anything abnormal, but he is still not awake. Erik, I need to say…"

Erik cuts her off again, "I know Dear and you will. But first things first, what can I do to help?"

"I'm not sure. I know I will need to make the arrangements for Mrs. Pitt's funeral, when I get back there. I need to let the hospital know where to take her body. Maggie and I have been talking about it. I think she should be closer to our home so the boys can visit her grave. She was their grandmother."

"Mary, if it is okay…I will call the hospital and have them bring her body back here to Jones Funeral Home. Once you are back, you can get with whomever you need for her final arrangements and last resting place. But you won't have to deal with it right this minute. You can concentrate on Ben, getting him well and getting him home with you, Glory May and Craig."

"Erik…Thanks. You don't need to do that. I just know I don't want her final resting place to be somewhere by herself. She was their grandmother."

"Mary, I'll call and take care of Mrs. Pitt's arrangements, you take care of Ben and yourself…we'll talk tomorrow. Now give me her full name and her doctor's name."

Hanging up the phone, Erik got out the telephone directory and looked up the number for Jones Funeral Home. The last time he had called them was to make arrangements for his wife, Nora. He placed the call and told them where Ms. Pitt's body was located. He gave them the information Mary had given him. "Thanks, no please, we will call when Mary gets back in town with the details for her arrangements. That's right," he said. "It will take several days before we can get back to you… Okay, thanks," he hung up the call. He then called the cemetery to reserve a final resting place. He knew right now everyone was mad at the old lady for taking the boys, but she was their grandmother and hoped they would show her a little respect with a final resting place. He would tell Spence and Jenny about the arrangements he had made hoping they would agree with him and that he had not overstepped.

When Erik finished with the arrangements, he decided to stop by The Bed & Breakfast Inn for a cup of coffee. The news around the inn was joyful because Mrs. Robins had won the grand prize for the Best Decorated Christmas Home in the county. He had not realized the prize had been awarded that very day. "That's why the town was so busy," he said.

With everything that had gone on with Mary and the new addition at the farm, he had forgotten today was the big luncheon. So, after his coffee, off he went to the Robin's Interior Design Shop to see Mr. and Mrs. Robins and gave them his best. He also wanted to make sure they were aware of what was going on with Mary.

The Robins were glad to see Erik. "Where's the 'New Vet'?" they questioned as Erik entered the shop.

Erik laughed. "So, you heard about the colt?"

Mrs. Robins wanted to know if Mary had called him.

He told her he just gotten off the phone with her.

"So, everything's okay with the two of you?"

"Not yet, but I'm hopeful! We will talk more after she returns."

"Good, I always knew you two would be good together."

Erik smiled, hoping Mrs. Robins would be right about this one. Erik said, he needed to get back out to Mary's farm. Cliff is still out there visiting. He would talk to them soon and gave them congratulations again. He made his way out the door and into his truck.

Thanksgiving, Christmas and now the New Year is right around the corner. For the most part the holidays came and went. Erik remembered he only received cards for Thanksgiving and Christmas addressed from Mary and Glory. Somethings never change. There were just seven simple words, "Have a Good Holiday... thinking of you" signed Mary and Glory. He was always hoping for a call or visit into his store or even a 'thank you' for the birthday picture or the Christmas tree. What is going on with this woman? Good thing he didn't know that the cards came from Glory, not Mary. That would have only added to his sadness and disappointment. Erik didn't know at the time what was behind her reasons for not calling. He thought, "there's a lot she's not talking about. I've met Craig, but that's not all of it." He was sure of that!

Cliff and Craig seemed to get along just fine. Erik's confusion was Mary didn't seem interested in him or not the way he wanted. Should he just stop trying? "No, I can't… I think I love this woman (shrugging his shoulders and shaking his head). You don't give up on love, not that easy," he thought out loud. "It doesn't come your way that often - maybe helping out with the arrangements for Mrs. Pitt will bring her around." Lost in his own thoughts, he finally realized he had been sitting in front of the ten single one room buildings created for gift shops in Perryville village. This is where Mary and he had come for the Oktoberfest. A smile came over his face as he remembered that wonderful day. She was carefree and seemed happy that day. He started the truck and headed down the country road, turning toward Mary's house. He wanted to check with Spence and see how Blacky and the new colt were doing today. He had also told the guys he would meet them to work on the barn.

Today Mary couldn't get Erik off her mind and his offer to help with the arrangements for Mrs. Pitt. It also put a grin on her face as she remembered their times together. How lucky she was to have a friend like Erik. Finally, she felt she should call him as she sat on the end of Ben's hospital bed. There were many times she had wanted to call. She had intended to call, but didn't know how or what to say about her feelings for him. She reached for the phone. No chance to change her mind as the phone rang. Standing with her hand clutched to the phone's receiver, she jumped when it rang. She picked up the receiver… "Hello…Glory May?" she said with a surprised look on her face and a crack in her voice.

"Mom…Are you okay? How is Ben?" Glory's voice also cracked. Mary was glad to hear her daughter's voice, but could sense the fear as she spoke.

Mary tried to speak, but no words came out. Her throat weakened to a whisper… "Hello…Hi, Dear." They talked for a few minutes. She let Glory know what was going on at the hospital. Mary told Glory she would call if there were any changes. The phone went silent.

Mary leaned over to hang up the phone thinking no one was there and Glory had hung up. Before she reached the cradle to release the phone again she could hear the words, "Mary…Mary please, won't you talk to me?"

Her heart raced. "Yeah…Hi Erik"

"Hi yourself." Then silence on both ends.

Mary thought he would be able to hear her heartbeat racing through the phone.

Erik began, "I had given up hearing from you… hoping some-time today you would have called." A thumping rattle sound was in his voice. He cleared his throat before saying, "Sooo… how are you doing?" Silence again… "Mary, are you there?"

"Yes, Erik. Better… It is nice to hear from you. I hope you and Cliff are good." Mary cleared her throat knowing she was going to lose the connection if she didn't try to get the words out. She thought at the same time how long was he going to continue to try to work out the unknown problems between them.

"We're working on the barn today. The repairs may turn into al-most a brand new barn by the time we're done. The snow has started to melt around here which helps. We were able to work for a while yesterday too. Everyone is praying for you and the boys. They miss you." Erik wanted to say, "I miss you." But again, he just kept talking. "And they can't wait for you to see the repairs. Oh yes, have they told you about the new addition to the farm? What color would you like to paint the barn?"

"Paint the barn? It will be several weeks before the barn will be that ready," Mary replied with a smile on her face. She was thinking please Erik, stop talking.

"Well we just may surprise you, Lady. If the weather holds out, you may see a new barn when you get back."

"Erik... ERIK!"

"Yes, Mary."

Mary caught herself before saying something she would later regret. "Good job, you guys have been working too hard on the barn. I don't know how I'll ever repay the town."

Erik thought to himself as he stopped talking, had Mary been listening to his rambling. He was so glad to talk to her. It had been months. He wanted just to hear her voice. Now he wasn't giving her a chance to say anything. He wanted to hit himself upside the head. 'What's with you?' he thought. 'You're not a high school kid having a crush on your first sweetheart. But Mary was his first sweetheart. He never told her so. How was she to know? Their lives went in different directions and now look at them almost fifteen years later.'

Mary's voice somehow seemed very distant. Maybe it was the pressure she was under being at the hospital, maybe not knowing where to find Mike and of course she still needed to make the final arrangements for Ms. Pitt. He could tell she was glad to hear from him. Erik knew it just wasn't the right time for them to get into the issues between them.

"I've got to go, Erik. Can we talk later?"

"Sure, call me anytime. See you soon."

Her voice soft and tender "Bye Erik and thanks for calling."

Mary sat by the phone with the receiver still in her hand, as she questioned herself. 'Why is it so hard for me to talk to him? Why can't I tell him how I really feel?' Mary leaned over and gave Ben a kiss on the forehead. She took one hand and brushed his hair which was sticking out from under the bandage and hanging across one eye. 'Maybe soon I will, once I get home with the boys,' she thought. She wondered if he could understand her reaction as they reached that response nearing the narrow borderline of attraction or just the natural lust of two adults needing each other's company. She stood there reminded of their last night together. She could feel that same tightness in her throat. With sweaty palms still gripped around the phone receiver she said aloud, "Look what this man does to me." She replaced the phone on its cradle.

"What man?" Maggie commented as she came into the room.

"No one."

"What's going on?"

"Maggie, I thought you and Billy were going home last night?"

"We decided to stay another day or two. We don't want you to be here alone."

"Thanks Maggie, but I know the two of you have jobs. You need to get back home."

"Stop Mary, friends help each other. Plus, we both had this week off for the holidays. We are not leaving you here alone. No more excuses! You know what you need…a good meal. Come across the street with Billy and me to the hotel dining room and have some dinner. You have been by Ben's side for days. The hospital will let you know of any changes. I'll make sure they know where to find us."

"Maggie, that's sweet but I want to be here if he wakes up."

"No, buts, you need to eat or you will be down sick and then who's going to take care of the boys? Come on… no more excuses!" Maggie was pushing Mary toward the door as she spoke. They walked into the hallway to the small waiting area where Billy had been patiently waiting for them. He had been watching the local news on the TV set hanging in the corner of the lobby waiting room.

"Mary, look, Mrs. Robins made the news. She won the Christmas contest. She took First Place for the county and runner-up maybe for the state! They are talking about showing the reviews on tonight's news at 11:00pm."

Mary smiled knowing the Robins had put a lot of work into the decorations. Mary was glad to hear she won. "I need to call maybe tomorrow after I have seen the review," Mary said.

"We are going to take this lady across the street and have a decent dinner, Billy."

Billy was up for that. The hospital food wasn't anything to write home about. It had been another long day. They knew Mary had to be exhausted and hungry. He hadn't seen her eat anything in several days - only one cup after another of black coffee, not even taking the time to put creamer in it before going back to Ben's room.

They walked into the dining room of the hotel. Mary had only been across the street to the hotel to take a bath and change clothes before going back to Ben's hospital bedside. The hotel was set up by the McDonald House with rooms for families who needed to stay near their children. But not once had she paid any attention to the dining area.

Fortunately, it was early afternoon and the dining room was not busy. Only two tables had someone seated at them. Mary looked around the room with an uncomfortable tension spinning around in her head. She seated herself facing the doorway. Maggie and Billy sat down facing Mary and a large picture window with the sun shining through the double panel of glass to give off a bright refection making their eyes water.

The waitress crossed the room drawing the blinds before coming to their table. She handed Mary a menu and in a soft voice asked, "What can I get you to drink?"

Maggie quickly said, "I will have an extra dry martini with olives. Come on Mary, have one with me."

Mary ordered a cup of coffee with extra cream. Billy also ordered a martini with pickled mushrooms, as he too said, "Mary, have just one. It will help calm you down."

The waitress waited to see if Mary was going to change her mind, but she still wanted the coffee. The waitress started to walk away when Mary called.

"No second thought Miss, can I have hot tea, fresh lemon, honey.

You do have some…and fresh cream on the side."

"Sure," said the waitress.

Mary looked around the room to see a gray-haired couple sipping on a chocolate-flavored drink with whipped cream and fresh cherries on top. They were laughing as a young boy stepped into the dining room on crutches. Mary could tell they weren't laughing at the boy, but his friendly invisible dog on a leash in his hand as he crossed toward the older couple's table. He seated himself. He told his invisible friend to be seated. The leash was moving back and forth like the animal was obeying.

Across on the other side of the room, Mary focused her attention on a woman in her forties. She was tall, thin, angular with skin the color of bittersweet chocolate and a marbled gray tint in her hair. Mary remembered seeing her at the hospital by the coffee machine several times. Her son was in the burn unit with 95% of his body fried from an electrical burn. Mary thanked God for Ben's injuries not being that serious. Although, it worried her that Ben had been unconscious for so long. The doctor said the tests and x-rays looked good. So why, why is it taking so long for him to come back to the real world? Mary's thoughts were interrupted by Billy laughing at the young boy playing around with the leash and the invisible dog.

"You like that, don't you?" Mary replied.

"He's just having so much fun with the leash. That's what I like - just the simple things of life."

"Maggie, you look like you could go to sleep."

Mary looked over to her dear friend Maggie with her eyes partly closed. "Yes, I'm tired today. You must be too!"

"Some - I will be glad to take Ben home. I have been thinking a lot about Mike too. I wish there would be some way to find him, before he gets into trouble. Not knowing where he could be is very upsetting."

"They'll find him, Mary," Billy replied. "Have faith."

"My faith is getting stretched to the max."

"We know how hard it has to be, Mary. Just stay focused on the positive things."

By this time the waitress came back with their drinks and was ready to take their orders.

"Mary, you first!" Billy directed.

Mary placed her order of ocean perch, listed as "The catch of the day" served with rice and garden vegetables.

Maggie decided on the pork loin served with mashed potatoes and side salad, house dressing, and another martini.

Billy went for the prime rib, cooked medium, baked potato, sour cream and lots of butter. He paused and decided he wanted the garden vegetables as well, with another martini.

"Ma'am, can I bring you another tea?"

"That would be great, thanks," Mary replied.

Dinner was a great idea. Mary realized after she had started to eat, just how hungry she was, remembering her last good meal had been Christmas dinner. Tomorrow would be a week. "Tomorrow is New Year's Eve," Mary replied. "Guys, you needn't stay with me. Go home… enjoy the New Year's Eve parties, but be safe."

Billy half laughing… "You kidding? Think about it: I have my girl with me, a nice hotel for dinner and music, maybe some dancing and the room to boot with no driving necessary. Why would I want to go home now? Maybe we need to see about finding you a date for tomorrow night?"

"No, Billy, I just want to stay by Ben's side. I'll watch the New Year come in by his bed."

Billy questioned that comment, but decided to wait. He wanted to run an idea by Maggie first before saying anything to Mary.

They finished dinner. Mary was ready to go back across the street to the hospital. Billy and Maggie decided to stay for another drink. The martinis were going down way too easy.

Mary excused herself and Billy told her they would be over to check on her in a little while. When Mary had walked out of sight through the large double doors heading toward the hospital corridor, Billy enlightened Maggie with his proposed idea. "Let's call Erik and have him join us here for tomorrow night. We can have dinner, some music, maybe some dancing and who knows maybe it will give Erik and Mary a chance to get back on track."

"Or maybe not, what if it explodes, Counselor?"

"Come on, she has been talking to him since she has been here... that's a start. She needs someone in her life. Erik is good for her. I'm going to call him and see how he feels about the idea."

Billy took out his cell phone and dialed Erik's number. On the second ring Erik answered. "Yeah, your dime my man!"

"Yeah guy... Erik, what's happening my man?"

How are Mary and her son doing?" was the first question out of Erik's mouth.

"Well that's why I'm calling...why don't you come join us tomorrow evening and find out for yourself?"

"Well, Mary hasn't really given me that okay yet."

"But the two of you have been talking, yes?"

"Well, yes!"

"Then come join us, I will make sure you have a room here at the same hotel where we are staying. They are having a New Year's Eve dinner with music and dancing. I will make sure there is a reservation for a table of four and we will surprise her."

"I don't know about surprising her? That could backfire. Maybe... I should call her and ask if she would care for me to join you for dinner, instead of just showing up."

"You think about it... I will make the reservations and you call me tomorrow to confirm you are coming. If you decide not to come, I can cancel the reservations. Deal?"

"Okay, let me think about it. Now - how is Mary really doing?"

Maggie sat listening to the guys. She really hoped this went the way Billy was planning. What if, Mary wasn't ready to see Erik, what then?

Billy was laughing at something Erik had told him, and the conversation came back to… "Okay, I'll see you tomorrow my man." Billy placed the phone back in his pocket.

"All set, but the hotel and dinner table… Excuse me." Billy got up walking toward the cashier. They spoke for a few minutes and Billy returned to the table. "Dinner reservations are set for 8:00pm. This will give us time for dinner and talking before the music starts at 9:30pm. Now let me go make him a room reservation."

Maggie catching Billy by the arm, "Are you sure about this?"

"I think this will be just what the doctor ordered," Billy said. "It could be an extremely good thing…maybe just what both of them need to put them back on track."

"Or… maybe not!" Maggie sighed. "It could blow up on all of us."

"Think positive, it could be a cure to yet another one of Mary's problems." Maggie laughed at the positive tone of Billy's voice and more so at his terminology.

Billy left the table heading toward the reservation desk of the hotel. Shortly he returned with the room information for Erik when he calls tomorrow. He tucked the paper into his pocket saying "We will make sure the New Year starts with a good promise of things to come for the upcoming year." Billy picked up his glass and gave a toast: "To a wonderful beginning of the New Year."

"The martinis are talking, aren't they?" Maggie replied. She couldn't help herself as she smiled at him. Billy did have good intentions and to think she would be alone with him. No town girlfriends to draw his attention she thought. Although he could have left to go home at anytime this week, he chose to stay by their sides. This told her a lot about this man she was becoming more and more attracted to.

They finished their drinks. Maggie wanted to go check on Mary and Ben. Billy wanted to catch a nap, telling Maggie, if she was still at the hospital when he got up from his nap, he would come over and sit with them. They agreed.

Chapter 33

MAGGIE WALKED TOWARD THE double doors going to the hospital corridor. Maggie stepped on the elevator and pushed the button for the floor going towards Ben's room. She watched as a young lady dressed in pink and white stripes pushed a hospital cart with library books into the elevator. Maggie said, "Excuse me... can I see what books you have?"

The young lady stepped back to let Maggie look. She found the book *The Adventures of Tom Sawyer.* This will do just fine. She signed a card for the candy striper with Ben's room number on it. When the elevator came to a stop, Maggie said thanks and stepped out into the hall walking toward Ben's room.

Mary was back in the corner chair, looking out the window onto the busy street below them when Maggie entered the room. Mary was watching the cars double-parked on both sides of the street and lost in her thoughts.

"Let's try something," Maggie said as she sat down on the corner of the bed. She opened the book to the first page. She began to read "The Adventures of Tom Sawyer." She turned the page naming some of the main characters Tom Sawyer, Huckleberry Finn and she stopped reading, "Ben, you remember this book, don't you? This has stories of boys like you and your brothers...Mike and Craig? I'm sure you would love to get into another adventure with them."

Maggie started to read again. "Remember your brothers, Mike and Craig?"

Mary stepped back to her seat in the corner again laying her head against the enforced glass as Maggie continued to read.

"Aunt Polly finds Tom in the pantry where he has been eating the forbidden jam. She gets a switch, but Tom convinces her that something is behind her. As she turns, he escapes, leaving her to contemplate how he constantly plays tricks on her." Maggie using a little Mississippi tone in her voice continues to read… *"That afternoon, Tom plays hooky from school, and at supper that night, Aunt Polly tries to trap him into revealing that he skipped school. Tom is able to avert her questioning, until Sid, Tom's brother squeals on him."*

Maggie laughs as she continued reading the story in her Mississippi drawl and glanced around to Mary who was looking out the hospital room window to the busy street below. "I forgot how funny this book can be," Maggie said. She turned the page and started reading again. *"Heading into town, Tom meets a stranger….a boy larger than himself. Who was dressed up like a city-slicker. He and Tom get into a fight,"* Maggie continues. *"Tom gets the better of the other boy and follows him home. The boy's mother appears saying Tom's a 'bad vicious, vulgar child' and orders him away. Tom gets home with his clothes torn and dirty. Aunt Polly decides as his punishment, he will lose his freedom on Saturday. He will have to whitewash the fence."* Maggie paused, "Oh, Ben, this sounds like something you and the boys would do." Maggie continued reading, *"Beginning the dreaded task of white-washing, Tom sees Ben Rogers approaching. When Ben teases Tom about not being able to go swimming and being forced to work, Tom points out that it is not exactly work if you are enjoying what you are doing. He was putting on a great show of applying the whitewash onto the fence. Some other boys show up, who came to jeer, but remained to whitewash and by the middle of the afternoon the fence is whitewashed by the other boys. Tom finds himself a rich man by collecting marbles, a part of a Jew's harp, a kite, and many other items as payment from the boys to enjoy the work of whitewashing…doing his work for him.*

Maggie stopped reading and said, "Ben, I think this story is about you and your brothers, Mike and Craig. It sounds like something the three of you would do.

By the end of the first chapter both Maggie and Mary are laughing at *The Adventures of Tom Sawyer* and relating the events with things the boys had done over the years. Maggie was glad she had chosen the book. Not only could it help Ben, but it was helping Mary as well with the long visits by Ben's hospital bedside.

Maggie had read for hours, but it didn't seem like it. She had gotten so overwhelmed with the book herself the time had flown by.

She looked up as Billy poked his head into the room. "How's things in here…Can I get anyone anything?"

"Hi Billy, come in. We are reading *The Adventures of Tom Sawyer* to Ben. Remember the book?" Maggie said.

"Sure, this is a great book." Billy began telling how his school class read this. "I thought oh no, I hate reading and I will have to give up a weekend to read this for a book report due on Tuesday. But after I got started, I didn't want to put it down."

"Wow… you want to take turns and we can read to Ben together?" asked Maggie.

"Sure, we can do that." Billy pulled up a chair and they sat across from each other, one on each side of Ben's bed. Maggie began to read again in her Mississippi joking tone.

Amy, the attending nurse came in to check on Ben and gave him a replacement IV bottle. Before long she too was enjoying *The Adventures of Tom Sawyer* laughing at the two readers, making jokes at the same time. The nurse finally said they needed to go and get some rest. Maggie asked Mary to join them back at the hotel. Of course, she said no she was going to stay by Ben's side. Maggie and Billy left saying goodnight.

Mary moved over to Ben's side, placed his hand into hers, kissed it and leaned her head on the bed as she began saying a pray. "Dear Lord, I know I haven't been the best mother, but could you see fit to give me one more chance? Let him wake up and let me take Ben home and teach him the ways of farm life. Let him be able to run through the fields, ride horses and play with his sister and brothers. Help me to give them the understanding of what and how a family stays together, works together, and may we grow old together." By this time Mary had tears running down her face. She finished her prayer with thanks for her good friends and family who were helping out at home and turned for a tissue to dry her tears. In doing so she saw her grandparents standing at the end of the bed. She heard a calm voice say, "It will be okay, My Dear." Mary wasn't sure if they were there to take Ben with them or to calm her after praying so hard. But a calm peaceful feeling came over Mary as she laid her head back on the edge of Ben's bed and drifted into a peaceful sleep.

Mary jumped as the head nurse came into the room about 7:00am. She walked around to the other side of Ben's bed, started checking on the machine still connected to his arm and took his blood pressure and pulse. "The doctor will be in around 9:00am today. He will be pleased to see Ben's vitals looking better today."

"Really" Mary replied.

"Yes, he seems much stronger today." The nurse stepped back to the window, "How about some sunshine?" She opened the drapes slowly. It's a beautiful day out. You should go get some breakfast and take a shower. You will feel so much better. Have you been here all night?"

Mary replied, "Yes."

The nurse again said, "You need to go get a cup of coffee, I'll stay with him until you get back, go on."

"You sure…Thanks, but I'll wait until my friend comes in and then I'll go get cleaned up. But I could use the coffee."

"Then go, I'll be right here until you get back. They just started a fresh pot down the hall."

"Thanks" Mary picked up her things that had fallen on the floor and placed them on the table beside Ben's bed. "Are you sure?"

"Go" replied the nurse.

Mary walked down the long hall toward the coffee machine. Today there was fresh coffee and donuts on a table beside the machine and a young lady pouring the coffee. Standing beside the table was the lady in the restaurant from last night. She was crying. Mary asked if she was okay?

She replied her son had passed. She knew he was better off, but it was still hard. Mary gave the lady a hug and asked if she could do anything.

The lady said, "Thanks, but you just go back with your son. I hope he will soon be talking and walking out of here."

Mary told her, "He will, I know he will. He just needs to rest for now." She got her coffee, asking the young lady if she could take an extra cup with her? Picking up the second cup Mary headed back to Ben's room. The nurse was still by Ben's bed just as she had said.

"Here, have a cup on me and thanks for staying with him."

The Tom Sawyer book was laying on the table beside his bed. The nurse picked up the book and said, "You been reading to him?"

Mary answered, "Yes, my two friends have been. They thought it might help."

"Great idea! You would be surprised how it helps. I have seen many cases like this. Sometimes it takes months and others just days. He's gotten stronger and that's a great sign. He possibly will be out of here in no time. Do we know anymore about what happened to him?"

"Not yet. The police are still working on it I was told."

"Well, he is in good hands with Dr. Howard." The nurse looked at her watch, "Well, time for me to get back to work. I will see you later when Dr. Howard comes in. I'm doing rounds with him this morning. Enjoy the coffee and thanks for mine." Out the door the nurse went.

Mary went over to the small sink next to the bed and wet her face. Leaning over to look into the mirror, she turned quickly at the shadow of her grandparents again standing by Ben's bed. "Grams, please don't take him from me, please!"

The tranquil voice spoke, "He will be running through the fields before you know it, My Dear. Teach him how to run the farm. He will be of good use."

Mary had a feeling of peace come over her (like someone had poured warm water down across her shoulders) as the shadow of her grandparents disappeared. Mary sat in the chair placing her head in her hands and feeling drained. Was she dreaming?

Dr. Howard came in around 9:15am and the head nurse was with him, as she had said. The doctor asked how she was holding up. "Ben looks like he is doing better today. His vitals are even stronger than two hours ago" as he checked the machine readings and looked into Ben's eyes. "Even his color is improving. These are all real good signs." The doctor was very positive with his visit. "I see you have been reading to him. That's good… keep it up. Watch for eye movement. Even if he doesn't wake up, he could be hearing you and the eye movement will tell us he can hear you."

"Okay" Mary replied. "So, he's doing better?"

"Oh yes, he seems to be getting stronger."

A warmhearted smile can over Mary's face as the doctor and head nurse left the room. Mary looked up toward the heavens and said, "Thank you."

Around 10:00am Maggie and Billy came into the room. They both gave Mary a hug and Billy handed a plate of food to her. "How are you doing today? I knew you would not go to get anything to eat so I brought it to you."

Mary laughed, "I really could use a cup of tea."

Billy turned to go back out the door.

"Where are you going?"

"To get Mary a cup of tea!" He was smiling like someone had just caught him in a big tale.

"Do you want lemon, honey and cream?"

"Sure"

"Okay, be right back!" Out the door he went.

Mary told Maggie about last night and seeing her grandparents for the second time today.

"Here?" Maggie was surprised but didn't question what Mary was telling her, because since Mary had been back into the farmhouse it seemed her grandparents were watching over her.

Mary told Maggie the book was a good idea. "The doctor says watch for eye movements when we are reading to him."

Maggie went over, picked up the book, and sat down beside the bed. Before she started to read again, she said, "Ben, what kind of trouble or mischief do you think Tom Sawyer will get into next? Let's read and see." She began to read in the tom-foolish mischief Mississippi voice. It wasn't long before she had Mary laughing with her as she continued to read. *"Tom struggles to learn his Sunday school lesson with the help of his cousin, who offers him a present if he can learn the lesson...later at church Tom remembering his wealth from swaps items with the boys for whitewashing the fence which paid off for his punishment. He decided to use the same idea and swaps items on tickets indicating how many verses in the Bible he had memorized. Soon Tom had collected so many tickets it appeared he knew around two thousand verses. In Sunday school class, Tom claimed the award for knowing the most verses. Tom had been introduced to Judge Thatcher, who asks him the name of the first two apostles. Tom blurts out David and Goliath!"*

Laughing Maggie continued to read... *"Tom on Monday morning tried without success to convince Aunt Polly that he was too ill to attend school.* "Well, Ben, I know you boys have tried this one." *Tom claiming he had a toothache. Aunt Polly quickly resolved this issue by pulling his tooth and sent him on his merry way to school. Tom meeting Huckleberry Finn, who was carrying a dead cat with the intent of taking it to the cemetery that night because he believed Satan would come for the cat and take Huck's warts with him."*

Maggie stopped reading for a minute. She thought she saw Ben blink. Watching she continued again… *"His encounter with Huck caused Tom to arrive at school late. His punishment is to sit in the girls section. Tom doesn't mind, Becky Thatcher was there. He drew pictures and wrote her a love letter. At lunch they agree to become engaged, even though Becky doesn't know what this means. Soon she spurns him and he is depressed and plays hooky for the afternoon."* Maggie watched Ben closely as she continued to read. It had been hours, there had been no other response from him. Billy had been back in the room for awhile now and told Maggie he would read to give her a break. She stepped back to the window and listened as Billy began to read. He too tried to make the story fun with the Mississippi voices. In a slow deep voice, he read… *"That night Tom and Huck took the dead cat to the graveyard. There they heard voices. The town drunk and Injun Joe were digging up a corpse for Dr. Robinson's research. The three men get into a fight, knocking the town drunk unconscious. Injun Joe stabs Dr. Robinson with the town drunk's knife. Huck and Tom flee and do not hear Injun convince the drunk that he is the murderer."* Billy stops for a minute watching Ben's eyes. "Look! Look at his eyes they're moving!" Mary jumped to her feet and was by the bed before her feet had time hit the floor.

"The doctor said this would be a good sign. Ben, can you hear us?" No other responses and his eyes went still again.

Billy started to read continuing for several hours, but nothing else was noticed. Around 5:00pm Billy's phone rang. He asked Maggie to take over and he walked into the hallway. It was Erik.

He had left Cliff with Spence and Jenny. They were going to do something with the teens through the church and had invited Cliff to join them, giving Erik a reason to get out of town. He had told Spence he was coming to Charlottesville, hoping this didn't upset Mary. Spence was glad he was coming to give her some support. He was about an hour away from the hospital since he was able to leave town earlier than planned. Billy gave him the directions to the hospital and the hotel room number. He told Erik to ring him when he got there. Billy moved back into the room and told Mary he had made reservations for them to have dinner at the hotel. Mary told Billy thanks, but she was going to stay with Ben.

Maggie looked at Billy and shrugged her shoulders. Then Maggie said, "Just have dinner and then you can come back and stay with Ben." After a little convincing Mary agreed she could eat something.

"Good," Billy said. "We will eat around 8:00pm. That's when I could get dinner reservations."

"Why reservations, Billy?"

"It's New Year's Eve. We needed a reservation."

"Oh yes, New Year's Eve." Mary walked over to the window and wondered how everyone was doing back at the farm and then her thoughts turned to Mike. "Where could you be tonight? Please, stay out of trouble, Mike," she whispered.

The hour past quickly and Billy's phone rang again. Billy again walked into the hallway to take the call. "Yeah man...are you here?"

Erik answered, "I'm downstairs. The hotel showed me how to get from the hotel to the hospital. How is Mary? Did you tell her I was coming? I have a dress for her to wear tonight. I didn't think she would have brought anything dressy with her. Jenny helped get it from her closet. You think she would wear it?"

"No, she didn't bring anything dressy with her and that's great you did. That was nice, but how are we going to get Mary to wear it, unless we tell her you're here? I think we will just have you come in after she is seated at the table for dinner."

"Okay. What about the dress?"

"Bring it to our room I'll have Maggie give it to her saying Jenny sent it to Maggie for us to take Mary out for New Year's Eve dinner."

"Okay, I'm going to my room now. Be over to yours shortly and then I can get a shower. Talk to you in a few. Later."

"Yeah guy" Billy snapped his phone closed with excitement as he went back into the room and waved for Maggie to come out into the hallway. Doing so Billy told her about the dress. Maggie told him to get the dress and she would bring Mary to their room to pick it up. "I hope this works!"

Erik went to the hotel front desk and asked if they had a flower shop?

"Sure do, sir." The desk clerk pointed to the corridor saying, "Go to the second floor and turn right."

"Thanks," Erik replied and walked into the corridor following the directions. He stepped into the flower shop looking around wondering why he didn't put together his own arrangement and bring it with him. He picked out red roses.

Took a card from the display and began to write:

> *May the New Year bring*
> *lots of good things,*
> *Erik*

Erik took the flowers, left the shop, and walked back to the hotel dining room. There he asked the waitress to put the flowers in the back and bring them out when he arrived for dinner around 8:00pm handing her a $10.00 bill. She agreed to do so and he went back to his hotel room.

At 6:15pm Maggie convinced Mary it was time to go to the hotel room and get a bath. "I have a dress for tonight. It is in my room."

"A dress?"

"Yes, it's for tonight, remember New Year's Eve dinner. Dressing up will be good for you. Ben will be in good hands and would want you to enjoy dinner."

Both ladies walked over gave Ben a kiss and left the room together. They stopped at the nurse's station to tell the nurse they would be at the hotel for dinner and to call them if there was *any* change.

"Sure will, Ms. Barnes," the second nurse replied. Enjoy dinner and try to have some fun. I understand the band at the hotel is pretty special tonight. Wish we could join you."

The ladies walked toward the hotel hand in hand, joking about the dinner plans.

"Ben will be fine, Mary. Let's enjoy the evening."

Chapter 34

THEY TURNED THE CORNER a couple of minutes after Erik had left Billy and Maggie's room. Billy had just closed the door not knowing how close the girls had come to seeing Erik.

Maggie went into the room and brought out the dress. It was Mary's black violet dress with a satin white boat style collar draped down over her shoulders into a bow in the back.

"Wow, Maggie...I didn't realize tonight was to be so dressy."

"Well, it is New Year's Eve." Maggie replied. Hugging her around the shoulders, they walked toward Mary's room reaching the door Maggie said, "We will stop and get you in about an hour and a half. Get a nice warm bath and try to relax."

Maggie quickly went back to Billy and her room. "What do you think she is going to think when you and I sit down to eat with her in our blue jeans?"

Billy is lying on the bed with a big ass grin on his face.

"No fear, My Dear, I have it covered." Billy had gone to the rental store and had a beautiful blue satin dress for Maggie and a black suit for him.

Maggie sat down on the bed, breathless. "You did this?"

"Sure, it is a special night."

Maggie was amazed by the effort Billy had taken to pull off this special evening hoping it didn't backfire. She went into the bathroom and started running the water into the tub. Billy came in behind her thinking the fun they could have before going downstairs to dinner.

Billy moved over to the water and turned it off as he turned toward Maggie where she had started to undress. "Here, let me help you." His hands moved slowly across her shoulders as the spaghetti strap dropped revealing the top firm portion of her breasts. He leaned over kissing the exposure as he gently touched the yet hidden areas of her breast through her knit shirt.

Stimulated Maggie could feel her breasts standing at attention as he cupped her shirt. In the excitement Maggie wanted more but played calm. Her hand moved to the front of his pants stroking gently. She could feel his swollen, firmness ready, but she wanted to play. Maggie took the initiative to slowly undo his belt and the zipper to his blue jeans allowing his baggy pants to drop to his knees revealing the large mass in his jockey shorts.

Now it was his turn, he gently opened the buttons on the front of her shirt, joking as one had gotten stuck. He told her just how much he had been looking forward to this. He admitted he thought it would be later in the night for this moment to happen.

She quickly put him at ease saying, "We can look forward to even more later tonight." The clothes continued to slip off their bodies with each of them touching, caressing, and kissing the exposed skin of their bodies, they were moving around to make it easier for the other. Before long both were totally undressed and their skin damp from their gentle kisses. Maggie took Billy by the hand and moved to the bed. There she enjoyed the naked body she had revealed. She took Billy's hand placing it on her exposed breast. He cradled it in his hand and began to run his tongue over the tip gently caressing the other, teasing her. She took his hand moving it between her legs as he acknowledged the hint to what she wanted. Teasing him with her tender sweet kisses from his nose across his chin to his lips where the kisses became more passionate. The anticipation grew as their mouths came together. Before long, his hand was wet from Maggie's excitement. She smiled as she moved on top, taking control of the foreplay. She stroked a fire deep within Billy as she touched and caressed his firm chest. She moved her hands out across his muscled arms holding his hand in hers and kissing, nibbling the tips of the fingers to the palm of his hand. A smile of enjoyment crossed her face from ear to ear.

His imagination was fired with excitement as she mounted him taking control of the depth of his manly thrust. Her movements again were intensified, she rode him like an untamed bull and before long she had exploded for the second time. Billy holding Maggie tightly moved to a seated position. Cupping her firm tight bottom in his hands, he began to move up and down embracing her tightly for their intimate explosion again - this time together. Their romantic emotions kindled a smile on their faces.

"Now for that bath," Billy replied.

"Should I help?" Maggie laughed as she removed herself from his lap noticing the time. "We need to get moving quickly. So, I had better get that bath alone or we won't be ready for our dinner date." She ran into the bathroom and started the bathwater once again. Quickly taking her bath she told Billy the bathroom was all his.

He joked, "Well, I liked it when it was ours." She gave a smile back as she continued to dress. Billy soon came out of the bathroom to see Maggie standing in front of the mirror wearing the blue satin dress.

She replied, "You did great, Billy.... I like it...Thanks!"

"You're beautiful," he replied.

Maggie moved into the bathroom to finish her makeup, while Billy got dressed. She returned to find Billy dressed in his black suit with a white muscle shirt and his gold cross hanging from his neck. Laughing as she looked down at his tennis shoes.

"I guess I didn't remember everything."

"We'll be just fine!"

"Are you, Maggie?"

"Yes. Let's hope this works!" Out the door they went to get Mary.

Mary was surprised to open the door when she heard the knock. Standing there were her two dear friends looking like they were dressed for the town ball. She told them she felt bad going out to dinner dressed like it was a special night while Ben was lying in the hospital.

Billy told her, "He wouldn't want you to miss out on New Year's Eve. "Come on… it will be good for you." He took her by the arm and down the hall the three of them went.

They entered the dining area. The room was full of busy happy faces. The band was setting up in the far corner of the room with the drapes open and with millions of lights twinkling across the mountain view. Mary was amazed the room sounded like honey bees humming around the honey jar.

The waitress greeted them and asked for their reservation name. Billy spoke up, "Watson table, please."

"Oh yes, right this way." As she guided them to the table, she commented on the tasteful shoes. Mary looked down at his shoes and began to playfully laugh.

"What! I couldn't remember everything!"

"You did fine, Billy." Maggie replied.

Billy pulled out the chair for Mary, placing her back to the door. He moved around and pulled out the chair for Maggie. Waiting for both ladies to be seated, he pulled out a chair to seat himself. "Well, nice idea…this is a good way to start the New Year."

The waiter dressed in a black long tailed tux with white shirt and black buttons down the front came over to take their order. "What can I get you to drink?"

Mary said, "Ice tea, please."

"Mary?" Billy questioned.

Just then a large bouquet of red roses was placed in front of Mary and she heard the words, "I hope you like them!"

Mary turned quickly to find Erik standing behind her dressed in a black suit, white collared shirt and very well-groomed haircut. Mary dropped her eyes to the floor and said, "Look Billy, he remembered his shoes." Joking she tried to hold back the panic of her heart suggesting it was in her throat instead of her chest. "Erik they're"…

Maggie quickly interrupted, "Well, come join us." Billy sprung to his feet to greet his friend. Then stillness came over the table, each looking at each other.

"Well, what a surprise," Mary finally spoke. "The two of you are in on this … I'm sure!"

Silence still had taken over the table as the waiter asked, "Can I finish the drink order?"

"Oh yes…please," Maggie replied. "I will have a martini, please in the long stem glass on the rocks, with olives with a glass of ice on the side. Well, guys what are the rest of you having?"

Mary was more than a little beside herself, eyeing her friend Maggie with a questioning eye.

"Maybe I shouldn't have come." Erik started to get up from the table.

"No, Erik, please be seated…. I'm sorry… I am totally surprised that the three of you pulled this off without a word to me. But I am glad to see you. Please stay!"

"Mary, we…"

Mary turned to Billy and said through gritting teeth, "I will talk to you and Maggie later about this. But for now, Erik came too far for these beautiful roses to go to waste. Thank you, Erik!" Mary added a warm smile across the table to Erik that grabbed his heart. "Now what are the rest of you drinking? This young man would like to be making his tips, instead of listening to us."

They each placed their drink orders and the waiter asked, "Miss, you still want the ice tea?

"For now yes"

The waiter disappeared behind the bar. Mary eyed her dinner partners one at a time. Erik leaned back in his chair with a lazy nonchalant attitude. One shoulder angled lower than the other as he rested an elbow on the table, circling the rim of his water glass with five fingertips. "Well, is anyone going to tell me how the boy is doing?"

"The boy?" Mary questioned.

"Mary, don't get all snippy with me...I don't remember his name... I'm sorry. But I am interested in how he is doing."

"His name is Ben. He is still unconscious and maybe that's where I need to be." Mary started to get up dropping the napkin on the place mat in front her.

"Mary please, sit down," Billy replied. "This was going to be a cheerful get-together and if you are unhappy about it, I'm very sorry. You can be mad at me - no one else. Erik and Maggie did what I asked them to do. Have dinner with us as friends and bring in the New Year on a pleasant note. Please, don't be angry with them. This was all my idea. I was trying to keep you from bringing in the New Year alone. I'm sorry if you are unhappy about it."

Mary dismissed herself from the table and walked toward the bathroom. Seeing that Mary wasn't leaving the hotel Erik got up and followed her.

Billy and Maggie questioned what they had thought would be a good thing and now look at their evening.

Mary went into the lady's room to collect herself, leaning on the wall just inside the small powder room thinking, "You fool!" She didn't mean to come across so mad at her friends. They did have good intentions. She was glad to see Erik. Why were angry words coming out of her mouth? Before she had a chance to answer her own questions...Erik walked in.

"Erik, what are you doing?"

Erik took her in his arms and his lips pressed firmly on hers. Mary tried to force him away, but she couldn't resist to completely give in, wanting his kiss. "I've missed you - don't you understand?" He whispered between the kisses. "You don't need to be alone." He had her by the shoulders. "You have someone that wants to share your bad times as well as the good times." Before she could speak someone came into the room. "We are sorry. Please, just give us a minute."

They backed out of the room closing the door behind them.

Mary started to cry, "Erik...I have wanted to call you."

"Then just pick up the phone."

"I couldn't. Each time I tried I only heard your voice saying the words "The man does the pursuing.""

"What? I had been pursuing and you didn't seem interested. What about the picture, the flowers, the Christmas tree?"

"I thought they were just my high school friend sending me gifts."

"It was with much more feelings than our high school days, Mary. I have missed your smile, your tea breaks, everything about you since you got back in town. Let's go out there, have dinner, enjoy some dancing and have a good time. Or if you just want to go up-stairs and be with your son, we can do it together, as long as I can be by your side. Here, dry the tears." Erik grabbed Mary a tissue from the box on the cherry dressing table.

They both looked into the matching mirrors hanging on the wall at the same time saying, "Look at us... you can dress us up, just can't take us anywhere." With smiles on their faces they both laughed. Erik took another tissue and dried the last of her tears from the rosy cheeks. Cupped her chin in the palm of his hand and said, "What do you think? Dinner and dancing or upstairs to see your son?"

Mary took a deep breath, trembling and said, "Let's have dinner and then I'll check on Ben before the dancing."

"<u>We'll</u> check on your son and it's a deal, Missy. By the way...
you're beautiful" as he kissed her forehead.

They walked out into the hallway where Billy and Maggie were
waiting.

"Mary?" with questioning looks on their faces.

"Don't say anything. Let us just go back and have dinner." Mary
put her arms around her friends, gave them a large hug and went
back to their table where their drinks were waiting. Mary sat down
and took a big drink of her ice tea. Waving for the waiter "Sir, could
you bring me something stronger?"

"Sure Miss...what would like?"

"I'll have what she's having," pointing to Maggie's drink.

"Well, now." Erik looked at Mary and said, "You don't need to, if
you don't want to drink. I know you want to go back upstairs."

"I'll go upstairs after dinner, but for now, I want to have one with
my friends."

Erik picked up his Manhattan taking a sip and told the waiter he
would have another Manhattan, please.

The waiter replied, "Should I just bring another round adding
the martini?"

"Sure...why not" replied Maggie.

Soon the waiter came back with their drinks. Once he had walked
away from the table Mary lifted her glass saying, "To good friends."

Erik eyed her over the rim of his glass, while Mary took a long,
sweet sip, slowly shaking her head from side to side. "Uh-oh!" He
studied the view of the woman he had loved for so many years and
had never told anyone until now. Now he wanted the world to know.
But instead, took a pull on his cocktail and enjoyed the view.

The waitress came to take their dinner orders and disappeared
into the kitchen again. The waitress soon returned with the first
courses, forgetting the salad dressing for each of them and asking if

anyone needed another drink. By the time they finished their salad and drinks they were finally joking about when they were kids.

Maggie looked up to find Billy's hands resting idly next to his plate. He was watching as they laughed at each other like who just got caught with their fingers in the cookie jar. He managed a smile to Maggie as his head shifted back and forward at Erik and Mary as the two chuckled. The sound brought a wash of relief to Billy. He took in a deep breath and exhaled. Their main course arrived and each dug in like they were starved.

"Can I get you anything else?" Everyone shook their heads. Erik waved his hand giving her the okay sign.

As dinner finished Erik wiped his mouth on a napkin and thought this is usually when he excused himself for a cigar, but he had stopped smoking. He found only when he drinks does he have the urge for one. He sat back in his chair and watched Mary. The room was full of beautiful women, but he was only interested in one: the lady seated across from him.

The waiter came over "Another drink anyone?"

Erik replied, "No, not right now…not for me…how about the rest of you?"

Mary said she would like to check on Ben before the music started.

"Okay," Maggie said. "I'll go with you."

"No Maggie, you stay with Billy and the two of you hold our table. Erik?" said Mary.

Erik didn't say a word, but pushed back his chair giving him room to stand and move around to assist Mary with her chair. Billy smiled.

Chapter 35

THE TWO WALKED TOWARD the corridor going to the hospital. When they reached Ben's door, Mary stopped before they entered the room. "He was doing much better today. His eyes moved while Billy and Maggie were reading to him. They have been reading *The Adventures of Tom Sawyer*. The doctor and nurses have told us this is good for him. If his eyes move, he may be hearing us and just can't respond yet."

As they entered the room, they asked the nurse who was just changing his IV bag, "How is he doing?"

"Ms. Barnes, he's getting stronger each day. His vitals are still good and strong." (She checked the chart.) "They have been improving for the better part of the day. How's the party? You look beautiful!"

"Thanks, dinner was good. This is my friend, Erik from back home. He came to see Ben."

"Okay, just for a minute and then I'm going to give Ben a warm bath. I thought while everyone was downstairs this would be a good time."

Mary walked around to Ben's side and spoke to him like he could hear them. "Ben, this is my friend, Erik. We came to see how you were doing and he's having dinner with me while you get a warm bath. You okay with that?" Ben's eyes blinked. Mary started to cry.

Erik placed his hand on hers and said, "Son, I will take good care of your mom and she will be back in the morning to see you. I think we need to make plans to get you out of this bed so we can go horseback riding. Would you like that?" Ben's eyes blinked with movement again.

"Erik, I think he understood what we are talking about."

"He sure did! He will be out on the farm before you know it." Still leaning on the bed, Erik took Ben's hand and said, "Son, get your rest now because we have a lot of work ahead of us this spring. We need your help to run the farm! Glory says hi and it's not fair, you getting all this rest and attention. But you know how the girls are. They like to have the attention." Ben gave no other acknowledgement to that statement.

The nurse asked if she could get started with his bath while there was floor coverage and things were quiet. Mary said goodnight to Ben giving him a kiss on the chin as she and Erik left the room.

Mary had a smile of relief on her face. She turned to face Erik, gave him a huge hug and said, "Thanks."

"For what?"

"You were good with him and he knew we were there. And..." she hesitated, "for coming."

"He's going to get better, Mary, just have faith. He will be out running up and down the fields. You'll see."

As they left to go to the elevator, the nurses at the desk told Mary how lovely she looked. They gushed over her beautiful dress and good-looking date giving her a thumbs up.

Mary smiled at them as the door to the elevator closed. Inside Erik leaned on his hands against the wall over Mary's head and gave Mary another kiss. "Feel better now?"

Mary just gave Erik a few pats on his chest as she responded to his kiss with a warm smile just before the elevator came to a stop and the doors opened. Erik was glad he came.

When they entered the dining room, the music was playing. Maggie and Billy were on the dance floor. Erik looked up at the clock over the band. It didn't seem like it but they had been in Ben's room for almost two hours. Maggie and Billy weren't sure if they were coming back to join them or not, but were glad to see Erik and Mary as they entered the room.

Erik took Mary by the hand and they joined their friends on the dance floor. They danced to several songs before coming back to the table. The men seated the ladies and everyone ordered another round of drinks. Billy ordered a bottle of chilled champagne. The waiter came with a silver bucket and a bottle of champagne packed in ice. He placed four long stem glasses on the table. "Champagne is included as part of the celebration tonight. Would you like me to open?"

"Not yet, we will let it chill a little longer." Billy replied.

"Sure, Sir" as he stepped away, placing his white folded towel back across his arm.

They danced several more times to slow grinding songs and fast songs where both ladies were not sure how to keep up with their fellows in their long dresses. As the music stopped the band leader announced that there were only ten minutes left of the old year. "Let's do one more song before midnight."

The music began to play. Billy started to uncork the champagne bottle. "I hope I remember how to do this." A few more turns and the cork came out with a pop. They handed him their glasses. He filled each one as bubbles ran down the side of the bottle. "Here's to good friends and our loved ones."

"Here! Here!"

They each took a drink and moved toward the dance floor. Everyone had their funny hats on and instruments ready as the band started the count-down. *"10, 9, 8, 7, 6, 5, 4, 3, 2, 1 Happy New Year."* Everyone screamed as the balloons fell from the ceiling and the band sounded their horns and drum rolls echoed down the hall.

Erik turned Mary to face him saying, "Happy New Year." They toasted to the new beginning just before he kissed her one more time. His strong arms lifted her up as his mouth slanted over hers. His tongue sweeping inside to duel with hers, his control damn near shattered when she made that seductive sound of pleasure.

Billy took Maggie into his arms and said, "I love you! Happy New Year!"

Maggie was speechless. This was the first time these words had been spoken between them. But she was pleased as she softly kissed him in return. His hand stroked her back moving slowly to press her up against his groin, both panting for breath when they finished the kiss.

Maggie looked over toward Mary to see her face pressed into the side of Erik's neck, as she placed another kiss gently on Billy lips. "You had a good idea... look."

Billy looked over to Erik and Mary now dancing, holding their bodies tightly together. He nuzzled the side of her neck and her sigh was filled with longing. She laid her head on his chest to hear the rapid beat of his heart.

"I did make that heart race," she said grinning at him.

"Yes," he admitted. "You cannot kiss me like that and expect to go on your merry way."

"What would you have me do?"

With a glint in his eyes, he slowly pulled her arms away from him and reminded her they were in a public place.

"Oh, that's right," she smiled slyly as they seated themselves.

Billy and Maggie were still dancing and smiling about their enthusiasm for each other. When the song ended, they didn't want to sit down. Both stood waiting for the next song to start.

Mary's anticipation of what the night would hold was almost more than she could control as she sat there watching Erik's eyes seducing her with each glance.

Erik wondered if tonight he would get to truly be with Mary in every way. He had longed for this night ever since the night she turned him away and he left her house. There were many sleepless nights he had dreamed of waking up with her body tucked beside him. How was he to control his feelings? His body ached for her as he gently stroked her chin.

Billy and Maggie came back to the table wet with sweat. Maggie seated herself and asked if they were having a good time. Both said yes at the same time laughing. "Me too! But I'm about played out. What about you, Billy?"

"You don't need to ask me twice. I'll get the check." He waved for the waitress to bring the check. "Erik, I'm glad you came tonight."

"Yes, Billy...I'm glad I came too." As he put his arm around Mary's hips drawing her close to him when they stood up, Mary's hand went into his back pocket.

"Go ahead, I'll get this. And you two can head to your rooms." Billy was thinking if they didn't walk with them, Mary may feel more comfortable inviting Erik to stay the night. Billy knew he was going to get lucky again tonight. He handed the unfinished second champagne bottle to Erik. "Go ahead take it to the room with you and Happy New Year, My Man!" Billy gave Erik a high five.

"Happy New Year to you guys as well and thanks for including me."

"Mary, goodnight...see you in the morning."

Maggie gave her best friend a big warm hug and kissed her cheek. "I hope you had a good time. Don't let it end." She handed Mary 2 fresh long stem glasses from the bartender.

"Thanks, Maggie."

Mary walked around the table and gave Billy a hug saying, "I'm not mad at you anymore." Smiling, she took Erik by the hand and they walked toward the elevator. The doors opened and Maggie and

Billy were pleased with themselves as their friends stepped inside.

In the elevator, Erik stood leaned against the wall, not knowing if Mary was going to ask him into her room or not. The door opened and they stepped off. Mary took out her key. Erik took the key to unlock her door. With the door slightly opened he handed the key back to her saying, "Goodnight…I had a great time."

"Me too." She leaned over tucking her head to his chest then feeling a bit uncertain, she battled her shyness. Then slowly she reached around his neck and buried her fingers in his hair drawing him closer. Her mouth touched his. Her teeth caught his lower lip and gently tugged on it. She heard a sharp intake of his breath and knew her boldness had pleased him. Tightening her grip, she tilted her head back, opened her mouth, and kissed him with uninhibited enthusiasm. His knees buckled but being a trained policeman, he couldn't let her have the upper hand. He picked her up. Their mouths engulfed each other. He kicked the door open with his foot and stepped into the room. He closed the door with the same foot. He released her legs, but her body clung to his. Their mouths were wet and their tongues were still embedded with each other dancing from side to side as she sounded with pleasure. God, she seemed so innocent he thought. Surely by the time he'd taken off her clothes, she would be ready to tell him where to go. Did he risk it? He wanted her so badly he ached. What if she panics and tells me to get out? He battled the wants and the what ifs, all running through his mind. "Oh God, I want you!" he yelled.

She said, "I need you, Erik" in a calm sweet voice of an angel. She dropped to her feet, taking him by the hand to the bed. She started undoing his shirt one button at a time kissing his chest with each opened button. He forced off his jacket. The anticipation of finally being united with the lady he has loved for so long was making him crazy.

Mary's hands shook as she continued to unbutton his shirt and move down to his pants zipper. Erik's stomach felt as though it were filled with butterflies.

He unzipped her dress and pressed the wide straps down over her shoulders causing the dress to fall to the floor. She was wearing a lace embroidered bra and panties to match. He worked his hands down holding her thin waist then he bent over and kissed her stomach. With the same movement she pushed him onto the bed, grabbing his pants legs and pulling the dark dress pants to the floor where they caught on his shoes. She laughed grabbing one shoe at a time and removing them as she threw them through the air. He watched her half-dressed body bouncing across the bed to rest by his side. He pulled her close kissing every inch of her body. The hot passion ran rampant through their veins. Mary moved over him and her hair dangled tickling his nose. He pulled her hair back for a full view of the enjoyable look of pleasure on her face.

"Don't worry you're not leaving tonight," she softly replied.

Erik was ready to explode **finally** holding his opinionated high school sweetheart in his arms and wanting to totally delight her. Once more her teeth caught his lower lip and gently tugged on it. She heard a sharp intake of his breath once again and knew her boldness was thrilling him. Seated over his stomach, he gently moved her body down placing her over his well enlarged manly area. She took a minute to arrange the lace panties allowing his organ to enter. A happy smile widened from ear to ear as she accepted.

He said, "I have needed you, Mary. I have dreamed of this moment."

She placed her hand over his mouth. "Just enjoy My Dear," immediately responding to his movement. Their movements became more intense as both expressed their desire for the other. Mary buried her fingers in his hair moving her hands down across his shoulders. Before long her petite figure of a body was moving uncontrollably, bouncing them across the bed as their bodies rolled from side to side. They rolled until Mary missed the bed landing on her back, legs and feet dangling in the air. Erik still had a tight grip around her hips and neither missed a stroke. They continued. Her voice repeated nearly in a shout of agreeable delight, "Yes... yes...don't stop...oh yesss....OH!" She grabbed his waist pulling him tighter, closer, wanting every inch of his manly tool as she exploded.

Erik began to whisper, "Oh God, Oh God, Girl...You ride me well." Suddenly his voice was no longer a whisper, "Oh God... I'm...I can't...I'm coming!" He grabbed her butt cheeks pulling her hard, wanting every inch deep inside her, trembling he held her tightly. "Oh, God, Girl," his voice was now a whisper. "That was great!" Neither wanted it to end, their bodies trembling and drained of all strength. He pulled her back onto the bed their bodies still connected. Her body was trembling and wet from his body. His hands were still tight around her hips and the satisfaction of delight was in his smile.

Mary wiped the beads of sweat from his chest, as she sat across his lifeless body. She bent to kiss the still trembling lips while violins still played in her head. Dizzy, she laid her forehead against his chin and the two drifted into a peaceful sleep.

Maggie and Billy had paid the check and left a good size tip for the waitress and waiter. Maggie picked up the bouquet of roses that Mary had forgotten to take with her. Both had wide smiles planted on their faces, hoping things went well with their friends.

"Should we check on Ben," Maggie asked.

"No, he's going to be resting and it's late. We're near if they need us. Let's get some rest ourselves."

Chapter 36

ERIK WOKE BEFORE DAYLIGHT and thought he was dreaming. The lady he had dreamed about for months was lying beside him. Her legs wrapped around him like a pretzel. The sweet smell of her cologne charmed the air. He leaned over kissing her forehead. She moved, drawing him closer and holding him tighter with her arm. A satisfying smile crossed his face and the sensation of wanting to climb on top of her again crossed his mind. He stroked her red hair from her face. Her eyes opened.

"Good morning, Blondie!"

She smiled at him moving her head against his shoulder, her arm drawing him closer, as if she could pull his rib from his chest. She flexed her body upward.

He asked, "Sleep well?"

"Heavenly. What time is it?"

"I don't know maybe five, five thirty, why?"

"I just wondered."

"It's still early."

"Good, want to play some more? That was great...even falling off the bed on my head."

They laughed together with Erik admitting, "Yes, it was!"

Erik leaned over kissing Mary gently on the lips. "Mary, will you marry me?"

He wasn't worried about her answer because last night had proven how much she cared for him and how much they had missed out on over the last several months. "Mary, you will get over your past, but let's do it together. I will help teach the boys to be good men and most of all I want to give you the most important thing you have always wanted… a family."

She looked him in the eye and said, "Yes… I know now I should have been honest with you from the start about my past, about my feelings and why. We have wasted so much time. I don't want to hurt anyone else, ever again. But you know I come with baggage, with a past that sometimes overwhelms my life and sometimes events click a bulb off in my head. But I promise I will love you like it is the last day of my life. We have had too much time stolen from our lives."

And she paused, taking a deep breath…"I cross my heart. You will never find a love truer than mine."

His hand gently touched her face. "So, let's make each day, each tomorrow the best we can make it. I promise to give you and your children a family, a father, and you a lover as true as my love for you."

They sealed their commitments with a gentle kiss of passion. Erik moved his hands gently to Mary's shoulders touching her soft skin with the tips of his fingers moving out across to the tips of her fingers, interlocking their hands together as he kissed her. Nuzzling his nose against hers, he answered her original question without words.

Things developed through their kissing and teasing each other with their licking. Erik began sucking on Mary's firm breast making even the other one stand at attention as he cradled them in his hands. His gentle touch stroked her naked belly, letting his fingers slip under the lace panties that never made their way off the night before. He explored the well-groomed private hairline. Erik was enjoying the moment just to be there with each other. He was savoring the touch of Mary's hand against his naked body as his hands peeled off her panties.

Mary's moves were letting Erik know she liked his touch and wanted more. Mary was enjoying the feeling she was having as he peeled away the panties from her skin like he was peeling the forbidden fruit one layer at a time. Edging the panties down a little at a time, he was stroking and squeezing her buttocks gently as he kissed and caressed her body all at the same time.

Mary knew her moves were heightening Erik's desires. He continued to grow as their body language signaled a desire for more without a word from either. The closeness Mary was feeling relaxed her. She wanted to show Erik through her caressing touches her enjoyment. The pampering sent chills across Mary's body giving her the desire for more. The intimate kissing and the warm, caring foreplay added to the sexual attraction and reflected their emotional closeness.

Erik gave Mary a playful kiss on the nose as his hands finally discarded the panties. In return Mary teasingly gave him a kiss around his chin moving to the jaw, down his neck and throat. She moved her lips back to his. Their lips energized the skin contact building the anticipation growing almost out of control. They both were trying to savor the deliciously intimate moments. The passion was heating up between them as their tongues embraced.

Mary could feel her body wanting to explode with emotion. She moved her body over his. Responding to his touches and his kisses were greater than any sexual foreplay she ever had before. Her body expressed the satisfaction and she made an appreciative sound of pleasure, "Oo..ohhh, Erik."

Erik, pleased with Mary's movement of pleasure and the smile on her face, enhanced his desire to deeply satisfy her every need.

Mary rolled to her knees, eyeing Erik, she stroked and caressed his groin. She moved her hand in long even strokes to the tip and back burying her hand against his leg as she continued to stroke back and forth. The enjoyment showed on his face and before long led to the peak of excitement as his leg became wet, but still hard he wanted more.

Erik rolled Mary over to her back kissing the soft roll of her belly as her body flexed wanting more. Tenderly he ran his tongue from her navel down her body working his way to her pubic area.

Stroking and rubbing her mons with his fingers and tugging gently on the pubic hairs while encouraging her body to move welcoming his warm lips. Her body arched inviting her partner for more making small sounds of enjoyment. She slowly was building to the intimate signal of pleasure one more time. "OH! God, Erik… Oh… Oh…I need you…Oh God, it's sooo good!"

The excitement of their lovemaking had enlarged Erik until he felt like he was going to explode. He moved on top entering Mary who was eager to share in the position. He began to move in and out slowly, gently, sharing in the enjoyment of their bodies interlocked. Mary embracing him wrapped her legs around his back and pulled him closer into her wanting him deep inside. They both could feel the pleasurable friction of each other at the same time each wanting to prolong their pleasure. Erik moved one of her legs down and the other lifted it above his shoulder as he asked if she was okay.

"Sure," as she stroked his shoulder.

Now he was able to thrust and move his body more easily while also increasing the pressure on her thigh and vulva. Mary relaxed wanting to enjoy him deep inside her. Before long she was totally engulfed in her movements, squeezing his leg against her thighs causing her body to arch. Now she pushed hard to demand his body, forced her chin to the ceiling and buried the back of her head into the pillow. Her body trembled with the final ecstasy. While his muscle fit tightly increasing the stimulation, she wiggled to exert extra pressure on his wanting body. Erik's hands firmly pressed on the bed, one of each side of Mary's hips. His arms straightened to support his weight as he rocked back and forth, in and out. Each movement of Erik's body teased her as he moved from side to side rubbing and stimulating her whole body for an even greater excitement. Suddenly the two surrendered and their bodies embraced, trembling. Erik's body shook with enjoyment. Mary screamed while she embraced him holding tight as she too had the most overwhelming satisfaction come over her body. Erik dropped his arms and rested his head on Mary's shoulder kissing her neck. Their bodies wet and his warm breath tickling her ear as they relaxed. Neither saying a word, their touch said it all.

Not wanting to get up the phone beside the bed started ringing. Mary reached for it, "Hello."

"Ms. Barnes...Mary Barnes, please!"

"This is Mary."

"Ms. Barnes, we need you to come to the hospital."

Mary jumped to her feet. "What is it? Is Ben okay?"

"Please, Ms. Barnes...I don't have any details...I was told to call and have you come to Ben's room."

"Okay. I'll be right there." Mary went to the suitcase pulled out pair of jeans and a t-shirt, trembling. By this time Erik was also on his feet and putting on the dress pants and shirt. Mary pulled her hair back into a ponytail and ran into the bathroom to brush her teeth, not even taking the time to see what she looked like.

"Erik...what if..."

"Mary, he will be okay!" He was putting on his shoes, not knowing what to think, but trying to stay calm for Mary.

Mary picked up the phone dialing Maggie's room.

"Hello"

"Maggie... it's Mary, the hospital just called asking me to come to Ben's room...no, I don't know anything...okay...I'll meet you there." Mary put the receiver back on its cradle.

Erik took Mary's hand and said, "It's going to be fine. Come on…let's find out what is going on." When Erik and Mary reached the end of the hallway, Maggie and Billy were coming out of their room. They all got into the elevator together. Holding hands, they prayed as the elevator went down. Entering the corridor from the hotel to the hospital, the long hallway seemed twice as long. When they reached Ben's floor, they could see Dr. Howard standing by the nurse's station. Mary stopped…frozen, afraid to take another step.

"Mary," Dr. Howard called. "Mary… Ben is asking for you."

"What?" Mary started to cry, running into his room. Ben was awake!

"He has been asking for you, Ms. Barnes" the nurse standing over his bed replied. She was holding a glass of juice in her hand. He has been awake close to an hour now. The doctor came in right behind Mary, Erik, Maggie and Billy. Mary moved over to the bed and brushed Ben's hair out of his eyes.

"Mom, I was fishing with Tom. Huck was upset with me for catching the largest one. He was going to throw me into the river, but Tom stopped him." Mary looked at Maggie and they all started laughing.

Dr. Howard checked Ben vitals again, told her to spend a little time with him and he was going to make his rounds. "I have ordered some tests and then I will be back to see how Ben is doing. I will keep you informed. But right now, things look good."

"Thanks, Doctor!" Everyone replied.

Maggie moved to Ben's side. "So… you have been fishing with Tom? What else do you remember?"

Ben took his hand placing it over his bandaged head. "Not too much, what happened…why am I here? Did Huck push me into river, I don't remember?"

Mary took his hand and replied, "That's okay, you will remember soon enough." She wanted to tell him just rest, but she didn't want him to go to sleep again. What if he went back into the deep sleep like before, so she kept talking to him asking questions about Craig and Mike.

"I don't remember, Mom. Please don't be mad! Who are all these people? Where's Dad?"

"What?" questioning with a puzzled look as she glanced around the room at her friends.

One of the nursing staff came in and said they were taking Ben down to x-ray. It would be for an hour or so if anyone needed coffee or to get cleaned up, smiling at Mary as she took the IV and hooked it to the head of Ben's bed pushing the bed toward the doorway. "I will keep you informed when he returns to his room, if that would help?"

Mary said thanks as the two nurses rolled Ben's bed out of the room and down the long hallway. Mary stood puzzled wondering what happened that he doesn't recall? How was she to relive Jack's going away and her losing her sons? How was she to explain taking him back to the farm? The people standing around his bed are their friends trying to help him. Mary started to cry not knowing what she was going to do.

Erik walked over to give Mary a hug.

"Not now" she said pulling away from him.

"Okay…I'll go for coffee. Anyone else?"

Billy said, "Hey, Man… I'll come with you, Erik. Maggie?

"I'm going to stay with Mary, guys…just bring us back something." Maggie pulled a chair over to Mary and told her to have a seat. "We will work this out. Don't worry."

"Don't worry? My life stays a mess! How am I going to explain to Ben about Erik or about us living at the farm, if he doesn't remember that Jack and I are not together? How do I find out about Mike, if Ben doesn't remember? Too many questions and not enough answers! What am I going to do?"

"We will fill him in as we need to Mary. We need to start with reminding him that he and the boys were living at Mrs. Pitt's. Maybe that will trigger something that he will remember. Let's be thankful he came out of the coma."

"You're right. I'm just so afraid, Maggie." They gave each other a hug.

The guys were back with their coffee. Erik handed Mary a cup, "I also brought you some tea with lemon, honey and cream. I wasn't sure what you felt like drinking."

Mary laughed and told him she was sorry for being short with him.

Erik replied, "Don't think another minute about it. You are under a lot of pressure right now. Coffee or tea?"

"Tea…thanks," she replied.

They all waited together to hear from the doctor or to see them bring Ben back into the room. An hour and a half had passed - still no answers. Mary had started to pace the floor back and forth.

"Mary, please sit down." Maggie went over and got her by the arm. "It will be okay, please sit down."

The guys trying to lighten things up, spotted the unusual cars double parked on the street below them as they looked out the window. They laughed at the brightly painted bug with bouncing black mouse ears.

"What will they come up with next?" replied Billy.

The nurse's aide came in with an arrangement of flowers in her hand. Mary quickly looked at Erik and said, "You didn't?"

"No, not this time."

Mary went over to read the card.

> *"Get Well soon.*
> *We look forward to you running*
> *around the farm."*
>> *Love from your family, Craig,*
>> *Glory May, Aunt Jenny and*
>> *Uncle Spence*

The flowers reminded Maggie that Mary's roses were in their room.

"Oh yes…Mary, I have your roses. I took them to our room for you last night."

"Thanks. I did forget them last night, didn't I? We had other things on our minds." Turning toward Erik she gave him a warm smile.

"What is taking so long?" Mary was starting to get very impatient. She walked out into the hallway looking for a nurse at the desk. Coming back inside the room, she said, "There's no one at the desk to ask if it will be much longer."

They started to bring in Ben's lunch, but stopped when they saw he was not back yet. "We will keep it warm until he gets back," said the nurse attending to the lunches.

The time turned into two hours. Mary went back out to the nurse's desk one more time. This time the nurse said they should be bringing him up the hall any minute now.

She stood tapping her feet on the shining tile floor. Finally, she saw him turning the corner down the hall.

They replaced his bed in his room and told Ben his lunch was on its way. "Are you hungry?"

"Sure," he replied.

Not wasting any time, he consumed the plate of food. Overwhelmed by the all people in his room he asked, "Mom, who are these people?"

Mary looked around the room and said, "Our friends, Honey. Let's work on how you got that blow to the head. What can you remember?"

Ben laid back on the pillow, "Only playing with the boys."

"Boys, what boys?"

"I don't know for sure, everything's a blur."

Mary stroked his forehead and said, "That's okay, Ben. We'll talk more later."

Maggie got up and walked over to Ben's bedside. "Ben, my name is Maggie. I would like to read you a story. Okay?" Maggie took out the book of Tom Sawyer from the side drawer of the table. She looked at Mary. Mary gave the okay. Maggie pulled up a chair and turned to the marked page, where they had stopped reading the day before.

She started to read… *"Feeling forsaken and friendless and like nobody loved him Tom decides to turn to a life of crime. He meets Joe Harper, 'his soul's sworn comrade,' and they begin to lay out their plans and decide to include Huck Finn as a member of their gang of pirates. Huck, having no qualms about which life of crime is the best, readily agrees, and the three plan to meet that night. "*

"Mom, this is what I remember. I was there playing with Tom and Huck," Ben replied.

Mary said, "You sure it's not Mike and Craig?"

Nurses came in several times during the afternoon to check on Ben making their notes to his chart each time. Around dinner time the nurse brought a message from the doctor. "Dr. Howard would like to see you in his office on the first floor, Suite 102 at 6:00pm if that would be good for you."

"Sure, I will be there," Mary answered. At 5:45pm Mary told Ben she was going to see Dr. Howard and get some dinner. After that she would be back to see him. By this time the guys were playing cards with Ben. Other than being weak when he stood on his feet, he seemed just fine. He had been laughing and was very impressed with Billy and Maggie's way of reading Tom Sawyer making it funny.

Maggie asked, "Mary, do you want me to come with you?"

Before Mary had a chance to answer Erik was on his feet. "I'll go if it's okay?"

"Maggie, do you and Billy mind keeping Ben company since he's enjoying your reading?"

They all agreed. Mary and Erik left the room. Mary stood outside Ben's hospital room, leaning against the wall, taking long deep breaths.

"It will be okay, Mary. Whatever Dr. Howard tells you we will get through it." He stroked her chin, "Come on, let's see what the doctor has to say."

The elevator ride seemed twice as long. Mary watched the lights as each floor number lit up. When it came to a stop, Mary thought her heart was going to stop with it. She stepped out on the shiny waxed tile and made her way to Suite 102. They entered and sat down on the plaid sofa, watching two children playing by the window with a stack of building boxes. They could hear the voices of two ladies behind the wall divider whispering about a chart misfiled. Dr. Howard stepped out into the lobby waiting area and said, "Ms. Barnes, please come in."

Mary's hands were wet with sweat. She took Erik's hand and entered the next room. They both sat down in the chairs facing the doctor's mahogany desk. Dr. Howard seated himself in his chair.

"Thanks for coming down to see me. I thought it would be better for us to talk about the testing we did on Ben. The good news is he seems to be fine. Most of the tests show things to be normal. But as you know he does not remember what happened. This may pass in a few days or it may take longer. His physical looks will heal faster than the amnesia will. The mind is a very funny thing. He could remember as fast as he woke up or it could take months or longer. I want to keep him several days to make sure he is resting good at night and I will have him up tomorrow going to the playroom with the others his age to see how he responds. If his daily activities show a reliable response he may go home soon. But we will still need to work on the loss of memory. Any questions?"

Mary sat looking at the doctor and turned to Erik, "What do you think?"

"Let's take one day at a time. It's going to be an adjustment for him. New people around him and new house when you take him home. Maybe when he sees Glory May and Craig things will resurface."

"I have a new medication I would like to try on Ben. It's to stimulate the brain cells. Studies have shown it to be very helpful on head trauma injuries. But I can only use it with your permission."

"Side effects?"

"It may cause some nausea, for some it lowers the blood pressure, but we would keep a very close eye on him and would start with a small dosage. In the meantime, bring pictures of family, friends, and places that he should know. If we could place him in the surroundings from the time just before the injury, it may help. That could be the hard part as I know he was living with his grandmother when the injury took place."

"I didn't have any contact with them. But if I need to, I will go to her house and see what we can find. I should go there anyway to look for his brother and any clues as to what happened or where he could be."

"Okay…with your permission we will start a small dose of the new medication and work from there. I will start Ben tomorrow in therapy with other teens his age and also start with Ms. Cook who is a children's therapist. When will you be going to visit his grandmother's home?"

Mary looked at Erik. "Can you go with me?"

"Of course, want to go tonight?"

"No, tomorrow morning…I don't think I want to sleep there and it will take at least an hour to drive there. In the meantime, I can spend a little more time with Ben. It's good to see him talking and laughing at the two of them reading the book."

The doctor added, "The reading was an excellent idea. Keep it up. If you finish one book, start another."

"Why does he seem to think he is with the characters from the book?"

"The mind can play games with us. Sometimes we go back several years in time and others go forward or talk about things that make no sense to us. But give him time he will start to remember things and put them in order. For now, he's awake and seems to be doing much better. All the tests look good. Maybe bringing something from where he had been living will trick his memory. It's worth a try. My rounds tomorrow will be covered by my partner, but I will be keeping an eye on his charts and meeting with the therapist after she has had a chance to sit with him. I have your number and will call you if there are any changes before you return. Good night and have a safe trip tomorrow."

They stood and walked toward the door. Mary turned and said, "Thanks, Dr. Howard for helping to bring my sons back to me." Erik shook Dr. Howard's hand and they left his office.

Back in Ben's room, he was busy talking with a boy about his age that had lost both legs in a train accident. They met in the hallway when the nurse had Ben out for a walk. The youngster was full of energy for having no legs. He was bouncing around in the wheelchair like he had been there all his life. "This chair's not going to keep me down," he said as Mary and Erik entered the room.

"Well, who's this?"

"Mom, this is Scoop. I met him in the hallway. He was in a train accident and lost his legs. He's going to run someday in the Miracle Run Race."

"Oh, he is now. Well, that's one big dream you have, son."

"No dream Ma'am. It will happen, you will see."

"Okay," Mary turned to see Billy and Maggie who had enjoyed the youngster's visit smiling from ear to ear. His determination was very good and he seemed very bright - not to mention how active he was in that wheelchair.

Ben looked up at his mom as Billy said, "He's a lot like Tom Sawyer - ready to take on the world! We all need to be like that, not afraid to take a chance sometimes."

Mary came to Ben's bedside and pushed his hair out of his face. "Well, I'm glad you have met a friend. I am going to need to go home and get you some things. The doctor says he will have plenty of activities to keep you busy until we get back. We are going to get some dinner and we will be back to sit with you for a while tonight. Then tomorrow we will be gone all day, okay?"

"Okay, Mom...But don't be too long."

Good timing as the nurse was bringing in Ben's dinner. "Scoop, off to your room now," the nurse replied. "Your dinner will be there by the time you get settled."

The four adults got up and moved toward the door. "Ben, have a good dinner," Billy expressed.

"Yes, Billy. Mom, you too."

"Okay, enjoy your friend. Scoop, give Ben some of that determination you have... okay?"

"Yes Ma'am, good to meet you." The boys were laughing as the door closed.

In the hallway Maggie asked about the doctor's visit. "We'll talk over dinner," Mary said.

Erik looked at both Maggie and Billy with a questioning expression.

They entered the dining room where the waitress remembered them from the other night. "Well. Hi. I see Mary hasn't frightened you away yet." Laughing she continued, "What can I get you to drink?" as she seated them in front of the picture window. She asked, "Mary, how is your son doing today?"

"Good, he's awake. Thanks for asking."

"Sure...we all become one big family here. I hope he continues to do well. Now, what are you drinking tonight?"

"Just hot tea for me, please," Mary replied.

Erik said, "I'll have the same. Billy, what are you having?"

"Well, sounds like no drinking tonight so I will have a cola."

Maggie turned and replied, "The same, please."

The waitress left the table. "Okay, Guys, what's going on?" asked Maggie.

"Well, Dr. Howard doesn't know why Ben's not remembering, but he going to run more tests and put him in therapy tomorrow. He wants to keep Ben for awhile longer to see if he starts to remember what happened. He wants me to bring some of his things to the hospital."

"How are you going to do that without going to Mrs. Pitt's house?"

"Well, I'm going to need to go there sooner or later anyway. Can you guys go with me or do you want to go home? Erik?"

"I'm going to take you. Billy and Maggie can go along if they like. You will need the support. I'm sure it's not going to be easy to go there."

Billy turned to Maggie, "Well?"

"Don't well me! I want to know what happened there too. We're in this together, that's what friends do."

"Good. Thanks Guys. I needed to hear that," as Mary sat trying to paste a smile over her worried freckled frown.

"It's going to be just fine. The police have the place under surveillance, so we don't need to worry. But Mary, you should call the detective and let him know we are going there."

"Right, let me find his number."

While Mary looked for the detective's number, Erik called Spence to see how things were going there. He told Spence to let Jenny know and to make sure it will be okay for Cliff to continue to stay with them. "How are the mare and colt doing?"

Spence filled Erik in about the repairs to the barn.

"Good... maybe talk to Craig, he may know something about the home that will be helpful when we get there. Okay, talk later, Man and thanks."

Mary was still digging in her purse. Erik laughed. "Everything but the kitchen sink in there," as she had now put everything on the table between them.

Mary finally said, "Here it is." She dialed his number. "Yes, Captain Williams, please. Yes, this is Mary Barnes. Okay...thank you." She left her number and hung up. "She's going to page him to call me."

"Okay, dinner. Now what are you going to have?"

"Just a salad."

"Salad? You haven't eaten a good meal all day."

"I know, but just a salad."

Everyone else ordered a full meal. The room didn't seem happy like last night when everyone was laughing and joking around. Tonight, everyone was back to the serious business for which they were here in the first place. Erik realized everyone here had a loved one next door as he read the sign above the entrance. "Remember your loves are in good hands!" Under it were several directional signs pointing toward the hospital...Burn Unit, Surgery Floor, Therapy, Emergency Treatment Unit.

Erik's fingers rounded the top of his glass without realizing what he was doing. The glass was making a whistling sound from his fingertips.

"Erik...you okay?"

"What? Oh sure...just thinking about something!" as his focus came back to the room.

"Well Mary, Maggie and I are going to call it a night. Ring us in the morning when you are ready to go. We'll be up and ready."

"Guys," Erik said, "Let get started early. We may need the whole day there."

"We can go tonight if you want."

"No, Mary didn't want to stay there."

"But Mary," Maggie replied. "Maybe we should, maybe Mike will hear that we are there and come to see you."

"I can't," Mary replied. "We'll go tomorrow."

Chapter 37

BEFORE SUNRISE THEY HAD left making the drive to Richmond. They were hoping to find something to help Ben's recovery. They were looking for clues to what happened and possibly to hear something about Mike. He might have some clues for them.

Captain Williams had returned Mary's call and was going to meet them there. They turned the corner following the directions to the house. Mary had not been there. Ms. Pitt had moved three times since she had taken the boys. Mary knew they were not living in a good area of the city. She remembered at one of her visits with Jack, he had told her that Richmond was the second largest crime area in the whole State of Virginia. She wondered how he knew so much about the violent crime of the area just by someone giving him the address. She never took the time to ask.

The truck turned the corner down the crime filled streets. Broken down cars were parked halfway out in street. Kids and adults filled the street and did not care to move out of their way as the vehicle passed them.

"Wow," Billy replied, "not like our little town."

"You think?" Erik said.

They drove around a large oak tree centered on its own island giving shade to the cul-de-sac. Erik's double cab truck came to a stop facing two large apartment buildings and a small house pushed between them. The faded blue house was stuffed like a peanut butter and jelly sandwich wedged between both apartment buildings. A chain link fence butted against the sides of the house and both apartment buildings. A narrow stained sidewalk was the only thing between them: no yard, no grass, just the broken cracked concrete stairs to the porch.

Captain Williams was standing at the gate waving his hand.

They got out of Erik's truck making their way across the street. Billy looked around as he locked the doors concerned about the neighborhood.

"I see you made it. How was your ride? Directions okay? Well, let's see if anything inside can be helpful. Watch your step."

They made their way up four steps and across the narrow weather-beaten porch just wide enough for two small cast iron yard chairs crying for a coat of paint. One was placed on each side of the door.

Mary took a deep breath before entering. Stacks of dirty dishes, used glasses and half filled cups, empty soda cans, and the smell of curdled food strongly took over the room. Medication bottles were on every table or stand. Mary walked around the room. There were no pictures of the boys, nor family or friends. Nothing to show the boys even lived there. She checked the kitchen still nothing but more dirty pots' n pans, etc. The place was awful and she had only made it through two rooms. The unpleasant smell made her cup her mouth. She ran from the room. How did they live like this?

The bathroom to one side off the kitchen wasn't any better. Dirty clothes were dropped across the tub and stacks of shoes were piled in one corner. A broken soap dish was hanging by one foot caught on a discolored towel. Mary turned backing her way out of the pit hole. She caught the narrow railing stairway and pulled herself toward the top entering a one room loft. There were three beds stacked on top of each other. The headboards were nailed to the wall and a homemade wooden ladder nailed to the foot of each bed with just enough space to crawl between them. To the other side of the room was a nine drawer dresser. Mary walked over looking at the things stacked on the dresser. She found framed pictures of Ms. Pitt, her son (the boy's biological father) and her two daughters (the boy's aunts). To Mary's knowledge only one of the daughters was still alive on that side of the family. She hadn't been seen in years. They heard she went back to somewhere in Colorado. She and Ms. Pitt never got along. Mary continued going through stacks of bills, papers, etc. Nothing here to do with the boys Mary thought. Maybe the pictures of Ms. Pitt would bring back something to help Ben remember. What happened here?

She pulled open the drawers. There has to be something she screamed. "What kind of person doesn't give kids anything!"

Each drawer had underwear, mismatched socks, torn t-shirts and faded jeans. They looked like the sizes of the boys. But no personal items…nothing!

Mary ran out of the room almost missing the step to the winding staircase. She couldn't wait to get Ben back to the farm and give him the life he had so greatly missed. Screaming she would give them good things to remember. "I will… I promise God… to give these kids a real home and a life with family and friends they can count on." Still crying she had made it to the front porch. Looking out across the dirty street she promised to give them a life to be proud of.

The others had followed Mary out of the house. "Captain Williams," Mary replied. "Thank you for meeting us. Please, call me if you hear anything about Mike or have any questions you may think could help to find him. I really am at a loss here. I need to get back to Ben and hopefully, take him home soon. The best place for him is to get him home with his brother and sister. Maybe things will start to come back and we can get some real answers. If I learn anything, I will call you." She walked toward the truck still in tears.

Erik and Billy took one more look through the house. They locked things up as they went, but were somewhat concerned if maybe Mike had been coming back here.

What Mary didn't realize since they had not gone into Ms. Pitt's bedroom was Mike was there. He heard someone coming and had gotten into the attic crawl space. If they had gone into her room maybe they would have seen the partly closed opening in the ceiling of Ms. Pitt's room. He wanted to call out to Mary, but he knew he was in trouble with Ms. Pitt. Thinking she was in the hospital but he didn't know she had died. There he stayed waiting, making sure no one else entered the house. He fell asleep.

Mary sat very quiet leaning back in her seat thinking about the fun times they all had as a family before Jack went away. Now things are so very different. 'Everything's upside down! Oh my God!' she thought wiping her tears running down her face. She would make sure each of the children knows how much she loves them. That remained the same, her love for her children, and they would all learn from this terrible experience.

Chapter 38

MARY STORMED INTO BEN'S hospital room like an Escap-
ologist. She felt like she needed to help Ben escape from the ropes
and chains that had entered his life. She backed out not seeing him
in his bed. "I need to speak with Dr. Howard," she informed the
nurse's station.

One nurse at the station said, "Ms. Barnes, please, quiet down."

Mary insisted she wanted to speak with Dr. Howard now! She
wanted to make sure there had been no setbacks. She wanted to take
Ben home today if possible.

"Ms. Barnes, he is in the therapy class Dr. Howard had ordered
for him."

"Where? I need to see him."

Mary followed the nurse to a large room with several sofas and
chairs where the youngsters were seated. Children from the ages of
8 to 18 were in a circle of at least a dozen wheelchairs. The kids
were entertaining each other. They were all laughing and having fun,
making friends and no one complaining or paying any attention to
their problems or injuries. Each one had their own story to tell. This
did not stop the eager caring smiles, all wanting the same thing…
to be kids. They would each have their turn to tell their own story
of pain.

Erik walked to the door looking into the room. "Come, Mary," he placed his hands on her shoulders. "Let's get a cup of tea until Ben has completed his session."

Hoping there would be no more setbacks he too was ready to take Mary and Ben home. Billy and Maggie were standing behind Erik.

"That's right, Mary, I could drink a cup of tea," Maggie replied.

That afternoon Dr. Howard gave Mary the okay for Ben to be released from the hospital. There were several things she would need to make sure he continued to do. If there were any problems, he gave her a number to call him day or night. Dr. Howard made his last official call on Ben while Mary signed his release papers.

Mary had a smile painted across her face. She couldn't wait to see the three children together again. Her sadness was not knowing where to find Mike and worrying if he'd be okay? Will he stay out of trouble? Is he living on the streets? Mary's worst nightmare was thinking about the streets of the second largest crime city itself and him being alone. "Oh God!" she prayed, "Please take care of him!"

Maggie pushed Ben's wheelchair to the restaurant. Mary holding Ben's few things asked for the table by the large picture window. The ladies excused themselves for the restroom. The guys ordered their hot teas. "Ben what can we get you? An ice cream soda?" Erik questioned.

"Can I?" Ben replied.

Billy being hungry himself went ahead and ordered some sandwiches for the group. They were going home tonight. They needed to eat before starting the long trip.

Mary looked drained as she walked across the room toward their table. With the sun shining across the room Mary looked like an angel coming through the glow. Erik smiled. He was taking his family home. He wanted Mary to become his wife and raise the kids together. He now felt there was hope.

The ladies were seated. Billy asked if they should call Jenny and

Spence. It would be late when they got into town.

"No," Mary said. "Let's wait until we get there. Erik, can Ben and I stay at your house tonight? We can take Ben to the farm in the daylight tomorrow after everyone is up."

"Sure. Whatever helps make this easier for you and the children."

They finished their first cup of tea and the ladies requested re-fills. The sandwiches were a great idea since everyone was very hungry. Even Ben ate at least one. Although, Mary was eating she didn't really taste the food. She was too full of thoughts. She had been given another chance to have her family. Would she prove to be the mother she always wanted to be?

They finished eating and headed to the rooms at the hotel to pack their things. On the way Mary and Maggie stopped at the front desk to settle their bills.

"Ms. Barnes, Dr. Howard has already called our desk. Your bill has been sent to The McDonald House office. They will send you a letter if anything is owed."

"Really? Thank you so very much for taking good care of us!"

"We are glad to help," the short overweight woman replied with a warm smile. "Please send us a card or two with pictures to add to our wall." She pointed to the wall across from the desk. They turned to see millions of families in pictures covering the walls from the ceiling to the floor up and down the hall on each side of the elevator.

Maggie said, "I never paid any attention to the wall before now. Did you, Mary?"

Mary replied, "NO...No I didn't."

Their ride home was quiet. Ben fell asleep on the back seat. Mary rested her head on Erik's arm and soon fell asleep herself. Erik knew there were lots of obstacles waiting for them when they got back to the farm. Each child is going to have lots of questions. Each will need to be addressed in different ways. Erik thought we need to make sure all get the love and attention they need. And of course, how will Cliff feel about his added family? He couldn't forget Glory already knowing she would be a handful, Mommy's girl. He smiles thinking of Mary Ann's grandparents, The Barnes. For a farmer Mr. Barnes was a good businessman when he had the farm running at full speed. What a business he did! Could he talk Mary and Jenny into doing this again? Could the guys work together as a team? He wondered if Billy, Spence and himself could work together. We could teach the children the ins and outs of the farm. We could make this work again, making family history. A bigger smile was pasted on his face as he looked down at Mary.

When they pulled into town, Billy stopped at Erik's shop. He got out and came to Erik's vehicle saying, "Maggie and I will head to her place tonight. We can talk tomorrow. Thanks for coming, Man."

Erik stepped out of his truck. "No, Billy, thank you for calling me." Erik gave his buddy a bear bounce hug and then they shook hands. "See you tomorrow, Man!"

Mary said, "Thanks, Billy! Tell Maggie we will talk tomorrow. Take care! Love you guys."

Billy returned to his vehicle and drove away flashing the lights. Erik pulled out behind him heading to his house.

When they got to Erik's house, Ben was still sleeping. Erik helped Mary with their things and carried Ben into the house. Mary opening the doors questioned could Ben sleep in Cliff's room. Erik said he would put her and Ben in his room. He would sleep in Cliff's room tonight.

When he put Ben down on the bed, he opened his eyes.

"Dad?"

"Ben, Mom is here. Just roll over and rest."

Erik gave Mary a kiss on the forehead and walked out of the room closing the door behind him.

In Cliff's room Erik dropped to the bed, exhausted, but couldn't fall asleep. He looked around the room at the many things Cliff had collected over his lifetime and couldn't believe they couldn't find anything belonging to Ben or the boys at Ms. Pitt's house. So many questions... with too few answers.

The sun began to come up shining into Cliff's bedroom window causing Erik to wake up. Still fully dressed he got up and brushed his teeth and hair. He picked up the phone and called Spence. "Good morning. Yes, we got back last night. Mary and Ben are with me. Sounds good. See you then." Erik started down the hall as Ben came out into the hallway.

"Good morning, Young Man. How did you sleep?"

He shrugged his shoulders.

"Bathroom is in here. Come on, I will get you a fresh toothbrush and washcloth. There's a comb on the table for your hair. Mom, still sleeping?"

"Yes!" Rubbing his eyes.

"Good, she needs the rest. Want to help me make breakfast?"

"Okay"

On that Erik waited for Ben to finish and they walked to the kitchen together.

Ben saw on the kitchen counter a rooster nested. "Mom likes roosters."

"Yes, she does, Ben. What else does Mom like?"

Ben rolled his shoulders then said, "Coffee, well sometimes tea."

"Sounds good, I like both too! Should we make a pot of coffee this morning? Do you know how?"

"Oh, yes... I'm good at making coffee."

"Okay." Erik placed the items out for Ben. "Here you go, let's see your stuff! When the coffee is ready, we will take Mom a cup!"

Ben replied, "Sure, where's the cups?" as he prepared the pot of coffee and waited for it to finish brewing.

Erik pointed and Ben reached for three cups from the cabinet. The top cup fell to the floor and broke. Ben quickly dropped to the floor crying, "I'm sorry! I didn't mean to break it! I'm sorry!" He was trembling sitting on the floor already in tears.

"Ben, it's okay. We have more cups. Don't cry."

Mary heard Ben and came running. But saw Erik had the problem under control. She waited by the kitchen door. "The coffee smells good, Guys."

"Mom," Ben ran to give her a hug. "I didn't mean to break it."

"It's okay, Ben." She smoothed back his hair as he buried his head into her chest like cub.

"Ben, it's okay!" She walked him over to the door. "Have you been outside?"

"No, can't go outside."

"Why not?"

"Grams wouldn't let us go outside."

"Well Ben, we can go outside today. Come on!" Mary opened the door and stepped out onto the porch. "Come on!" Down the steps she went running into the yard. "Come on! What are you still doing in the doorway?"

Ben turned looking at Erik.

Erik said, "Son... go ahead have some fun with Mom." Down the steps he went. He chased Mary across the yard until both fell to their knees laughing and rolling from side to side. Mary held him so tight not realizing her hug was starting to hurt. Ben said, "Mom, stop." They sat up facing each other.

"Mom... Where are Glory and Craig?"

"Oh, Ben, you will see them in just a little while. I promise you."

Erik shouted, "Anyone for breakfast?"

Mary said, "At the farm - we'll have breakfast at the farm!" They walked up the stairs.

Erik handed them both their coffee. "Mary, I did call Spence this morning. He knows we are in town. He and the youngsters were going to check out Blackie and the colt. Said they'd be back at the house in about an hour. All three kids were going to be with him."

"Three?" Ben replied.

Mary said, "I have been so worried about Ben, I forgot about Blackie and her baby."

"I guess Spence and Cliff will be the ones to answer that question," replied Erik. "You will know soon. More coffee? Ben more coffee?"

"Sure" Mary held out her cup too.

But Ben was already back out in the yard with a stick in his hand.

"It's going to be a beautiful day!" said Erik.

"It already is," replied Mary watching Ben in the yard. Mary went inside collecting their things. When she stepped back out onto the porch, she shouted, "Ready to go home, Ben?"

In a flash he was beside Mary. "Come on, Erik. Take us home." She walked toward the truck.

Ben asked, "Can I ride in the back?" He was already standing on the back bumper.

"Not today, Son. Come on. Get in beside Mom."

Erik closed their door tapping the truck gate as he rolled around the truck to get into the driver's seat. He looked back at Ben who had moved to the back seat. "Ben, ready to see everyone and your new home?" He started the truck.

"I am ready to see Glory and Craig," he quickly replied.

The drive was nice. It was warm and sunny for a January day. The snow was almost gone. It didn't seem like it was the middle of the winter season. They crossed the narrow bridge and their farm house was in site.

"Ben, remember this place?"

Ben now perched across the seat between them replied, "No."

The two-story house had a welcome home feeling to Mary as they turned into the driveway. Mary noticed all the work that had been done to the barn. "Wow! It will soon be completed," she said.

"Yes, Ma'am. It will be just in time for the Spring festivals."

"Mom," Ben replied pointing at the colt jumping across the yard.

"Oh, my word!" Mary said, "What a beautiful sight!"

The small three and a half foot colt having more legs than a body was jumping around full of life. Cliff, Craig and Glory were running behind him. The colt would stop like he was waiting for them to catch up. Before they could reach him, he was off again kicking his heels. The youngsters were laughing not paying any attention that the truck was sitting in the driveway. Mary got out.

"Kids!!!"

Glory came running and jumped into her mom's arms. "Oh, I have missed you."

"What about ME?" Ben said, coming around the corner of the truck.

"Ben!" she screamed. "Oh Ben, look! Look at the addition to our farm family. Come let me introduce you to Chance."

The two walked out into the yard. Glory called, "Chance. Come to me." She stood silent. Chance looked up... nose in the air. He could smell Glory's treat. Her arm out in front of her palm up and open, she had some finely ground oats in her hand. "Here Ben," she gave him a small handful. Ben stood frozen as Chance checked out the new arrival. The colt would take a few steps toward the young-ster and back up two.

Mary laughed watching the kids. "Oh, Erik, they're home!"

The boys, Craig and Cliff, were standing by the fence chatting as they gave Mary and Erik the thumbs up.

Erik replied, "Yes, Mary, they are." He put his arm around Mary's shoulder... full of smiles, thoughts and dreams for his new family. What Erik didn't realize was all the **Road Blocks** he would endure.

Books By Judy

Must read series II (ROAD BLOCKS)
Fiction, Romance and Suspense
Author has composed Anniversary, Birthday, Get Well, Special Occasion, and Sympathy cards which at one time or other you may have read or purchased.

Books: Special Moments (Dedications by short stories)
Short Stories for Reader's Digest

Poetry Books:
Inspirations By Judy Kay series I
Inspirations By Judy Kay (Take Time to Listen) series II

CPSIA information can be obtained
at www.ICGtesting.com
Printed in the USA
BVHW082224140521
607267BV00004B/384